Dear Reader,

Romances featuring Native American heroes and heroines have a long history at Silhouette Books, which is why we are delighted to bring you this special collection featuring three brand-new stories about a Native American legacy and the hope it brings to three different couples as they fall in love.

The legend begins with an historical romance set on the Western frontier, "Wolf Dreamer" by Madeline Baker. In this dramatic story, a woman's spirit is restored by the proud Indian warrior who saves her life. And her happiness is secured by a cradleboard created to protect the lives of her future children.

The amulet from this cradleboard find its way into a cowboy's hatband in the contemporary story "Cowboy Days and Indian Nights" by Kathleen Eagle. And it is this amulet that puts the rugged rodeo man in touch with his Native American roots as he finds his own future with a sweet woman looking to open her heart again to love.

The cradleboard itself is the only legacy the hero of "Seven Days" has left from his Native American parents. And the single mom he falls in love with helps restore his faith once more when she creates a new amulet and makes the heirloom—and her life—whole once more.

We hope you enjoy these wonderful stories!

All the best,

The Editors
Silhouette Books

MADELINE BAKER

has written over twenty historical novels, half a dozen short stories under her own name and over seventeen paranormal novels under the name Amanda Ashley as well as Madeline Baker. Born and raised in California, she admits balancing her love for historical romance and vampires isn't easy—but she wouldn't like to choose between them. The award-winning author has now found another outlet for her writing with Silhouette Romance. Readers can send a SASE to P.O. Box 1703, Whittier, CA 90609-1703 or visit her at her Web site http://madelinebaker.net.

KATHLEEN EAGLE

published her first book, an RWA Golden Heart Award winner, with Silhouette Books in 1984. Since then she has published more than thirty-five books, including historicals and contemporaries, series and single titles, earning her nearly every award in the industry, including the Lifetime Achievement Award from *Romantic Times* and RWA's RITA® Award. Her books have consistently appeared on regional and national bestseller lists, including the *New York Times* extended bestseller list. Ms. Eagle live in Minnesota with her husband, who is Lakota Sioux and a public school teacher. They have three children.

RUTH WIND

is the award-winning author of both contemporary and historical romance novels. She lives in the mountains of the Southwest with her two growing sons and many animals in a hundred-year-old house the town blacksmith built. Her only hobby since she started writing is tending the ancient garden of irises, lilies and lavender beyond her office window, and she says she can think of no more satisfying way to spend a life than growing children, books and flowers. Ruth Wind also writes women's fiction under the name Barbara Samuel. You can visit her Web site at www.barbarasamuel.com.

MADELINE BAKER
KATHLEEN EAGLE
RUTH WIND

Lakota Legacy

Silhouette Books

Published by Silhouette Books
America's Publisher of Contemporary Romance

SILHOUETTE BOOKS

LAKOTA LEGACY

Copyright © 2003 by Harlequin Books S.A.

ISBN 0-373-21810-9

The publisher acknowledges the copyright holders of the individual works as follows:

WOLF DREAMER
Copyright © 2003 by Madeline Baker

COWBOY DAYS AND INDIAN NIGHTS
Copyright © 2003 by Kathleen Eagle

SEVEN DAYS
Copyright © 2003 by Barbara Samuel

This edition published by arrangement with Harlequin Books S.A.

® and TM are trademarks of Harlequin Books S.A., used under license. Trademarks indicated with ® are registered in the United States Patent and Trademark Office, the Canadian Trade Marks Office and in other countries.

Visit Silhouette at www.eHarlequin.com

Printed in U.S.A.

CONTENTS

WOLF DREAMER

Madeline Baker

* * *

For Luke,
Because he always comes running to meet me;
His arms open wide to welcome me;
A smile on his face.

Dear Reader,

I was thrilled when I was asked to be a part of this anthology. Kathleen Eagle has long been one of my idols, and sharing a book with her and Ruth Wind is a dream come true.

As some of you may know, I'm always working on more than one story at a time because my Muse isn't always reliable. Sometimes she takes a vacation, and sometimes she insists on doing things Her way! That's what happened with "Wolf Dreamer." Originally, this story was going to be a fantasy set in the mountains of a distant planet. However, my Muse didn't like that idea, and the next thing I knew, my hero was no longer a wizard but a warrior. But as they say, all's well that ends well.

Thanks to all of you who wrote to tell me how much you enjoyed *Dude Ranch Bride,* my very first Silhouette Romance novel. Thanks to my wonderful agent, that was another dream come true. My second Silhouette Romance book, *West Texas Bride,* will be out in November.

Best,

Madeline Baker

Prologue

She stood on the edge of a high mountain meadow, hiding behind a tree, captivated by the sight of a tall copper-skinned man dancing in the cool silver glow of a full moon, his waist-length hair his only covering. He chanted softly as he danced, his voice low, the words foreign to her ears, his steps graceful, elegant, intricate. She had watched him dance before. Always the same steps, always the same chant. He danced for what seemed like hours, untiring, his voice lifted toward heaven in what she was certain was a prayer.

She watched until her eyelids grew heavy and she sank down to the ground.

It was then that the mist came, rising from the earth, enveloping the dancer in a sparkling golden-brown haze.

It was then, between one breath and the next, that the miracle occurred. Copper-hued skin became thick black fur, his body changed, transformed, until the man was gone and in his place stood a huge wolf with golden-brown eyes. Lifting his head, he sniffed the air and then he turned, ever so slowly, toward her hiding place.

Startled, frightened beyond words, she leaped to her feet and began to run, her heart pounding, her pulse racing.

He was behind her. She knew it without looking, knew if she dared glance over her shoulder, she would see the wolf chasing her, gaining on her. She ran and ran. Ran until her sides ached, until her legs were weak and she couldn't run any more. With a sob, she fell face down in the tall grass, her heart roaring like thunder in her ears as she felt the wolf's hot breath blow across her cheek like the hot breath of a desert wind. She tried to tell herself there was nothing to fear, that wolves did not attack humans, but she knew, deep in her heart, that his teeth would soon rend her flesh.

She opened her mouth to scream....

And that was when she always woke up.

Chapter 1

He watched her as he did every day, drawn to her, to this place, without knowing why. Crouched behind a screen of tangled vines and wild blackberry bushes, he watched the white woman make her way down to the river. Her name was Rebecca Hathaway and she came here each day just before dusk. Sometimes she swam in the slow current, sometimes she just sat on the grassy bank and gazed into the clear water, her expression pensive, often sad.

He had watched her off and on since she had come here five summers ago as a new bride. He had seen her eyes light with joy as she watched a brown-and-white calf struggle to take its first step, heard her laughter as she danced in the rain, listened to her sing, her voice soft and sweet, as she worked in the vegetable garden that grew behind the house.

He had watched her belly grow round with child, had listened to her tears when she stood over her husband's grave. He did not know why the man had died and though it grieved him to see her in tears, he was pleased that she no longer shared her bed or her body with another.

This evening she had again come down to the river to bathe. A low growl rose in his throat as she stripped off her dress and petticoat and stepped into the water.

It pleased him to watch her.

It pained him to watch her.

The setting sun caressed her skin, making it glow like pale gold. Her eyes were the bright green of new grass in the springtime. Her hair, which was the color of the rich dark red earth of his homeland, caught the fading light, emphasizing the red highlights, turning the long silky strands to burnished copper.

She reached for the chunk of homemade hard yellow soap and began to wash. The soap smelled of flowers. The lather slid down her arms, down the valley between her breasts. Watching her, he was sorely tempted to join her there in the river, to feel her skin against his own, to lick the drops of water sliding down her slender neck and rounded belly...

He lifted his head and sniffed the wind, then slowly eased back into the shadows, his nostrils filling with the stink of unwashed bodies.

Strangers were coming.

Rebecca's first warning that she was no longer alone was the jangle of horse harness, a sound she would forever associate with the day her husband had been killed, and with the army deserters who had killed him. Fear rose up within her, hot and swift and overpowering.

Scrambling out of the water, she grabbed her clothes and ran for the house, her heart pounding with fear. Fear for her own life. Fear for the life of her unborn child.

She screamed as three men on horseback rode into view, blocking her path.

Breathless, she stared up at them, covering her nudity as best she could with her crumpled dress and petticoat.

One of the men crossed his arms on the pommel of his saddle and leaned forward. He leered down at her, exposing a mouthful of crooked yellow teeth.

The second man nudged his horse up beside her and dragged a hand through her wet hair. He was young, even younger than she was, with wavy brown hair and blue eyes. She thought he might help her, until he smiled. It was a cold, cruel smile.

The third man laughed as he dismounted. It was a sound filled with menace, not humor. "Told you, I did, that this would be our lucky day."

Rebecca shook her head and backed away. "No. Don't." She placed her arm over her swollen belly in an age-old gesture of protection. "Please."

"I like a woman what says please," the third man said. He winked at his companions, then reached out to grab her arm.

With a strangled cry, Rebecca twisted out of his grasp. Throwing her dress and petticoat in his face, she turned and began to run back toward the river. And even as she ran, she knew she would never get away. She heard one of the men shout, heard the sound of running feet behind her as all three men gave chase.

Please, oh please, oh please…

The cry echoed silently in her mind as she raced toward the river. A large flat rock jutted out over the deepest part of the water. If she could just make it to the rock…it would all be over. She would hurl herself into the river. Better to drown than be at the mercy of these barbarians.

I'm sorry, so sorry… Unspoken words, meant for her unborn child.

She wasn't going to make it. She could feel the earth vibrate beneath her bare feet as the three men drew closer. Almost, she could feel their breath on her back…

She screamed as another man burst out of the cover of the trees. They had her surrounded!

Images planted themselves in her mind—lean copper-hued flesh, long black hair, piercing golden brown eyes.

In movements that were almost too fast for the eye to follow, he nocked an arrow to his bow and let it fly. Once, twice, and two of the men chasing her were dead. The last man managed to fire his rifle before her rescuer let a third arrow fly. With a sharp cry of pain, the man fell backward to lie motionless in the dirt. For a moment, she stared at the bodies, astonished, as always, at how quickly lives could be snuffed out.

Taking a deep breath, she turned around to thank the man who had come to her rescue, but he was gone, leaving nothing behind but a faint trail of blood. Had he been wounded? Was he dead, too?

Concern for his welfare overcame her fear of what she might find and she followed the blood droplets until they disappeared.

It was only when she turned for home that she remembered that she was naked. Retracing her footsteps, she picked up her dress. She shook out the dirt before slipping it over her head, then stepped into her petticoat, smoothed her skirts, and took a deep breath. She would have to dispose of the bodies. But how? And where?

Walking up the path to the house, she was surprised to see the horses of the three men gathered in the yard. They had run away when the fighting started; now they were back, standing close together, ears twitching as they watched her.

Speaking softly, she walked toward them. Her own horse had died not long ago. Taking up the reins of the three horses, she led them into the small corral behind the house. The pen was in need of repair, but it was the only one she had. One of the horses, a pretty little bay with a star on its forehead, nuzzled her arm as she removed the saddle. She stood there a moment, scratching the bay's ears. It calmed her somehow, and for a few minutes it kept her from thinking of what had almost happened.

Leading the bay out of the corral, she closed the gate. Going to the barn, she found a shovel and a pair of heavy work gloves. She would bury the bodies in the woods where the dirt was soft, where she could cover the graves with pine needles and deadfall.

The bay shied at the scent of blood and death, but Rebecca finally coaxed the mare to drag the bodies into the woods, one by one.

It was dark by the time she managed to dig a grave large enough for all three of the men. She covered the shallow hole with pine needles and branches and rocks, then stood back, her hands resting on her belly. She knew she should offer a prayer for their souls, but she simply couldn't do it. *Rot in hell,* she thought. *I've buried you, and that's enough.*

Later, lying in her lonely bed, her back and shoulders aching, she wondered what had happened to the mysterious man who had saved her life.

He crawled toward the river on his hands and knees. His body burned with fever; the bullet lodged in his side throbbed with every movement, every breath. He had tried to remove it with his knife, but to no avail. It was lodged under a rib and he hadn't been able to pry it out.

He sighed as he slid into the water. It felt like winter rain against his heated skin. He drank deeply, hoping to cool the fire raging within him, clawed at the shore as his empty belly rebelled and he began to vomit up the cold water.

He felt a faint vibration in the earth beneath his hands, looked up to see the woman walking toward him. He crawled out of the river, head hanging as he tried to gather his strength to rise, to run, but his legs refused to hold him and he pitched forward, a wave of dizziness sucking him down, down, into darkness...

Rebecca stared at the man sprawled face down on the riverbank. The early-morning sunlight glistened on his broad back and shoulders and long,

long legs. His hair gleamed wetly, a mane of thick black that fell almost to his waist.

Curious, she took a step forward, and then another. Who was he? What was he doing here? And where were his clothes?

He groaned softly as she rolled him over. Ribbons of bright crimson oozed from a ragged hole in his side.

She recognized him instantly. It was the man from her nightmares. The man who had come to her aid the day before.

His eyelids fluttered open, and she found herself staring into a pair of golden brown eyes clouded with pain.

"Can you stand up?" she asked. "I can't lift you."

He stared at her for a moment, his gaze unfocused, and then he nodded.

Rebecca slid her arm under his shoulders and after several false starts, managed to get him to his feet. He swayed unsteadily and then, step by slow step, they walked toward the house. He towered over her. Heat radiated from his skin. She managed to get him inside the door before he collapsed.

Rebecca stared down at him, watching as blood pooled beneath him, staining the raw plank floor.

With a sigh, she went into her small kitchen, wondering if she wouldn't have been better off to leave him where he was. For all she knew, he could be one of the men who had killed her husband. She shook the thought aside. Had he been one of those men, he would not have aided her yesterday.

She gathered the items she needed, tied an apron around her waist, filled a bowl with water. Moments later, she knelt at his side. Taking a deep breath, she washed the area around the wound, then picked up a slender-bladed knife and began to probe the area.

At her touch, the man growled low in his throat and began to thrash about.

"Don't." She placed a firm hand on his shoulder. "You've been hurt. I'm trying to help you."

His eyes opened at the sound of her voice.

"It will be all right," she said soothingly. "Don't move. I'll be as quick as I can."

He continued to thrash about, reminding her of a wild animal trying to bite the hand that wanted only to help.

Removing the sash from her robe, she drew his hands up over his head, bound his wrists together with the sash and secured them to the leg of the heavy wooden table her husband had made.

The man stared at her, his eyes narrowed with anger and pain, as she straddled his legs and bent her head to her task.

Sweat beaded his forehead and chest and his breathing became shallow and rapid, but he didn't make a sound as she cut the misshapen slug out of his side.

She blotted the blood with a clean rag, applied a coat of pungent salve to stop the bleeding. She placed a square of cotton cloth over the wound, then bound it in place with a length of soft cloth and tied off the ends. When that was done, she wiped his body with a cool cloth, gave him a cup of warm willowbark tea to help him sleep, then covered him with a thick wool blanket.

Rising to her feet, she stared down at him, knowing, somehow, that he was going to be a lot of trouble.

Chapter 2

He woke slowly, aware of the hard floor beneath him, of the warmth of the scratchy wool blanket that covered his nakedness, of a presence in the room. Heat emanated from the hearth a short distance away; the air was filled with the scent of freshly baked bread.

He opened his eyes.

"How are you feeling?"

Her voice was soft with a slightly husky quality that he found appealing.

He searched his mind for the right *wasichu* word, frustrated when it eluded him. He licked his lips, then glanced at the water jar on the table.

Her gaze followed his. "You want something to drink?"

He nodded, and she smiled as she poured him a cup of water. Kneeling, she slid her arm under his head, lifting him a little as she held the cup to his lips. "Slowly," she admonished.

It was cool and sweet, and he drank it all. With a sigh, he closed his eyes, letting sleep claim him once again.

When next he woke, it was dark. Sometime during the night, the woman had freed his hands. A single candle lit the room. The woman stood near the hearth, her back to him as she stirred something in a large black kettle.

His stomach growled loudly and she glanced over her shoulder. Seeing that he was awake, she filled a bowl, then knelt on the floor beside him and offered him a spoonful of the savory broth.

It pricked his pride that he was too weak to sit up and feed himself.

She accomplished the task quickly and efficiently. When he had eaten his fill, she examined his wound, nodding as she ran her fingers over his skin.

"It's healing," she remarked. She placed her hand on his brow. "I think your fever has gone down a little." She regarded him for a long moment. "Do you think you can stand up? I'm sure you would be more comfortable in bed."

He nodded, and she helped him to his feet, seemingly unbothered by the fact that the blanket slid over his hips to pool at his feet when he stood up.

Her room was small, furnished with only a bed and a chest of drawers covered by a lacy cloth. An earthenware vase held a bouquet of dried flowers.

She pulled back the covers and helped him lie down on the straw-filled mattress, then drew the covers up over him. "Can I get you anything?"

He shook his head.

"Rest," she said. "You'll feel better in the morning, I'm sure."

The bed was far softer than anything he was accustomed to. The pillow and blankets surrounded him with her scent. He slept and woke and slept again, his dreams hazy and confused.

The sound of the woman's footsteps woke him later that night. She placed her hand on his brow, nodded, and moved toward the door. "Call me if you need anything."

He watched her leave the room, realizing, too late, that he needed to relieve himself. He tried to ignore it for a moment, then tossed back the rough woolen blankets. He slid his legs over the edge of the bed, groaning as the movement renewed the ache in his side.

He closed his eyes as a wave of nausea swept

through him. When it passed, he stood up. Swaying unsteadily, he took a step toward the door.

"What are you doing?"

He paused in midstride at the sound of her voice.

"You shouldn't be out of bed," she exclaimed, stepping into the room.

He licked dry lips, searching his mind for the *wasichu* words. "Me...I...need to..."

"You need to what?" She moved up beside him, her gaze searching his.

He pointed outside. "Need to..."

"Oh."

He watched a tide of red sweep up her neck and into her face, amused by the fact that, while she did not seem to be affected or offended by his nudity, his need to perform an act of nature made her blush.

"Here, let me help you."

Taking the blanket from the bed, she draped it over his shoulders, then slipped an arm around his waist and helped him outside. A short distance from the back of the house, she left him alone, one hand propped against a tree for balance.

He watched the gentle sway of her hips as she walked away. Her hair, unbound, fell to her waist in shimmering chestnut waves. In spite of her pregnancy, she was thin. Too thin. When he regained his strength, he would fill her larder with venison.

His gaze moved to the corral, noting the broken rail, the way the gate sagged. The house needed repairs, as well. The roof looked as though it would blow off with the first winter wind.

He shook his head ruefully, wondering what his father would think if he could see him now, naked as a newborn babe, relieving himself against a tree.

She returned for him a short time later. He would have shunned her help, but he was too weak to make it back to the house on his own. He was panting and out of breath when they returned to her room. When they reached the bed, he collapsed on the mattress, cursing the nausea and weakness that swept through him.

The woman covered him with the blankets, offered him a cup of cool water. She left the room, returning with a bowl of the broth she had cooked earlier. She sat beside him, feeding him a spoonful at a time, as if he were a child. It humbled him as few other things had done.

Utterly weary, warmed by the broth, he fell asleep once again.

When next he woke, it was dark. No lights burned in the house. All was quiet. He lay still and silent, listening, wondering what had awakened him. And then he heard it again, a muffled groan edged with pain.

Summoning what little strength he had, he slid out of the bed. For a moment, he stood there, one hand grasping the bed frame. And then he made his way into the other room.

Peering into the darkness, he saw the woman lying on the floor in front of the fireplace, her body curled in on itself. The scent of blood reached his nostrils.

She became aware of his presence then. "Help me," she whimpered. "My baby…"

He crossed the room and knelt at her side. Closing his eyes, he reached deep down inside himself, drawing on the indomitable strength of will that was his heritage. He felt the power within him come to life, infusing him with the strength of his wolf spirit. Lifting the woman in his arms, he carried her into the bedroom and lowered her onto the cot.

It was too early for the child to be born.

He stripped her of her soiled dress and covered her with one of the blankets. His insides clenched as she cried out, her hands clutching her stomach.

He stood beside the bed, his own pain forgotten as he watched the woman writhe in agony as she sought to expel the child from her womb. She looked up at him, her eyes dark, tormented, and he knew he could not let her suffer. She had saved his life. He could not let her die, not when it was in his power to save her.

Kneeling by the bed, he took her hand in his. "Woman."

She clutched his hand in hers, her nails digging into his skin, her body convulsing with pain.

"Woman, will you trust me?"

"What...what do you mean?"

"I can help you."

"How?"

"Look into my eyes."

She hadn't been afraid of him before, but she was now. He could smell the sharp scent of her fear.

"Look into my eyes, woman. Do not be afraid. Only trust me, and I will take your pain."

"How...how can you do that?"

"Will you trust me to help you?"

She nodded weakly.

His gaze locked with hers. Putting everything else from his mind, he concentrated on the woman, listening to the sound of her breathing. Gradually, his body took on her rhythm, so that his heart beat in time with hers, his breathing mimicked hers. When his body was in tune with hers, he reached deep within her and drew her pain into himself, absorbing the knife-like contractions that engulfed her, amazed that such a frail creature could endure such agony. The pain was worse than anything he had ever experienced. It started low in her back and wrapped around to the front. He sucked in a deep breath, feeling as though he were about to be torn in half. He concentrated on the pain, made it a part of himself.

Panting softly, he looked into her eyes, eyes now empty of pain, and wished he could spare her the heartache to come, but only time would heal the sorrow that awaited her.

He wiped the sweat from her brow, wondering how he would find the words to tell her that the child she had so gladly anticipated was dead.

Chapter 3

The infant was born a short time later, a tiny scrap of humanity with a thatch of wispy red hair. Even knowing the child was dead, he tried to revive it, but to no avail.

The woman watched him in tight-lipped silence, tears dripping like rain down her pale sunken cheeks.

When he had done all he could, she held out her arms. ''Give me my baby.''

As tenderly as if the child lived, he wrapped the tiny infant in a length of swaddling cloth and laid it in her arms.

The woman gazed down at the stillborn child, her

tears dripping onto the waxen cheeks. "Poor little girl," she crooned. "How pretty you would have been." She held the child close to her breast, her tears coming harder and faster. When he tried to take the infant from her, she shook her head. "No! No!"

While she cried over the child, he disposed of the afterbirth, then went into the kitchen to warm some water. He sat at the table while he waited for the water to heat, his head resting on his folded arms. How strange it felt to sit where the woman had sat. He had never sat at a table before. His wound throbbed dully; he felt weak and light-headed and wanted nothing more than to lie down in front of the fire and sleep, but that would have to wait. The woman needed help.

When the water was hot enough, he poured it into a bowl and carried it into the bedroom.

The woman looked up at him, a wildness lurking in the back of her eyes. "What are you going to do?"

"Wash you," he said.

She didn't argue. She clutched the lifeless child to her breast while he washed her body from her waist down to her feet, then he stripped the soiled bedding from the mattress and spread a clean sheet beneath her.

When that was done, he held out his arms. "Give me the child."

She shook her head weakly. "No."

"The child is dead. She must go to join her ancestors."

"No!" She held the baby tighter still. "Please don't take her from me. She's all I have left. I can't be alone again. Please."

"You are not alone, woman," he said quietly. "I am here."

She looked up at him, her eyes wet with tears. "Why are you helping me? Who are you?"

"I am Wolf Dreamer, son of Cloud Woman and Catches Thunder, shaman to the people of the high mountains."

Her eyes widened in disbelief. "You're an Indian?"

He nodded.

She shook her head. "I've never seen an Indian with eyes that color."

A muscle worked in his jaw. Once, his eyes had been as black as midnight. Only after he had gone to seek his vision had the change taken place. It was the sign that he was truly the chosen one, destined to be the shaman of his people when the time came.

He had gone to the pinnacle of a mountain to seek his vision. Three days and nights of fasting and prayer. When he woke the morning of the fourth day, he had awakened to find a large gray wolf standing over him, and standing behind the great cat was the shadowed image of a woman with hair the red of an autumn leaf and sun-kissed skin.

Lying on his back, he had stared up at the wolf, certain he was about to be killed. *So,* the wolf said, his voice like the echo of thunder over the mountains, *you are the chosen one.*

Before he could reply, the gray wolf sank its teeth into his left arm; he still bore the mark of the animal's teeth. And with that bite, the wolf had given him the mystical healing powers that caused some to fear him and some to hunt him.

For the next four days, the gray wolf had taught him the ways of the shaman, the prayers, the chants, the healing arts. On the last day, the gray wolf had told him that he would now wear a new name, Wolf Dreamer, and that he would one day have a son who would lead the People to their final destiny.

Wolf Dreamer shook the memory from his mind. "And you are called Rebecca Hathaway."

"How do you know that?"

"It does not matter. Rebecca." He said her name quietly, liking the way it sounded.

It was then that he heard the voice of his old friend, the gray wolf, speak to his mind and heart. *She is the one. The other half of your soul.*

Wolf Dreamer stared at the woman. He recognized her now. She was the red-haired woman he had seen in his vision.

It was only when the child grew cold and stiff in her arms that the woman let him take the infant from her. He wrapped it in the blanket she gave him, one made by a mother's loving hands, and then he carried the tiny body outside. He found a shovel in the barn and after a great deal of effort, he managed to dig a suitable hole beside the grave of the woman's husband. He was breathing heavily by the time he finished. Blood leaked from the wound in his side.

He was about to lower the tiny body into the ground when he looked up and saw the woman walking slowly toward him. Her hair fell in a tangled mass over her shoulders; her face was almost as white as her gown.

"You should not be out of bed," he told her.

"Neither should you."

They stared at each other from opposite sides of the grave. For the first time, it occurred to him that he was still naked, but the woman didn't seem to notice. She was staring at the blanket-wrapped body.

"It doesn't seem right, to bury her without a proper coffin."

He frowned at her. "Coffin? What is coffin?"

"A box to put her in."

"She will rest more comfortably in the arms of mother earth than in a box."

His voice, low and filled with compassion, brought fresh tears to Rebecca's eyes. She bit down on her lip as he began to shovel dirt into the grave. She glanced at Gideon's final resting place. A tin can filled with a wilted bouquet of wildflowers marked his grave. And now their daughter lay beside him.

With a sigh, she sank down on her knees beside her child's grave and bid a silent farewell to her last reason for living. Soon, she thought, soon she would join them.

She wondered who would put flowers on the graves of her husband and her daughter when she lay in the ground beside them.

She had set her face toward death. Wolf Dreamer recognized the look in her eyes. He had seen it before, on the faces of Old Ones who had lost the will to live. They refused food and water, growing weaker and weaker, until their spirit left their body to travel the long road to the Afterworld. Sometimes, to spare their loved ones the sight of their dying, they walked away from the village, never to return.

He had stood at the woman's side as long as he could, and then he had taken her by the arm and lifted her to her feet. They had trudged back to the house, their arms wrapped around each other for support. And now she lay on the bed, staring up at the ceiling, her eyes blank, her face as pale as the covering on the pillow.

Though he wanted nothing more than to sink down on the floor and sleep, he knew they both needed food to sustain them, to strengthen them for the journey ahead.

He filled a bowl with broth from the iron kettle, but she took one look at it and turned away.

He ate because it was necessary, then stretched out on the bed beside her and closed his eyes.

Deep in the night, he woke to find her curled up in his arms, her cheeks damp with tears. The sight of her tears touched an aching place deep within him. Was there no relief for her, even in sleep?

He placed his hand over her heart. It beat slow and steady. Closing his eyes, he called to the pain that engulfed her, felt it flow into him. He groaned as he took her grief into himself. How did she survive such anguish? His hands clenched as her agony washed through him, a pain that was deeper than that she had endured in the hours of childbirth, more excruciating than any pain he had ever known. He felt her sorrow, her loss, the aching emptiness in the deepest part of her soul.

With a sigh, he drew her closer, his hand stroking her hair. Gradually, she relaxed in his arms.

He held her all through the night, his heart speaking to hers in the ancient tongue of his kind, soft words that soothed her troubled soul and cocooned her in layers of sweet forgetfulness until the dawn.

Chapter 4

When he woke, he was alone in the woman's bed. He went into the kitchen, thinking she might be there, but there was no sign of her. He had watched her make tea, and he put the kettle on, then, gazing out the window, he raised his arms over his head and offered his Dawn Song to the Great Spirit Who Ruled Over All, praying that he might quickly regain his strength so that he could care for the woman.

The woman. Rebecca.

She is the one, the gray wolf had said. *The other half of your soul.*

Had he known it all along? Was that why he had

been drawn to this place all these years, the reason why he had been compelled to watch her, why he had struggled so hard to learn her language? She was not of his people. Would they accept her? Would they accept *him* after so long an absence?

Taking the kettle from the stove, he made himself a cup of the hot bitter brew.

He was staring out the window when he heard the voice of the wolf speaking in his mind again.

You have been gone long enough. It is time to go home. Time to accept who and what you are. Time to meet your destiny.

He drained the cup, then left the house in search of the woman.

He found her where he had expected, lying across her child's grave. She was asleep, her arms outstretched as if to encompass the child. There were tear tracks on her cheeks.

Bending, he lifted her into his arms and cradled her against his chest. "Rebecca." He murmured her name, liking the sound of it, the taste of it on his tongue.

Her eyelids fluttered open. She looked at him a moment, her eyes filled with grief, then buried her face against his shoulder. He felt the warmth of her tears against his skin as he carried her back to the house.

Inside, he placed her on the bed, then sat down beside her. Her skin was pale. Dirt clung to her arms, her feet, her cheek. Her eyes were swollen and red.

Leaving her, he went into the kitchen and warmed a pot of water. When the water was hot, he poured it into a bowl and returned to the bedroom. Setting the bowl down, he began to remove her sleeping gown.

"Leave me alone."

"I am going to wash you."

She started to protest, then sighed in resignation, as if it didn't matter what he did to her.

He removed her gown, washed her gently, found clean cloths to absorb the after fluids of the birth. When he was finished, he put her gown on her again and covered her with a blanket.

He had to find a way to revive her spirit, but how?

Returning to the kitchen, he warmed the tea, filled a cup, insisted she drink it.

She did so reluctantly, then turned on her side and closed her eyes.

She slept all that day.

He bathed in the river, found an ax and chopped wood for the fire. The exertion left him breathless and sweating and he sank down on the ground, cursing his weakness. The wound in his side was still tender.

Stretching out on the ground, he closed his eyes, his mind filling with images of the woman. Since the first time he had seen her, she had never been far from his thoughts. He had carried her image with him wherever he went, held it close when the weight of who he was grew too heavy to bear. Time and again, he had been drawn back to this place, this woman.

He rested for an hour, then went into the house to check on her. She was still asleep, one hand beneath her cheek. Unable to resist the lure of her soft flesh, he caressed her cheek. Her skin was smooth and warm beneath his fingertips.

A sob escaped her lips. A tear rolled down her cheek. The sight tore at his heart.

"Ah, Rebecca," he murmured, and sitting down on the bed, he drew her into his arms.

Rocking her gently, he stroked her hair and back, singing to her as he did so. It was an ancient lullaby, handed down from mother to child, a song that spoke of love and hope and the beauty of the human spirit. He sang it in the ancient tongue of his people, hoping it would soothe her even though she could not understand the words.

Gradually, her sobs lessened and she relaxed against him. He continued to hold her, content to do so. Content to hold her as long as she needed.

The sun was setting in a blaze of crimson and gold when his stomach growled.

Rebecca sat up, blinking at him. "You're hungry."

He nodded.

"I'll fix you something to eat."

"I can do it."

She shook her head. "No." Rising, she left the room.

His arms felt empty, bereft, without her. He listened to her move about the small kitchen. Soon, the scent of venison stew filled the air. His stomach growled again.

A short time later, she called him into the kitchen. Her eyes widened, and a blush stained her cheeks. He frowned at her, then realized he was still naked.

She moved past him, her gaze averted. She returned a short time later and handed him a pair of woolen trousers.

He looked at her askance.

"They were my husband's."

He nodded, then stepped into the trousers. He was not comfortable in them, and not just because they were a little too snug, a little too short. She offered him a shirt, as well, but he waved it away.

"Sit down." She gestured toward a chair, then turned to the stove and filled a bowl with stew. She placed it on the table in front of him. "Careful, it's hot."

"You are not eating?"

"No."

"You must eat."

She shook her head.

He stood up, pulled out a chair, and pushed her, very gently, into it. He filled a bowl and set it before her. "Do you want me to feed you?"

"I'm not hungry."

"You want to die," he said. "But you will not. I will not allow it."

She looked up at him through eyes filled with sorrow. "Please, just let me go." She made a gesture that encompassed the house. "I have nothing left to live for. No reason to go on."

He picked up his spoon, scooped up some broth, and offered it to her. "Eat."

It was not a request this time.

She stared up at him, somewhat taken aback by his tone. Their gazes held for several moments, and then she took the spoon from him and began to eat.

Wolf Dreamer sat down across from her. Lifting his bowl to his lips, he drank the broth, then picked the meat out with his fingers.

Rebecca finished eating a few minutes later. She carried her bowl to the sink, rinsed it out, then left the room.

Wolf Dreamer sighed heavily. He had to find a way to make her fight, a reason to make her want to live.

Rebecca drew the covers up to her chin and closed her eyes. She was weary, so weary. Her breasts were heavy with milk. Her arms ached to hold her child. Her heart ached. Her very soul ached.

She listened to Wolf Dreamer moving about in the other room. As soon as she was sure he was asleep, she would leave the house and find a place to hide, a place where she could be alone. A place to die...

She blinked and blinked again, surprised to find that it was morning. She bolted upright at the jangle of horse harness, fear running cold through her veins. Soldiers! Had they come looking for their comrades? She should never have kept the horses! They would find the animals in the barn and they would blame her for the deaths of the three men.

She slid out of bed, grabbed hold of the bedpost as dizziness swept through her. She glanced wildly around the room. She had to hide, but where?

And then it was too late. Two men wearing the dark-blue uniforms she had come to associate with death and destruction burst into the room, weapons drawn.

She backed away, her heart pounding with terror, but there was nowhere to run, no place to hide.

She cringed as one of them grabbed her by the arm, his fingers digging painfully into her skin.

"Let's go," he said gruffly.

"No." She shook her head. "Please..." She looked at the second man. "Please?"

But they didn't listen, only dragged her outside and lifted her onto the back of a horse. A horse that had belonged to one of the dead men. Resigned to her fate, she offered no resistance as the man tied her hands. She had wanted to die, she thought dully. Soon, her wish would be granted.

The two men mounted their horses. One of them held her horse's reins, the other man held the lead ropes of the other two horses. She wondered briefly where the Indian had gone, bade a silent farewell to her loved ones, and then, closing her eyes, she blocked everything from her mind.

They hadn't gone far when she heard a high-pitched shriek. Opening her eyes, she saw that the man in front of her had an arrow protruding from his back. Even as she watched, he slid off his horse's back to land with a dull thud in the dirt. The other man was sprawled facedown on the ground a short distance away.

She glanced over her shoulder to see Wolf Dreamer striding toward her. He carried a bow in one hand. A quiver was slung over his back.

She looked back at the two men, at the arrows protruding from their flesh.

A dark abyss rose before her. With a wordless cry, she tumbled into it, reaching for oblivion.

Chapter 5

Filled with a sense of urgency, he untied her hands, then carried her back into the house. He cradled her to his chest. How light she was! And how good it felt to hold her in his arms. Lowering his head, he breathed in the scent of her, felt his desire stir to life.

He had never had a woman.

Filled with a sense of urgency, he carried her back into the house, laid her gently on the bed and covered her with a blanket. They had to leave this place, now.

Going into the kitchen, he laid his quiver and bow on the table, then packed everything he could carry into a sack. He left the bundle by the front door, then went into the bedroom. He gathered her few articles of clothing, rolled them into a tight bundle, and tied them with a cord he had found in a drawer in the kitchen.

Leaving the house, he looked over the horses standing in the yard. He picked out a pretty little bay mare for the woman and a big, wild-eyed gray gelding for himself and tethered them to a tree, then unsaddled the rest of the horses and turned them loose.

Returning to the house, he gathered the sack of food and the woman's clothing, carried them outside and shoved them into the saddlebags lashed behind the gray's saddle.

By the time he finished, the wound in his side was aching, and he was breathing as though he had just run up the side of a mountain.

Cursing his weakness, he rested in the shade a moment, then went into the house. The woman was awake when he entered the bedroom.

He held out his hand. "We must leave this place."

She shook her head. "Go...go away."

"I cannot leave you here alone," he said patiently. "Other soldiers will come. I cannot kill them all."

"No. Go on and leave, if you want to. I must

stay here." A sob caught in her throat. "My baby is here. I cannot leave her."

"You cannot stay here alone," he repeated, his patience growing thin. "If you wish, I will come back for the child when it is safe to do so."

She shook her head, her eyes wild. "No, I will not go. I will not!"

Wolf Dreamer took a deep breath. He was weary in mind and body. His wound ached with renewed ferocity. Steeling himself to withstand whatever resistance she offered, he scooped her into his arms, blankets and all, and carried her outside.

"No!" She screamed the word, her small fists pummeling his chest and shoulders. "No, no, no!"

She continued to strike out at him until he lifted her onto the back of the mare and tied her hands to the saddlehorn.

"Let me go!" she shrieked. Tears welled in her eyes and rolled down her cheeks. "I hate you! Let me go!"

Turning a deaf ear to the woman's cries, he eased himself into the saddle and took up the reins. Clucking to the horse, he circled around, picked up the mare's reins and turned his horse north. He knew a secluded valley, far from here, where the woman would be safe. He would take her there until she was strong enough to travel further.

And then he would take her home to the People.

Gradually, the woman's tears subsided and they rode in silence. Wolf Dreamer let his thoughts drift toward home. How many years had he been gone? Two? Three? He had lost track of the time, aware only of the changing seasons as he roamed the land, yet always drawn back to this place, this woman. Why was he the one who had been cursed? The old shaman had said it was a blessing, but Wolf Dreamer had not seen it as such. Enemy tribes had sought to capture him, wanting him to use his healing power in their behalf. Those of his own tribe had come to him for help. They treated him with honor and respect, but he had seen the fear lurking in the backs of their eyes. He had used his power for healing, but he knew their unspoken fears, knew they were afraid that some day he might turn that power against them.

Summer Moon Rising had not wanted to share him with the tribe. She had been jealous of the time he spent with the people, afraid of his power, and she had turned her back on him and married his best friend, Elk Chaser. Hurt and angry, his pride wounded, Wolf Dreamer had fled down the mountain, determined never to return. But he would go back now, for Rebecca's sake. She would be safe there.

Rebecca rode slumped in the saddle, her head bowed. She was empty inside. Cold. Dead.

Dead…like her husband. Her daughter. Fresh tears stung her eyes. Born and buried without a name, without so much as a stone to mark her grave. Such a tiny grave…

Her grief and pain poured out in a long wordless cry.

Wolf Dreamer reined his horse to a halt. Dismounting, he untied the woman's hands. Lifting her from the saddle, he drew her into his arms and held her close, one hand lightly stroking her hair while his mind spoke to hers, not in words, but in thoughts and images. He assured her that her daughter's spirit was at peace, that her soul had traveled safely along the bright path of the Milky Way to a place of rest and beauty where she would be welcomed by her father and by all those who had gone before.

He felt peace enfold Rebecca's heart as his words took shape in her mind.

She leaned against him, small and warm in his arms, as delicate as a wildflower. A wave of protectiveness swept over him, and he knew in that instant that he would live and die for her if she would let him. But it was too soon to speak of that now. She needed time to grieve, time to heal.

He closed his eyes and drew in her scent, wondering if she would ever be able to accept him for

what he was. They came from different worlds.
Could she ever learn to love and trust him?

Later, concerned for the woman's health, plagued
by the constant ache in his side, Wolf Dreamer
drew rein sooner than he would have liked.

It was late afternoon when he reined his horse to
a halt in a shallow draw. Dismounting, he spread
one of the woman's blankets on the ground.

Rebecca was limp in his arms when he lifted her
from the saddle. He carried her to the blanket and
she curled up on it. Moments later, she was asleep.

He covered her with the other blanket, then
stripped the saddles and blankets from the horses
and tethered the animals to a bush.

When that was done, he eased down on the
ground, his back propped against one of the saddles. He would rest for a few minutes while she
slept, and then he would find some wood for a
fire…

Rebecca woke with a start. She glanced around,
confused. Where was she? And then she saw the
Indian. He lay facedown on the ground, his face
turned toward her, his eyes closed, his breathing
slow and steady. Who was he? He frightened her,
this strange man with his black hair and his extraor-
dinary golden-brown eyes. Yet there was something
about him…something he had done while she was

in labor. Somehow, he had taken her pain away. If only he could do that now.

She pressed her hands to her breasts. They were heavy with milk, a constant reminder of the child she had laid to rest. Tears burned her eyes, tumbled down her cheeks. So much hope, so much pain. Her empty arms yearned to hold her child.

She had to get away from this man, whoever he was, now, before it was too late. If only she wasn't so tired, so weak. She glanced at him again. He was still sleeping soundly. She would never get a better chance.

He knew as soon as he woke that she was gone. Foolish woman, did she think she could survive out there alone? Perhaps, if she had been stronger, but not now, when she was still weak from childbirth. Too weak to even saddle her horse. She must have stood there, on a rock, to mount.

Rising, he stood with his feet braced apart, his head lifted while he scented the air. South. She had gone south. Foolish woman, he thought again. That was the direction the soldiers had come from. That was where their fort lay.

With a sigh of exasperation, he vaulted onto his horse's bare back and set out after her.

He could have followed her in the dark with his eyes closed. Her scent filled his nostrils, a lure he

was powerless to resist. Her helplessness stirred his
protective instincts, her quiet beauty beckoned him,
the pain in her eyes made him yearn to comfort her.
He had never felt this way about a woman before,
not even Summer Moon Rising, whom he had once
hoped would be his woman. Now, he was grateful
that Summer Moon had refused him. And yet, what
made him think Rebecca would be any different,
that she would be able to accept him for who and
what he was, or that her heart would heal enough
to let her love again?

The horse moved steadily onward through the
darkening night, the sound of its passing muffled
by the thick grass beneath its hooves. Clouds whispered across the sky; lightning flashed in the distance.

He shivered in the rising wind as he urged his
horse into a lope.

Rebecca huddled against the side of the tent, her
whole body trembling with fear, her gaze fixed on
the three men sitting across the way. They were
gambling. Gambling to see who would get her first.
She had begged them to let her go, to be merciful,
but they had only laughed. From time to time, as
they passed a bottle between them, they looked over
at her, their gestures lewd, their eyes filled with lust.

She had never been so afraid. Why had she run

from Wolf Dreamer? He frightened her, too, but not like this. He had treated her gently, cared for her, comforted her. These men would use her, abuse her and kill her when they were through.

Tears stung her eyes and dripped down her cheeks. She had wanted death, but not like this.

She prayed for help, for deliverance. Prayed to die before they defiled her.

Their laughter sent cold shivers down her spine. The bottle was almost empty now. She trembled uncontrollably. She had been married only a short time before her husband was killed. She had married Gideon to escape the restrictions placed upon her by her father. Her parents had predicted she would regret it, and they had been right, but, being young and rebellious, she had refused to listen. Gideon had been handsome and dashing and filled with the fire of youth. Too late, she realized she had made a mistake, that she had only escaped one taskmaster for another. Her husband had been her first and only lover. She had never found pleasure in the intimate side of marriage, a lack he had assured her was due to her own cold nature. Their lovemaking had always been hurried, a duty rather than a pleasure. It was an act she had barely endured with her husband. She could not imagine suffering through it at the hands of these rough strangers.

She watched in terror as the bottle was tossed aside and the dice were rolled again.

Outside, the wind began to howl, keening like a soul in torment as the last man threw the dice.

"I win!" he exclaimed.

The other two muttered good-natured obscenities, and then they all three gained their feet, their gazes hot with hunger as they stared at her.

"I need to take a piss," one of them said, and staggered out of the tent.

The other two paid no attention to his going as they advanced toward her. Scrambling to her feet, she looked wildly from side to side, but there was no escape. She screamed as one of the men grabbed her by the arm and pushed her down on the ground. He held her arms over her head while the other man sat on her ankles, then lifted her skirt.

She writhed beneath them in a last desperate attempt to free herself. Revulsion rose deep within her as the man sitting on her legs began to unfasten his trousers. Bile rose in her throat as his hands brushed the skin of her thigh.

He was bending toward her when he made a horrible gagging sound. His body went limp and he fell across her.

It was then she saw Wolf Dreamer. Fury glittered in the depths of his golden-brown eyes as he jerked the knife from the dead man's back, flipped it in his hand and, with a flick of his wrist, sent it spinning through the air. There was a horrible gurgling noise behind her, and then a thud.

Wolf Dreamer scooped her into his arms, gained his feet, and carried her out of the tent and away from the camp. He moved through the darkness without making a sound.

She wept silent tears as he carried her through the night. Tears of relief. Tears of horror.

Shortly, he came to a stop and placed her gently on her feet. "Woman," he said, and there was a hint of laughter in his voice, "you are a great deal of trouble."

She stared at him, not knowing what to say.

He did not seem to expect an answer.

"Stay here," he said, and disappeared into the darkness.

She glanced around, only then noticing that their horses were tethered nearby. She moved toward the bay mare, lightly stroked the mare's neck.

She never heard the sound of his footsteps, but he returned a short time later leading a horse.

In the back of her mind, she knew the horse belonged to one of the dead men, knew that it carried supplies Wolf Dreamer had taken from the tent. But she was too numb to care. There had been too much killing, too much death, and she turned away from it, seeking escape deep inside, where no one could hurt her, and no one could find her.

Wolf Dreamer felt her spirit withdraw, and understood. She had seen too much, been through too much. He spoke to her softly, assuring her that all was well, and then he lifted her onto the back of his horse. Vaulting up behind her, he drew her against his chest. She tried to resist, but then, with a sigh of resignation, she slumped against him.

"Rest, *wastelakapi*," he said quietly. "You are safe now."

Gathering the reins of Rebecca's horse and that of the pack animal, he rode into the darkness. They would reach the valley by morning.

Chapter 6

She woke to the sound of birds singing and the warmth of the sun on her face. She should get up, she thought, there were chores to do, but she didn't care.

She stared at the vast blue vault of the sky and wondered what had happened to the roof.

She heard the soft snuffling of horses grazing and wondered why they were in her bedroom.

She felt the heat of a body beside her and wondered how that could be when Gideon had been dead for almost a year.

She felt the warmth of milk leaking from her breasts and remembered that her child was dead.

The memory was too painful and she turned away from it, withdrawing once more into that place deep inside where there was only darkness and forgetfulness...

Wolf Dreamer watched her from the corner of his eye. Although he could not read her thoughts, he sensed her pain, sensed the moment when she again retreated into herself.

Rising, he bathed in the shallow pool, then, lifting his arms above his head, he offered his Dawn Song to *Wakan Tanka,* beseeching the Great Spirit for the courage to return to his people, as well as the patience and the wisdom to guide them if they would again accept him in their midst. He prayed for the woman, that she might regain her strength. He prayed that he might win her trust, that she would accept her destiny.

Returning to the campsite, he built a fire with the wood he had gathered along the way. Rummaging through the goods he had taken from the white men, he cut several thick slices of bacon and dropped them into a pan and placed it on the edge of the fire to cook. He filled a coffeepot with water from the river, added a handful of coffee, and set it on the opposite edge of the fire.

In minutes, the air was filled with the tantalizing aroma of frying bacon and coffee.

The woman stirred. Her eyes opened, but she

made no move to rise, simply lay there staring up at the sky, her expression blank.

"Rebecca?"

There was no response. He called her name again, louder this time, and still she did not respond.

Grunting softly, he filled a plate with bacon and some hard biscuits he had found in the soldiers' tent. He poured a cup of coffee and carried both to the woman's side.

Slipping his arm under her, he lifted her into a sitting position. "You must eat."

She stared at him blankly.

"Rebecca. You must eat now." He picked up a piece of bacon and offered it to her.

Obedient as a child, she opened her mouth and took a bite. He fed her half of the bacon and biscuits, then held the cup to her lips so she could drink.

She sat there, unmoving, while he ate, then put out the fire.

Taking her by the hand, he drew her to her feet and led her down to the pool. He removed her clothing and then his own and then led her into the water where he washed her from head to foot.

Awareness flickered in her eyes. She stared at him and then at his hands moving over her skin. Her eyes widened in alarm and she stepped backward, putting herself out of his reach.

"Rebecca, do not be afraid. I will not hurt you."

Crossing her arms over her breasts, she took another step backward.

He held out his hand, palm up in a gesture of appeal. "Come, the air grows cool."

"Don't touch me! You killed those men. So much blood! So much death!" Her voice rose in anguish. "My baby...it was you! You killed my baby!"

He stared at her in horror. "You know I did not! The child was born dead. If not for me, you would have died, too."

"Why didn't I die? Everything you touch dies. Why not me?"

He moved toward her, stunned by her accusations. Was that what she thought? That he had killed her child? How could she think such a thing?

"Don't touch me!" Turning, she tried to run from him, only to stumble and fall as the water swirled around her ankles.

He caught her arm and drew her up against him. Her skin was smooth and cool against his. "Rebecca!"

"No, no!" She beat her fists against his chest. "Let me go! It's all your fault! My baby's dead, oh, my poor poor baby..."

He held her close, willing her to be calm, soothing her with the power of his mind and heart.

She looked up at him, her eyes filling with grief

and with the horror she had suffered at the hands of the cruel men who had killed her husband and sought to defile her.

His gaze met and held hers as he stroked her hair, his mind speaking to hers, comforting her, soothing her tangled thoughts and emotions.

"I'm sorry." She whispered the words as her memory cleared. "I was wrong to blame you."

With a nod, he swung her into his arms and carried her to their campsite where he wrapped her in a blanket. When she was sitting in the sun, he filled the coffee cup and handed it to her, then walked back to the pool.

He pulled on his trousers and even though he had his back to her, he could feel her watching him all the while. Gathering her clothing, he returned to the camp.

She looked at him over the rim of the coffee cup. "Where did you learn to speak English?"

"I learned a little from the white trappers who trade in our village. I learned some of it from listening to you."

Her eyes widened at that. "From me? How? When?"

He hesitated, but decided there would be no secrets between them. "I watched you and your man for several years."

"You spied on us!"

He shook his head. He had not been spying on

her, though he wasn't sure how to convince her
otherwise. "I was drawn to you."

"Drawn to me? Why?"

"I saw you in a vision."

Rebecca drew the blanket closer as a chill ran
down her spine. "You saw me?"

"Yes."

She stared at him for a long moment and then
she drew in a deep breath. She pointed her finger
at him as she released a long shaky sigh. "It's
you." She shook her head. "It can't be, but it is.
You're the man in my dreams."

He frowned at her. "You have dreamed of me?"

She nodded slowly. "You were dancing high on
a mountain. You danced for a long time beneath a
bright yellow moon. And then you turned into a
wolf. A black wolf."

Wolf Dreamer stared at her. No one knew what
he had seen in his vision save Roan Horse, the old
shaman in the village. But this woman knew. Truly,
she was the other half of his soul.

They spent three days in the valley while the
woman recovered her strength. She watched him
warily, careful not to touch him, careful not to let
him touch her. She spoke only when spoken to until
the morning of the fourth day.

He was packing their belongings when he looked
up to find her watching him curiously.

"Do you have family where we are going?"

"My cousin, Red Otter, is there."

"What about your parents?"

"They are dead, and my brother with them, killed by our enemy, the Crow."

"I'm sorry." She paused, then blurted, "You can't really change into a wolf, can you?" she asked.

Wolf Dreamer shook his head. "No, but the wolf is my spirit guide."

She frowned. "Spirit guide?"

"When a warrior comes of age, he seeks a vision to guide him through life."

"How can a wolf guide you through life? Especially a spirit one."

"Wolves are held in high regard by my people. The wolf mates for life. He is a good hunter. He is wise and strong and yet mysterious. His heart is filled with courage. Among my people, it is considered a good thing to follow the ways of the wolf. It is from the wolf that I draw my power."

"So, you worship the wolf?"

"No. We worship *Wakan Tanka*. The Great Spirit. He is the Giver of Life."

"You mean God?"

"Is that the name of the white man's power?"

"Yes. And there's only one God."

"There must be two," Wolf Dreamer said. "For

surely the *wasichu* and the Lakota do not worship the same god.''

''Do you pray to your god?''

Wolf Dreamer nodded. ''Yes, every morning and every evening.''

She mulled that over for a time, her expression pensive. ''Do you believe in heaven?'' At his frown, she said, ''You know, an afterlife?''

''Yes. *Wanagi Yatu,* the Place of Souls. It is a land of many lodges. The hunting is always good there.''

''Do you think...'' Her gaze searched his. ''Do you think I'll see my baby there?''

''Yes.''

He left her to ponder that while he finished packing their gear and saddled their horses.

She looked at him askance when he led her horse over to her. ''Where are we going?''

''I am going back to my people. I have been away too long.''

She felt a twinge of regret at the thought of never seeing him again. He had been kind to her, had saved her life, defended her honor. ''Thank you for helping me.''

He studied her face a moment, then grunted softly. ''This is not goodbye, Rebecca. You are coming with me.''

''No.'' She shook her head vigorously. ''No. I'm going back where I belong.''

"You cannot go back to your house. It is not safe for you there."

"I'm going home," she said. "Back east, where I came from."

"Back east? Where is back east?"

"It's a long way from here. My people are there." The east. She was overcome with longing at the thought of all she had left behind. Proper houses with green lawns and flower gardens. Wide streets and boardwalks. Churches and schools. Stores where she could buy the things she needed. She never should have let Gideon Hathaway talk her into going west. She wasn't cut out to be a frontier woman.

She held out her hand. "I wish you all the best."

He looked at her hand a moment, then lifted her onto the back of her horse. "I cannot let you travel to this back-east place alone," he said, handing her the reins. "You will come with me."

"No. I'm going home."

"You are my destiny, Rebecca. You will be the mother of my son."

She stared at him, her eyes wide. "I am not your destiny! I never heard of such nonsense."

"I saw you in my vision."

"I don't care."

"You saw me in your dreams."

"I...but..." She shook her head and squared her shoulders. "It doesn't matter. I don't believe in

dreams. I'm going home and you can't stop me."
She said the last defiantly, and even as she said it,
she knew it wasn't true. He could easily stop her.

She knew it.

And so did he.

With a sigh of mock resignation, she followed
him out of the valley. For now, she would pretend
she had no choice. But only for now.

Chapter 7

"Tell me more about your people," Rebecca said. They were crossing a wide stretch of grassland. A pair of eagles soared effortlessly overhead, making lazy circles in the sky.

"What do you wish to know?"

"Are there other spirit guides besides wolves?"

"Of course."

"Like bears and mountain lions?"

"Mountain lions are bad signs and mean you are being stalked."

"I see. What about other animals?"

"Badgers are good signs. They offer protection and warn of danger. Bears are good signs. They represent wisdom and strength. The buffalo is also a good sign. He possesses strong power. Coyote is a trickster, now good, now bad. You cannot trust him. The elk is a strong protector of women. It is a good sign if a woman sees an elk. Fox is a bad sign and warns of danger or sickness, but there are shamans who can use the power of the fox for good. Raccoons are good signs. When one needs help to solve a problem, it is a good idea to make a prayer to the raccoon.''

Rebecca shook her head. Pray to a raccoon! Was he serious?

''Skunks are bad signs. Witches use the power of the skunk to cause conflict and sickness.'' Wolf Dreamer glanced up at the sky. ''Eagles are always a good sign. They represent wealth, wisdom, strength and spirituality. If an eagle comes near you when you are praying, your prayer will be answered.

''Owls are bad signs. They are messengers of evil, sickness and death. If you hear an owl hooting near your lodge, it means someone will die. Like the skunk, the power of the owl is often used by witches.

''Ravens and crows are good signs and bring good luck. Ravens can travel between this world and the next. Hawks warn of danger.

''Antelopes are messengers. If you see many of them together, it often means you will soon meet many people. A doe means that you will meet a new woman. If you see antelope fighting, it is a warning that you may soon find yourself in conflict with another.''

Rebecca shook her head. ''You don't really believe all that, do you? It's just a lot of superstitious nonsense.''

''Are there no superstitions among your people? Is there nothing you believe in?''

Rebecca thought about that for a moment, remembering that whenever her mother spilled the salt, she threw a pinch over her shoulder to counteract the bad luck, and how her father always had a horseshoe nailed above the door of the barn to avert bad luck. And then there was the notion that black cats and broken mirrors brought misfortune. They had moved into a new house when Rebecca was nine and she recalled that her mother had bought a new broom for good luck.

''Yes,'' she admitted, ''I suppose we have our own superstitions.''

''My people believe that we are all related,'' Wolf Dreamer said. ''Animals, birds, fish, insects, the earth itself. If I can pray to the Great Spirit, why should I not also speak to my brother the wolf?''

She had no answer for that and silence fell between them once more.

They rode for hours. The sun was warm on her

back. A sea of grass spread out before them, stirred by a gentle summer breeze. A trickle of sweat rolled down her back; milk stained the front of her dress. Her breasts were heavy, a constant reminder of what she had lost. She blinked back her tears, but they would not be stayed.

At the sound of her tears, Wolf Dreamer reined his horse to a stop. Dismounting, he lifted Rebecca from the saddle and wrapped her in his arms.

She rested her cheek against his chest and let the tears flow. She had lost everything she had ever loved, everything she cared for, and now she wanted nothing more than to return to the place of her birth, to her family, to the people who knew and understood her.

Wolf Dreamer's hand, big yet gentle, stroked her hair. His voice murmured to her, soft words of comfort, and though she did not understand his words, she understood the meaning, and cried all the harder, knowing she would miss this strange man when they parted ways.

They rested often after that. Wolf Dreamer silently cursed himself for not being more considerate of the woman's weakness. She had given birth not long ago, laid the child in the ground. She could not be expected to ride from sunrise to sunset without resting.

He made camp far earlier than he would have normally, insisted she rest while he gathered wood for the fire, then filled their canteens from a nearby stream. He prepared the food and served it to her, then sat across from her, the fire between them.

When they finished eating, he added wood to the fire and insisted she lie down. She was asleep within minutes.

He watched her for a long while. Her hair gleamed like bright mahogany in the light of the flames. There were dark shadows under her eyes.

They were different in so many ways; he knew in his heart she was meant to be his and yet...what if the People would not accept her? She was *wasichu* and therefore the enemy. But she had saved his life, and he was counting on that to make the difference. The People would honor and respect her for her courage if for no other reason.

After checking on the horses, he crawled under the blankets, content to lie beside her, to feel the warmth of her body, inhale the scent of her hair, her skin, listen to the soft sound of her breathing.

He closed his eyes. Soon, he thought, soon she would be his.

They traveled for several days across the prairie, seeing no one. Each day, upon rising, Rebecca told herself that she would find a way to escape before nightfall, but somehow she could never summon the energy. Lethargic and depressed, she ate and slept when she was told, too lost in her own grief to give heed to anything else.

It was only when they reached the foot of the mountain that Wolf Dreamer called home that fear took hold of her. His people lived here. People that believed in an alien god and prayed to animals.

She thought of her dream, of the huge black wolf that pursued her. She had always considered it to be nothing more than a nightmare that came to her time and again, but Wolf Dreamer believed dreams were more than just dreams. He believed in spirits and visions. If such things indeed foretold the future, and he was the wolf in her nightmare, didn't that mean her life was in danger?

She shook off the apathy that had held her in its grasp since her baby died. If she was ever going to get away from Wolf Dreamer, it would have to be now, before it was too late. Before they arrived at his village.

Tonight. It would have to be tonight.

She went to bed right after dinner. Huddled beneath the blanket, she closed her eyes. Heart pounding, she pretended to sleep. She listened to his footsteps as he moved around the fire, heard him speak softly to the horses as he checked on them. A tingle of awareness washed over her as he slid under the covers beside her. She could feel the heat of him, smell the acrid scent of smoke in his hair.

How long would it take him to fall asleep? How would she know when it was safe to leave? How would she travel all the way back east alone? She had no money, no clothes except what she was wearing now...

Suddenly, striking out on her own didn't seem like such a good idea after all and yet, what other choice did she have if she wanted to get back east, where she belonged?

Wolf Dreamer would not take her, so she had no choice but to go alone.

She could do it. She had lived alone in the middle of nowhere for six months and survived. She would find her way to a town, then telegraph her parents. They would send her the money she needed to get back home.

She smiled into the darkness. All she had to do was find a town.

It seemed like hours passed before Wolf Dreamer's breathing grew slow and steady. Moving carefully, she slid out from under the blankets and gained her feet. As quietly as she could, she saddled her horse, hooked one of the canteens over the pommel. Inch by slow inch, she eased one of the blankets off Wolf Dreamer, rolled it into a cylinder and lashed it behind the saddle. Feeling guilty, she picked up the bag of foodstuffs and tied it to the saddle horn, then gathered her horse's reins and walked away from the camp.

Her heart was pounding with excitement and the thrill of success as she pulled herself onto her horse's back and turned it toward the east.

"Home." She whispered the word over and over again as a talisman to fight off her fear of the dark. "Home." Back to Mama and Papa, where she belonged.

Wolf Dreamer sat up and stared into the darkness, listening to the sound of hoofbeats fade into the distance.

Foolish woman, to strike out on her own in the middle of the night.

Foolish man, to chase a woman who did not want him.

Rising, he saddled his horse and went after her.

He was coming. She didn't know how she knew it with such certainty. She heard nothing. When she glanced over her shoulder, she saw nothing. But she knew he was there.

Panic bubbled up inside her. If he caught her now, she would never get away. Leaning low over her horse's neck, she drummed her heels into its flanks.

"Hurry!" she whispered. "Hurry! Hurry!"

The mare lined out in a dead run, her hooves

skimming over the ground as she fairly flew over the dark prairie.

Rebecca held fast to the reins in one hand and the mare's mane in the other. She knew it was dangerous to race through the darkness. A rock, a slight rise, a prairie dog hole, all could spell disaster and yet she raced onward, away from the strange man pursuing her, away from feelings she did not want to acknowledge, away from a future that was more frightening than the thought of being lost in the dark.

The moon slid out from beneath the clouds that had gathered at sundown. She felt a surge of relief as silver moonlight lit her way across the vast grassland.

It was a good sign, she thought, and then, to her horror, she saw a large gray wolf silhouetted in the moonlight.

Moments later, she heard the sound of hoofbeats coming up rapidly behind her and knew that her illusion of freedom was just that, an illusion.

She urged her horse to go faster, looked for a place to hide, but to no avail.

Resigned, she put up no resistance when he rode up alongside her and grabbed hold of her horse's bridle.

When they came to a stop, he looked at her. "Why, Rebecca?"

"Because I want to go home."

"Your home will be with me from now on," he said.

"I will live with you, because I have no other choice," she said dully. "But it will never be home."

Chapter 8

Rebecca stared at the Indian lodges that were spread in a wide circle in a high mountain meadow. A winding river made a dark ribbon of blue against the green grass. Stands of tall timber provided wood for their fires. She saw men and women engaged in a number of activities. Children ran between the lodges or swam in the river. Dogs slept in the shade. A little boy was throwing a stick for a puppy. Thin columns of blue-gray smoke rose from several conical tipis. Horses grazed on the thick grass, or stood head to tail, heads drooping in the sun.

It was a peaceful scene and yet it filled her with trepidation. She would be a stranger here, an outsider. The enemy.

She glanced at Wolf Dreamer, surprised to see that he, too, seemed filled with trepidation. While she was wondering at its cause, he urged his horse forward.

Taking a deep breath, she followed him toward the village. She looked down at her dress. The hem was torn and dirty, the bodice was stained with milk. She lifted a hand to her hair. It was dirty and hung in a tangled mess down her back and over her shoulders. She wished suddenly that she had a clean dress, that she could wash and comb her hair, and then wondered why she cared. She didn't want to be here with them, and she was certain they would not want her here.

Men, women and children looked up as they rode into the camp. Most of the people looked surprised, a few merely curious. As though drawn by the same string, they fell into step behind Wolf Dreamer's horse and followed him through the camp.

He pulled up in front of a large tipi that was decorated with stars and moons and a brilliant yellow sun. A faint whisper of gray smoke rose from the smoke hole.

Wolf Dreamer had no sooner dismounted than a man stepped out of the lodge. He was a very old man. His face was lined and wrinkled, his hair completely gray.

He stared at Wolf Dreamer through watery black eyes.

Rebecca's gaze moved over the people who had gathered around. No one spoke. Even the children were quiet.

A long sigh escaped the old Indian's lips. "*Wolf Dreamer* has returned to us. Truly, *Wakan Tanka* has answered my prayers this day." Taking a step forward, the old man embraced Wolf Dreamer. "*Hohahe, le mita kola.*" Welcome, my friend.

"*Pilamaya, leksi.*"

"Your lodge awaits you."

"How did you know...?"

"The spirits told me you were coming." The old man looked up at Rebecca. His gaze moved over her for a long time and then he nodded. "So, you have found her."

Wolf Dreamer nodded. "It is as the gray wolf foretold. She is the other half of my soul. She will be the mother of my son."

"She does not want to be here."

"No."

Rebecca frowned. It was obvious they were discussing her; she only wished she knew what they were saying.

The old man lifted his arms. "My people, Wolf Dreamer has returned to us. Make him welcome. He has brought a stranger into our midst. She is the woman of his vision and must be accorded respect and honor."

At his words, all the people looked at her, their

expressions guarded but not unkind save for one
woman who stood on the edge of the crowd. She
was tall and slender, with finely shaped features and
thick waist-length black hair tied with a bit of red
cloth into a single braid that fell over her left shoulder. When the Indian woman looked at Rebecca,
her eyes were filled with hatred.

The old man placed his arm across Wolf
Dreamer's shoulder. "Wolf Dreamer has returned
to take his rightful place among us as shaman to
the People of the High Mountain."

A ripple of noise ran through the crowd as the
people came forward to grasp Wolf Dreamer's
hand. Some embraced him. The woman with the
braid did not come forward to greet him. Hands
clenched at her sides, the woman stared at Wolf
Dreamer, her black eyes filled with such longing it
made Rebecca's heart ache.

Wolf Dreamer introduced her to his cousin, Red
Otter, and his wife, White Deer Woman. Neither of
them spoke English. Rebecca nodded at them and
smiled. How would she ever feel at home here? The
Lakota didn't speak her language, and she doubted
she would ever learn to speak theirs.

When the people dispersed, Wolf Dreamer lifted
Rebecca from the back of her horse.

"What did that old man say about me?" she
asked.

"Roan Horse told the people to make you welcome. Come, let us go down to the river and bathe. My cousin's wife will bring us soap and a change of clothes.''

"Who was that woman?"

"What woman?"

"The one standing by herself. She was the only one who didn't come forward to welcome you home. Why?"

An expression she could not read flitted across his face and was gone.

"Her name is Summer Moon Rising."

"She's in love with you, isn't she?" Rebecca asked, surprised that the notion caused her a sharp pang of jealousy.

"I thought so, once."

"What happened?"

"She married my best friend."

"Why?"

"I wish to bathe," he said, taking her hand. "Come."

The thought of bathing with him chased everything else from her mind, though why she should feel embarrassed at the idea, she could not say. She had seen him naked before. He had watched her give birth. But bathing together...it implied an intimacy she did not wish to pursue.

He led her away from the village to a bend in the river that was screened from view by tall shrubs and cottonwoods.

With no concern for his nudity or the fact that it was broad daylight, he began to strip off his moccasins and trousers.

Rebecca turned her back.

She heard a splash as he waded into the river.

A few minutes later, White Deer Woman appeared carrying a pile of clothing. The plump woman smiled at Rebecca as she placed the clean clothes on top of a rock, waved at Wolf Dreamer, and went back the way she had come.

"The water is warm," Wolf Dreamer called.

"I'll wash later, after you get out."

"It is common for my people to bathe together."

"Well, I'm not one of 'your' people, and it isn't common for me."

"Come, Rebecca, I have already seen all of you there is to see."

The thought brought a hot rush of blood to her cheeks, but she stood her ground, trying not to remember that she had seen him naked before, trying not to remember the breadth of his shoulders, the long clean lines of his arms and legs, the smooth copper color of his skin.

"Rebecca," he called softly. "Will you bring me the soap?"

"Soap?" She glanced around, then saw a small yellow lump on top of the clothes the woman had brought.

Picking it up, she walked backwards toward the river. "Here," she said, and tossed it behind her.

The sound of his laughter filled the air.

She stared into the distance, trying not to imagine what was going on behind her. She heard splashing as he walked out of the water and fought down the urge to turn and look at him, to see if he was as beautiful as she remembered.

She didn't hear him move, but she sensed he was standing behind her. His arm reached around her waist and she saw the soap in his hand. Careful not to touch him, she picked it up.

"Go away," she said.

"As you wish." His breath was warm against her cheek. "For now."

She waited until he was out of sight, then undressed quickly and waded into the river. The bottom was smooth and sandy and squished between her toes. The water was indeed warm and she lingered there, enjoying the feel of it against her bare skin as it swirled around her.

It was a pretty place. Sunlight filtered through the leaves of the trees and glinted on the surface of the water. Birds flitted from branch to branch. A small gray squirrel starred down at her, chattering loudly. She gave a little shriek, then laughed self-consciously as a small silver fish darted past her leg.

Time and again, she glanced at the shore to make

sure she was alone. She was wading out of the river when she saw someone making off with her dress and petticoats.

She shouted, "Hey! Come back here!" then stamped her foot when she realized the thief probably didn't understand English and probably wouldn't have stopped if she did.

Rebecca stared after the woman. It had been Summer Moon Rising, she was sure of it.

The whisper of the wind across her bare breasts reminded her that she was naked and she backed up until the water again covered her up to her shoulders. Now what? She wasn't about to go traipsing back to the village stark-naked.

She lost track of the time as she huddled there, felt a surge of relief when she heard Wolf Dreamer call her name.

"I'm here!" she shouted.

He strolled into view, a pile of clothing over his arm. "I am sorry," he said. "She will not bother you again."

Wolf Dreamer dropped a doeskin dress and a length of cotton cloth on a rock, then turned his back so she could get out of the water. He was sorely tempted to glance over his shoulder, but he restrained himself, knowing she would not approve. He puzzled over her modesty. He had watched her in childbirth. What could be more intimate than that?

He heard the whisper of cloth against her skin, wished he had the right to take her in his arms and caress her. For years, she had filled his thoughts and haunted his dreams. Knowing she belonged to another had cooled neither his ardor nor his desire. Many times he had been tempted to swoop down and steal her away from her *wasichu* husband, but always he had restrained himself, knowing the time was not yet right for them to be together.

But there was nothing to keep them apart now.

Slowly, he turned to face her. He had never seen anything more beautiful, he thought, than Rebecca as she looked now, clad in a simple, ankle-length dress of sun-bleached doeskin. There were moccasins on her feet. Her hair, still damp, fell over her shoulders in dark red waves. The setting sun tinged her skin with a faint golden glow.

She flushed under his steady regard.

"Come," he said. "The wife of Roan Horse has prepared food for us."

She smoothed a hand over her skirt, then followed him back to the village. The doeskin felt strange against her bare skin. She felt naked without her chemise, petticoats, stockings and shoes.

She followed him back to the village, aware that she was being scrutinized by everyone she passed.

Wolf Dreamer stopped in front of a large tipi. Rebecca perused the drawings on the lodgeskins. There were several scenes, all depicting wolves—a wolf howling at a bright yellow moon, a wolf sitting on a pinnacle, staring out over a broad valley, a wolf standing over a kill, teeth bared.

Lifting the flap, he gestured for her to enter, then followed her inside.

A fire burned in a small round pit in the center of the lodge. Buffalo robes were spread on the ground around the firepit. Several hide containers were stacked in the back of the tipi. A shield hung from a pole in the back of the lodge, together with several rawhide bags and pouches. Wood was stacked beside the door.

"My shield is sacred," Wolf Dreamer said, pointing to it. "You must not touch it."

Two bowls and two cups rested near the edge of the firepit.

"Sit," Wolf Dreamer said, indicating a willow backrest on one side of the fire. "Your place is always there, to the left of the fire."

"Why can't I sit on that side?"

"It is customary for women to sit on the south side of the lodge. When entering a lodge, men go to the right and women to the left. If possible, you must not pass between a seated person and the fire."

"Whose tipi is this?"

"It is mine. Sit. Eat."

"Yours?" She sat down where he had indicated, noting, as she did so, that there was a quiver of arrows hanging from one of the lodgepoles in the back of the tipi. "I thought you said you'd been away for a long time. Has your tipi been waiting for you all the while you were gone?"

"No. Roan Horse's spirit guide told him we were coming today."

"Of course," she said skeptically, yet she couldn't deny the tipi had been here, waiting for them. She picked up one of the bowls and stirred it with the spoon. "What is this?"

"Venison stew." He lifted a small piece of meat from his bowl, murmured something she did not understand, and placed the meat in the fire.

"What are you doing?"

"It is an offering to the spirit of the deer." He took a bite. "From now on, you will be expected to do the cooking. You will also gather the wood and the water."

"Oh I will, will I?"

He nodded. "It is woman's work."

"You did it before."

"Because it was necessary. It is not necessary now."

"How long are you going to keep me here?"

"The ways of my people will seem strange to you, but we are not savages, as the *wasichu* believe. Though our customs are different from yours, you will soon get used to them."

"I don't want to get used to them. I want to go home."

"No. Your destiny is here, with me."

"Isn't that for me to decide?"

"I saw you in my vision..."

"And I saw you in a dream. A nightmare! That doesn't mean anything."

The look in his eyes told her it meant everything.

She dreamt of the black wolf that night. It was the same dream as always save for one difference. This time, when he chased her, he caught her. She felt his weight bear her down to the ground. She rolled over and found him standing over her, his forelegs on either side of her shoulders. His breath was hot on her face as she stared up into his deep golden-brown eyes. She tried to tell herself that there was nothing to be afraid of. It was only a dream...only a dream. She closed her eyes and when she opened them again, it was Wolf Dreamer bending over her, his face close to hers, his eyes alight with desire....

She woke, breathless, her body warm with wanting. Sitting up, she glanced across the floor of the lodge. In the faint light of the coals, she could see him on the other side of the lodge, sleeping. He had thrown off his sleeping robe; her gaze moved slowly over his broad back and shoulders. She knew an overpowering urge to run her fingertips over his skin, to delve into the thick blackness of his hair, to trace the line of his jaw.

She curled her hands into tight fists, turned on her side, and stared at the wall of the tipi. Even when she closed her eyes, she couldn't escape him. It was all too easy to summon his image from memory, to imagine her fingertips playing over his copper-hued skin, to imagine his mouth on hers, his hands caressing her...

She groaned softly. Why did he tempt her so? Though she would never admit it, he was constantly in her thoughts, making her yearn for that which was forbidden, making her wonder what it would be like to hold him, to touch him, to be held and touched in return. Perhaps it was only because it was forbidden that he consumed her thoughts and troubled her dreams.

He was awake. She knew it without knowing how. He had made no sound, spoken no word, yet she knew he was awake. Awake and watching her.

Her heartbeat quickened and she sucked in a deep breath, loosed it in a long shuddering sigh.

"Rebecca."

His voice moved over her, soft as dandelion down yet filled with longing.

She didn't move, didn't reply. Only waited...

There was a faint whisper of cloth over skin as he eased out of his sleeping robe and padded toward her. She sensed him looming over her, waiting.

Unable to resist, she rolled onto her back and gazed up at him.

Taking that as leave to do so, he knelt beside her and slipped under the covers beside her.

His nearness made her tremble. Did he mean to ravish her? The thought filled her with panic. It was too soon, too soon.

"Do not be afraid," he said quietly. "I want only to hold you close, nothing more."

He slid his arm beneath her neck and drew her body against his. Unwilling to lie naked in a strange place, she had worn her doeskin dress to bed. He wore nothing save for a breechcloth. Despite the clothing that separated them, she felt the heat of his arousal.

"Go to sleep, Rebecca." He lifted a lock of her hair and wrapped it around his finger. "You have nothing to fear from me."

She was certain she would never be able to sleep with him so close beside her yet her eyelids felt suddenly heavy, so heavy.

When she opened them again, it was morning and she was alone in the lodge.

Chapter 9

Wolf Dreamer was returning to the camp when Summer Moon Rising stepped onto the path, blocking his way.

"I did not have a chance to welcome you home yesterday." Her voice was as low and throaty as he recalled.

"You could have come forward with the others."

"I could have," she agreed, "but I wanted to save my welcome for a time when we could be alone."

"I did not see Elk Chaser yesterday."

She lowered her gaze. "Elk Chaser has gone to the land of his ancestors."

"Was it a good death?"

She nodded. "It was a brave one. He was killed while defending our village from an attack by the Crow."

With a nod, Wolf Dreamer took a step forward, intending to move past her.

She stayed him with a hand on his arm. "Wait."

Slowly, deliberately, he removed her hand from his arm. "We have no more to say to each other."

"Do not hate me, Wolf Dreamer. I was wrong to refuse you. I know that now, and I am ready to be your woman."

"I have a woman."

"That *wasicun?*" she asked scornfully. "She is your woman?"

He nodded.

"Get rid of her. The People will never accept her. She will never be one of us."

"She is mine. I will have no other."

"I lost you once," Summer Moon Rising declared, her dark eyes flashing. "I will not lose you a second time."

"Listen to me. You will not touch her. Do you understand?"

"I said nothing about hurting her."

"If any harm comes to her, you will regret it."

Summer Moon Rising made a derisive sound low in her throat. "She is not worthy of you."

"You will return that which you took from her."

"I took nothing."

"I can read the lie in your eyes. Return her clothing by nightfall."

She stared at him, her expression defiant, yet he read the fear in her eyes, the uncertainty. Everyone knew he was destined to be the next shaman and that, as such, he possessed power over good and evil.

Without another word, she turned and disappeared into the woods that lined the path.

Wolf Dreamer stared after her. Once, he had thought to share his life with her. Now, he felt nothing but pity for her and relief that she had refused him.

Banishing Summer Moon Rising from his mind, he walked swiftly up the path toward the village and Rebecca.

Rebecca looked up as someone raised the lodge flap, felt her heart skip a beat as Wolf Dreamer stepped into the lodge. He was so incredibly handsome, she couldn't stifle the quiver of excitement that slid down her spine whenever she saw him, but it was more than that. Even though he was keeping her here against her will, she felt safe with him. He had saved her from death and worse. He was the only constant in her life, the only protection she had in this strange new place.

He paused just inside the doorway, his gaze meeting hers.

Warmth flowed between them, made her skin tingle and her toes curl. Her mouth was suddenly dry and she licked her lips, clenched her hands at her sides to keep from reaching for him.

He took a step toward her, his golden-brown eyes glowing, until she saw nothing but him. Wanted nothing but him.

There was an ache deep within her, a need she'd never known before, a hunger that frightened her.

She gazed up at him, her heart beating so loudly in her ears she was surprised he didn't hear it, too.

He lifted his hand, then hesitated, giving her time to back away if that was what she wanted. When she stayed her ground, he slipped his arms around her waist and drew her up against him.

"Rebecca, can you not feel that this is right, that we were meant to be together?"

"I'm not sure what I feel," she replied quietly. "All I know is that I'll die if you don't kiss me."

"Kiss?" He frowned at her. "What is kiss?"

"Don't you know?"

At his look of confusion, she drew his head down and touched her lips to his.

Startled, he jerked his head back. "That is a kiss?"

"Yes."

He grunted softly, then lowered his head and covered her mouth with his.

He learned very quickly.

She was breathless when he drew back. She had been fighting her attraction to him since the first time they met, but she couldn't fight it any longer. Right or wrong, she cared deeply for him.

"I think we should do that again," he remarked. "What do you think?"

"Oh, yes," she murmured, her hands clutching his shoulders. "We should definitely..."

His kiss cut off the rest of her words, but she didn't mind. Going up on her tiptoes, she pressed herself against him, loving the way they fit together, loving the way his hard muscular body cradled her softer one.

Her hands slid down his back, skimmed his taut buttocks, then slid up to cling to his shoulders once again as her knees went weak.

He held her tight with one arm, letting his free hand slide up and down her back before he cupped her breast.

She moaned softly and leaned into him.

"Rebecca..." He took a deep breath and put her away from him. She had given birth only a short time ago. As much as he yearned to possess her, he knew it was too soon. Her body had not yet recovered from childbirth. And yet, even if the time had been right, he knew in his heart he would not take her to his bed, not until she was his woman according to the custom of his people. She would be the mother of his son. He would not bed her until she was truly his wife.

He grinned wryly as she released a long shuddering sigh. It was good to know she wanted him as badly as he wanted her.

He clasped her hand in his. "Will you be my woman, Rebecca?"

"What do you mean?"

"Will you share my life and my lodge? Will you bear my children?"

"Are you asking me to marry you?"

"Yes."

"Oh, my." She looked deep into his eyes, those strange golden-brown eyes. Marry him. How could she? He was an Indian; she was a white woman. His ties were here; hers were in the east. He was a warrior, a man destined to be a leader among his people. His people would never accept her. Even if she learned their language, adopted their customs, she would never be one of them.

How could she marry him?

How could she refuse?

He squeezed her hand. "Rebecca?"

"I don't know. I'm afraid…"

"Of me?"

"No!"

"My people?"

She nodded. "I don't belong here. I never will."

"If I accept you, my people will also accept you." Yet even as he said the words, he wondered if he spoke the truth.

* * *

Early that afternoon, Roan Horse summoned Wolf Dreamer to his lodge.

"What do you think he wants?" Rebecca asked.

Wolf Dreamer shrugged. "I will go and find out."

Roan Horse's woman left the lodge when Wolf Dreamer entered.

"Come, sit." Roan Horse gestured for him to sit down. Lifting his pipe, he puffed on it and handed it to Wolf Dreamer, who took a puff and handed it back to Roan Horse. They passed the pipe back and forth four times, then Roan Horse set it aside.

"It is good to be back with the People, yes?" Roan Horse asked.

Wolf Dreamer nodded.

"I knew you would return, when you were ready."

"Did you?"

"I saw you in a vision. You were searching for the red-haired woman. I knew you would return when you found her, and you did."

Wolf Dreamer nodded.

"It is time for you to take over as shaman for the People of the High Mountain."

"No. You have many years left."

Roan Horse shook his head slowly. "I waited only for your return. Tomorrow, I will travel *Wanagi Tacaka* to the Place of Souls. My ancestors will be waiting for me there. We will smoke the pipe and talk of the good old days."

Wolf Dreamer stared at the old man, speechless. He did not doubt Roan Horse's words for a moment. He had known too many Old Ones who had set their faces toward death and gone to meet it. "I am not ready."

"You will do well, as long as you do not stray from the Life Path of the People. Tonight, we will have a sweat. Tomorrow, you will be ready."

With a nod, Wolf Dreamer left the old man's tipi.

Rebecca was waiting for him outside when he returned to his own lodge. "What did Roan Horse want? Is everything all right?"

"I am to meet him later for a sweat."

"A sweat?"

"It is a ceremony of purification."

"Oh."

"It is a sacred thing, not to be taken lightly." As a child, he had learned that the sweat lodge represented the womb of Mother Earth. The darkness within was man's ignorance. The hot stones represented the coming of life, the hissing sound of the water hitting the stones was the power of creation. Earth, air, water and fire were all represented within the lodge.

"What else?"

He shook his head.

"What else did he say? Why do you look so sad? Is something wrong?"

"Roan Horse will die tomorrow."

"How can you know that?"

"He has set his face toward death."

"But...people don't die just because they want to." If they did, she wouldn't be here now, she thought, remembering how she had yearned for death when she learned her baby had been born dead. "That's impossible."

"You will see."

Rebecca walked slowly along the edge of the timberline, pausing now and then to pick up a piece of wood for the fire. Wolf Dreamer had left to meet Roan Horse over an hour ago. She wondered exactly what went on in a "sweat" and why it was considered holy and if he would tell her about it when he returned.

She bent down to pick up another piece of wood and when she turned around to start back toward the village, Summer Moon Rising was blocking her path, her eyes filled with anger and jealousy.

Refusing to be intimidated by the other woman, Rebecca lifted her chin, squared her shoulders, and started walking up the path. Summer Moon Rising stood her ground and as Rebecca drew alongside, Summer Moon Rising gave her a hard push. She was thrown off-balance and the wood tumbled from her grasp.

With a malicious laugh, Summer Moon Rising turned and ran down toward the river.

With a sigh of frustration, Rebecca began picking up the wood she had dropped.

Wolf Dreamer closed his eyes as Roan Horse's wife poured cold water over the hot stones. It had been years since he had participated in a sweat. He had observed it all as if it were the first time. A small pit called *iniowaspe* had been dug to hold the heated stones; the floor of the lodge was covered with sweet sage. The earth that had been removed from the *iniowaspe* was formed into a small mound, which was called *hanbelachia,* or the vision hill. An area between the vision hill and the pit was cleared and this was known as the smoothed trail, which was a representation of a vision quest.

Roan Horse had placed offerings of tiny bundles of tobacco on the hill, along with the pipe that would be used during the ceremony.

And now Wolf Dreamer sat across from Roan Horse while Roan Horse's wife ladled cold water over the hot stones. A great hissing sound filled the air; great clouds of steam filled the lodge.

Perspiration poured from Wolf Dreamer's body. The bitter taste of sage was on his tongue, sweat stung his eyes.

Roan Horse chanted softly.

The pipe was passed between them four times.

Water was ladled on the hot rocks four times.

The sacred songs were repeated four times.

Reality faded into the distance as he was swallowed up in the thick steamy blackness. And then, out of the dark mist, a gray wolf appeared. Tail wagging, tongue lolling out of the side of its mouth, it stared at Wolf Dreamer through amber eyes.

You need not fear to lead the People, the wolf said. *They will accept you as their shaman. They will accept your woman. Only be true to the lessons you have been taught and all will be well.*

Wolf Dreamer nodded.

The gray wolf shook his head and bared his fangs. *Beware Summer Moon Rising.*

With that warning, the gray wolf faded into the mists from whence it had come. At the same time, Roan Horse lifted the door flap, admitting a blast of fresh sweet air.

Wolf Dreamer followed Roan Horse out of the lodge, where they rubbed themselves with sweet sage, then plunged into the river.

The cold water should have come as a shock, but it didn't. Coming up out of the water, Wolf Dreamer felt at peace, light in heart and mind.

Until he started for the shore and found Summer Moon Rising standing there.

Chapter 10

She watched him as he stepped out of the water. Roan Horse's gaze flickered between them, and then he followed the narrow path that led back to his lodge.

"What are you doing here?" Wolf Dreamer asked when they were alone.

"I wanted to see you." Her gaze traveled boldly over his body as she walked toward him, his clout swinging from one hand. "I know you are angry with me for marrying Elk Chaser, but you must forgive me."

"I am not angry with you." He snatched his clout from her hand. "If it is my forgiveness you want, you have it."

"I want to be your woman," she said, her voice low and husky. "Let us be together, as we were meant to be."

He shook his head. "It we were meant to be together, we would be together now. You did not want to be a part of my life when it was offered to you. Nothing has changed, Summer Moon. I possess the same powers that once frightened you. Tomorrow, I will become the shaman of our people, and those powers will grow stronger."

"I was wrong to refuse you. I know that now. I am older now, and wiser. Will you not give us another chance?"

"I cannot. I saw Rebecca in vision. She is to be my woman."

"If you care for her, send her away before it is too late. She will never be happy here," Summer Moon Rising remarked. She placed her hands on his shoulders and looked deep into his eyes. "She will never belong here."

The words cut into his heart. They were the same words Rebecca had said.

"I cannot send her away."

"Then keep her as a slave, if you must have her, but do not let her come between us."

A muffled footstep caught Wolf Dreamer's attention. Looking past Summer Moon Rising, he saw Rebecca standing a few feet away, her eyes wide as she took in the scene before her.

Knowing how it must look, he felt a rush of guilt, even though he had done nothing wrong.

Summer Moon Rising glanced over her shoulder, a malignant smile curving her lips when she saw the white woman. She let her hand slide down Wolf Dreamer's bare chest in a gesture that was boldly possessive before clutching his shoulders again.

Muttering an oath he had learned from the whites, Wolf Dreamer pried her fingers from his flesh and took a step backward.

Summer Moon Rising grabbed his arm. "Do not go."

He shook off her hand. "Leave me! You have caused enough trouble for one day."

Summer Moon Rising sauntered up the path that led to the village. When she drew even with Rebecca, she paused long enough to give her a smug smile, then continued on her way.

"Rebecca."

She turned her back to him. "Get dressed."

He frowned, then looked down at the clout in his hand. He donned it quickly, then went to Rebecca. When he placed his hand on her shoulder, she slipped out from under it and turned to look at him.

"Rebecca…"

"I thought you said there was nothing between the two of you?"

"You do not believe me?"

She lifted a skeptical brow. "I think there's

plenty going on between you. I suspect if I had gotten here sooner, I would have found her naked, too.''

His eyes widened in surprise. ''You think that we...'' He shook his head. ''I would as soon sleep with a wounded she-bear as share my blankets with that woman.''

''What did she want?''

''She wants to be my wife. She said I could keep you as my slave, if I could not let you go.''

''Slave!'' Disbelief and fury blazed from the depths of her eyes. ''You expect me to be your slave?''

He had thought to make her laugh with the foolishness of it. He had not meant to arouse her anger. ''Rebecca...''

''I will not stay here and be your slave!''

He closed the distance between them, his hands folding over her arms. ''Listen to me...''

''No! I'm leaving, and don't you try to stop me!''

''Rebecca!''

His hand tightened on her forearm, his grip like iron. ''I want no other woman. I will have no other woman. If you will not be mine, then I will live my life alone.''

She blinked up at him, her anger fading in the face of his declaration. ''I know you care for me, Wolf Dreamer, but do you love me?''

''How can you doubt it?''

"I guess I was just jealous, seeing the two of you together...you..." Heat climbed into her cheeks. "You with no clothes on. I thought...never mind what I thought."

"I think we must marry soon," Wolf Dreamer said.

The thought excited her almost as much as it frightened her.

Wolf Dreamer spent the rest of the afternoon instructing her in the ways of his people. All living things had spirits of their own—animals, trees, the mountains, rivers, the tall grasses that covered the prairie, even the earth itself. The people worshipped *Wakan Tanka.* He was the Great Spirit, the creator of all living. Four was a sacred number, as there were four other gods under *Wakan Tanka: Inyan,* the Rock, *Maka,* the Earth, *Skan,* the Sky, and *Wi,* the Sun. There were four directions to the earth, four seasons to the year.

He told her that, once they were married, the lodge and all its belongings would be hers, save for his clothing and his weapons. Her duties would be to keep the lodge clean, cook the meals, keep the fire going, sew and mend their clothing, gather the wood and the water, rear their children.

"And what will *you* do?" It was a foolish question, but one she could not resist. Her duties as the wife of an Indian man were the same ones she had shouldered as Gideon's wife.

"I will fill your lodge with meat and protect you from our enemies."

"And what will you do when you are shaman?"

"I will guide the people. I will heal their wounds. I will interpret the dreams of those who have had visions and determine when it is time to move the camp. I will make courting flutes for the young men..."

"Courting flutes?"

Wolf Dreamer nodded. "Flutes are *wakan,*" he said. "Holy, when made by one with power..."

"Someone like you?"

"Yes. When a young man is in love, he goes to a holy man for a flute. The shaman makes him a flute and gives him a song that will win the heart of the woman he wishes to court."

"So," Rebecca said, grinning, "it's like magic?"

"Yes," Wolf Dreamer agreed. "Magic."

"Did you play a magic flute for Summer Moon Rising?" Rebecca asked, unable to keep the jealousy out of her voice.

"No."

"Why not? What happened between you? Why did she marry someone else?"

"Soon after we agreed to marry, I went to seek a vision. It was then that my spirit guide came to me..."

"The gray wolf?"

"Yes. It was then I learned that I would be the next shaman. Powers I had sensed before grew stronger. One day, when Roan Horse was away from the village, a war party returned home. One of the young men was badly hurt. I laid my hands on him, and he was made whole again.

"Other tribes learned of my power to heal. Our enemy, the Crow, attacked our village and tried to take me captive. Many warriors were killed.

"Summer Moon Rising was frightened by this and she turned away from me. She was afraid of my powers, afraid of what it might mean to be my woman."

"So she married your best friend."

He nodded. "Soon after, another tribe attacked us. Again, there were many deaths. I felt responsible and I ran away from the village."

"Why did you decide to come back?"

"It was time."

"How did you know?"

"My spirit guide told me."

Rebecca thought about all he had told her while she prepared the evening meal. She didn't believe he spoke to a gray wolf, but there was no point in mentioning it because it was obvious that he believed it.

She went to bed early that night, wondering if she would ever get used to cooking over an open fire, eating with utensils made of buffalo horn, sleeping on the ground under a furry robe. Living with a man who spoke to animals…

Wolf Dreamer woke to the high-pitched cry of a woman wailing and knew that Roan Horse's spirit had left his body to follow the spirit path to the place of souls.

Sitting up, he glanced over at Rebecca. She was also sitting up, clutching her sleeping robe to her breast. "What is that?"

"Roan Horse has gone to his ancestors. Lark Song is crying for her husband."

During the next few days, Rebecca again had cause to doubt her ability to accept the Lakota life style. She watched Roan Horse's kinfolk as they mourned his death. The men gashed their flesh. His wife cut off her little finger and hacked off her hair. The other women also cut their hair short.

"It is a way to show their grief," Wolf Dreamer told her. "The physical pain is an outward sign of the pain they feel within."

They mourned him for four days, then wrapped the body in a buffalo robe and carried it away from the village to the burial ground and lifted it onto a scaffold. His weapons hung from the poles, together with a small bundle of food—so that he might have food on his journey to the next life, Wolf Dreamer said. His favorite pipe and his shield were also placed on the scaffold. She watched with horror as a horse was killed.

"So that he may ride in comfort to the After-world," Wolf Dreamer explained.

Rebecca thought the killing cruel and barbaric.

As they left the burial ground, she caught Summer Moon Rising staring at her with ill-disguised loathing. The Indian woman was just one more reason why living here would never work. Summer Moon Rising would always be there, watching, sneering, trying to cause trouble, making sure Rebecca was never accepted.

She looked up as Wolf Dreamer touched her arm.

"You are far away," he remarked, falling into step beside her.

"Yes."

"You are feeling uncomfortable and afraid."

"How do you know that?"

He shrugged. "You will grow accustomed to our ways, in time."

"What if I don't?" she asked, ducking into his lodge. "What if I never do?"

Chapter 11

Rebecca sat apart from the other women and children who had sought to cool off at the river's edge. She watched them laughing, talking, playing in the water. Some of them looked her way now and then. A few of the younger women offered tentative smiles, the children stared at her curiously.

Three weeks had passed since Wolf Dreamer had brought her here. She spent most of her days alone while he was busy doing whatever it was shamans did. He spent his evenings teaching her Lakota ways, teaching her to speak the language which she thought was rather lovely. She was rarely bored, as there was always something to do...wood and water to gather for cooking and bathing, food to prepare. She was trying to learn how to make moccasins, using one of Wolf Dreamer's old ones for a pattern.

Still, for all that she managed to keep busy, she couldn't help feeling lonely, an outcast among strangers.

"You will never belong here."

Rebecca glanced over her shoulder, startled to hear a female voice echoing the words in her heart.

It was Summer Moon Rising.

"You speak English!" Rebecca exclaimed.

"When I wish."

"Did Wolf Dreamer teach you?"

"No. My grandfather was *wasichu*. He taught me." Summer Moon Rising crossed her arms over her breasts. "Why do you not go away from this place? We do not want you here."

"I would if I could," Rebecca retorted.

"I could help you."

"Really? How?"

"I will guide you down the mountain. Once you reach the bottom, you have only to follow the river south. After two days, you will come to a small *wasichu* settlement."

"What about Wolf Dreamer? He's sure to come after me."

"He is going hunting with my brother and two

of his friends tomorrow morning. They will be gone for several days.''

Home. The very word filled her with excitement. This was her chance to go back to Philadelphia, to see her parents again, to return to civilization. It would be wonderful to live in a real house again, to shop in the city, to wear nice clothes and sleep on a feather bed. Home. Even the thought of facing her father and hearing him say, *I told you so,* couldn't dull her excitement.

She stared up at Summer Moon Rising. Dared she trust her? She shook off her doubts. This might be her only chance to get away. Taking a deep breath, she said, ''All right, I'll be ready in the morning.''

Wolf Dreamer sat cross-legged in front of the fire, surreptitiously watching Rebecca. She had been unusually quiet this evening, ever since he had told her he was going hunting in the morning. He had thought her silence might be due to anger that he was leaving, but she had assured him she wasn't angry, had smiled and said she would get along just fine without him. He had told her they would marry when he returned. She had stared at him, then looked away, but not before he saw the tears in her eyes. Were they tears of joy, he wondered, or tears of defeat?

With a shake of his head, he continued to hone

his skinning knife. Women. Who could understand them? He could read the signs of the moon and stars, track a buffalo across the vast prairie, find water in the desert, but he could not find his way in a woman's heart.

That night, he slid under her blankets and drew her into his arms. "Rebecca, what is it that troubles you?"

"Nothing."

He stroked her hair, loving the feel of it, the way it curled around his hand as though it had a life of its own. He yearned for the day when she would truly be his, when he could love her as he longed to do.

He was surprised, but pleased, when her arms crept around his neck and she kissed him. He drew her closer, his body stirring in reaction to her nearness. Of all *wasichu* customs, he liked kissing the best.

She didn't protest when he caressed her, only whimpered softly. It was not a cry of pain, but of pleasure and his body quickened still more, encouraged by her response.

Rebecca clung to him, her emotions in turmoil. She would never belong here, she knew that, just as she knew in her heart that she had fallen in love with Wolf Dreamer. But sometimes love wasn't enough. The thought brought tears to her eyes and filled her with a sense of desperation. After tonight, she would never see him again.

But she had tonight.

She ran her hands over his strong shoulders, down his arms, over his chest, delighting in the smooth heat of his skin, the way he responded to her touch, the husky tremor in his voice when he murmured her name.

She burned for his touch, for his kiss, his caress. He wanted her, too, of that there could be no doubt. She knew he didn't intend to make love to her until they were married, but that day would never come and she wanted him now, wanted to spend one night in his arms, loving and being loved.

When he started to pull away, she wrapped her arms around him and kissed him, her tongue stroking his lower lip, slipping inside to duel with his. He moaned softly as her caresses grew more bold until, with a low growl of surrender, he rose over her. He gazed down at her for a long moment, his face illuminated by the glow of the coals, and then his body merged with hers and there was no more time for thought of anything but the wondrous pleasure of being in his arms, of feeling his body moving deep within her own...

Before going to sleep, Rebecca wondered how she would face him in the morning, not only because they had made love but because she was leaving. Would he see it in her eyes?

But all her worrying was in vain. He was gone when she woke in the morning. He had told her he would be leaving early, but somehow, she had thought he would awaken her and kiss her goodbye. She put her disappointment aside, telling herself it would be easier this way.

Rising, she dressed, smiling a little as her body reminded her of what she had done the night before. Her smile quickly faded with the realization that it would never happen again.

She pushed the thought aside, braided her hair, slipped on her moccasins, and she was ready to go.

Summer Moon Rising appeared at her lodge a short time later.

Rebecca felt a deep and surprising sense of loss as she rode away from Wolf Dreamer's tipi. Though she had never felt that she belonged here, she couldn't shake off the feeling, however wrong it might be, that she belonged with Wolf Dreamer.

Thrusting that wayward notion out of her mind, she concentrated on following Summer Moon Rising out of the village toward the narrow, tree-lined trail that led down the mountain. Because she didn't want to think about Wolf Dreamer, she thought of her parents instead. In a month or so, she would be home again, but for some reason, even that thought failed to cheer her.

As they left the village further behind, the misgivings Rebecca had had earlier crept into her mind. Had she been foolish to put her life into the hands of a woman who was so openly her enemy? Her own vulnerability struck Rebecca like a blow as her gaze lingered on the knife stuck in the sash of the other woman's tunic. If Summer Moon Rising attacked her, she had nothing but her own strength with which to fight back. It was a frightening thought. Summer Moon Rising was a head taller and outweighed her by perhaps thirty pounds. She would be able to overpower her by size alone.

What would Summer Moon Rising do if Rebecca decided to return to the village?

Dare she even try?

Wolf Dreamer sighted down the shaft of his arrow, released his breath, and let the arrow fly. It was a good, clean kill, his first of the day, and yet his thoughts were not on the hunt, or the buck he had just brought down, but on Rebecca and the night he had spent in her arms. She could be carrying his son, even now.

When he returned home, they would be married.

Walking toward his kill, he smiled as he imagined Rebecca's belly rounded with his child, Rebecca cradling his son in her arms.

The sun was warm on his back as he gutted the deer, skinned and quartered it, then wrapped the meat in the hide. Rebecca had much to learn of living with his people. Her ways were not his, but she had a quick mind. Already, she knew several words in his language. Once she could speak his tongue, he hoped she would feel more at ease among his people, and they would be more at ease with her. They would accept her as one of them, in time.

After loading the carcass onto his pack horse, he swung onto the back of his own mount and rode back to where the other warriors were butchering their own kills. One more day, and they would return home.

He smiled at the thought of returning to the village, of Rebecca waiting for him there.

Chapter 12

Rebecca reined her horse to a halt alongside Summer Moon Rising. She had been apprehensive about following the Indian woman, but her fears had proven unfounded. Summer Moon Rising had said little on the way down the mountain and now their journey was at an end.

Summer Moon Rising handed Rebecca the parfleche that held their food supplies. "The town is two days to the south," she said, pointing downriver.

Rebecca nodded. "Thank you for your help."

With a curt nod, Summer Moon Rising clucked to her horse.

Rebecca watched the Indian woman ride away until she was out of sight, torn by the knowledge that Summer Moon Rising would soon be with Wolf Dreamer. Would he take her as his wife? The thought of another woman sharing his lodge, sharing his bed, was like a knife in her heart

She told herself it was foolish to be jealous, that she had left him of her own free will and should not be jealous if another woman desired him, but she couldn't help it.

She looked back up the mountain. Could she find her way back to the village?

With a shake of her head, she touched her heels to her horse's flanks. She hadn't come this far to turn back. She was going home, where she belonged.

But she couldn't block out the little voice in the back of her mind that whispered she belonged here, with the tall, copper-skinned man she had seen in her dreams.

She rode for an hour, stopped to rest her horse and drink from the river, then moved on. The surrounding countryside was lush and green and beautiful. The sound of the water tumbling over rocks filled the air. Birds flitted from tree to tree. She saw a bushy-tailed squirrel looking down at her from a low branch.

She rode until dusk, and it was only then that a

sense of unease began to creep over her. She had lived alone after Gideon passed on, but she hadn't been out in the open like this.

She found a place a short distance away from the river to bed down for the night. She watered her horse, then slipped a rope around its neck and tied it to a nearby tree. Summer Moon Rising had given her a blanket and she spread it on a flat stretch of ground. Summer Moon Rising had also provided her with enough food to last three days.

Now, sitting on the blanket eating a hunk of dried venison, she listened to the sounds of the night. She had never been afraid of the dark before, never realized how *dark* dark really was until she found herself alone in the midst of the prairie. She was suddenly glad for the company of her horse. At least she wasn't totally alone.

She started at every strange sound, heard danger in the rustling of the leaves overhead. What was she doing out here? What had made her think she could make it all the way back east on her own? For the first time, it occurred to her that she was in danger not only from wild animals, but from other Indians, as well. The Lakota were not the only tribe on the Plains.

The full consequence of her foolishness struck her like a blow. She had only the word of Summer Moon Rising that there was a settlement ahead. What would she do if there was no settlement

there? Or worse, what if there was an enemy camp?
She lacked the knowledge and the skills to survive
in the wilderness alone. She could die out here, and
no one would ever know what had become of her.

Her parents had been against her marriage to
Gideon Hathaway from the start. Her father had
told her bluntly that she was making a mistake, that
she would never be happy living in some rough-
hewn cabin in the middle of the untamed west, but
she'd been young and restless and eager for a little
excitement and Gideon had seemed like the answer
to a prayer. He had made it all sound so wonderful,
the journey west, nights under the stars, helping to
settle a new land.

In some ways, her father had been right. She had
been unaccustomed to hard work, and it had been
difficult, those first days and months as they built
a house and planted a garden, but there had also
been a strong sense of satisfaction in the work. She
loved the wild beauty of the land, the vaulted skies,
the endless prairies....

She stared into the distance. The land did not
seem so beautiful now, not when she was alone in
the dark.

"There's nothing to be afraid of," she murmured. And so saying, she wrapped up in the blanket and closed her eyes. The sooner she got to
sleep, the sooner morning would come.

* * *

She woke to the sun in her face and the sound of birds singing. Staring up at the sky, it took her a moment to remember where she was.

Rising, she walked down to the river, washed her hands and face, combed her fingers through her hair. She saddled her horse, then rolled her blanket into a cylinder and lashed it behind the saddle, together with the parfleche of supplies.

She would eat later, she decided, since she really wasn't hungry now.

Riding along the river gave her plenty of time to think...about her mother and father, about Gideon, about the baby she had lost, about going home, about what she wanted in the future.

About Wolf Dreamer.

His image sprang quickly to mind, a tall copper-skinned man with long black hair, golden-brown eyes that could warm her with a look, a voice that made her shiver inside.

Wolf Dreamer. He had said he had watched her for years, that he was drawn to her, that she was his destiny.

Thinking back, she realized there had been times when she had felt she wasn't alone, when she'd looked up from weeding the garden or doing the laundry, fully expecting to find someone standing behind her. Had she known, on some unconscious level, that he had been there?

Thoughts of him, of all they had shared in the

past weeks, filled her mind while she rode, when she stopped to eat and rest her horse. She was so preoccupied with reliving the time she had spent with Wolf Dreamer that she was somewhat surprised to look up and see the settlement Summer Moon Rising had promised laid out before her.

She glanced down at her Lakota tunic and moccasins. She wished she had her own clothes to wear, but there was no help for it. Smoothing a hand over her hair, she urged her horse into a trot.

The settlement had a transient air about it, as if it might be blown away by the first winter winds. There was a combination general store and saloon, a hotel, a small restaurant, a stable and a stagecoach depot. She was relieved to see a telegraph office, though she had no money to send a wire. Perhaps they would send her message on credit.

Men turned to stare at her as she rode down the dusty street. Most were only curious; a few looked at her in ways that made her blush. It took her a minute to realize there were no other women to be seen.

She stopped in front of the restaurant. Dismounting, she tied her horse to the hitch rack, smoothed a hand over her tunic, and entered the building. She felt a rush of relief when she saw a woman wiping off a table.

"Hi, honey," the woman said, looking up. "What can I get for ya?"

"I...I need a job."

"Some man run out on ya?"

"No, no, nothing like that. I..."

"That's all right, honey, no need to explain. I reckon I could use some help in the evenings. I suppose you need a place to stay, too?"

Rebecca nodded.

"Well, there's a cot in the storage room out back. You can stay there, if you like."

"Thank you."

"Here," the woman said, pulling out a chair. "Sit down and I'll see what I can find for you to eat in the kitchen."

"I can't pay..."

"Don't worry about it. I'm Minerva Shellcroft, but everyone calls me Shelly."

"Rebecca Hathaway."

"Welcome to River Bend."

Rebecca waited tables that night, something she had never done before. Shelly had lent her a dress to wear and assured her that although the men might flirt and make outrageous propositions, most of them were harmless.

Rebecca ignored their ribald remarks as best she could. They were a rowdy lot, rough of dress and speech and though they did flirt shamelessly, they treated her with respect when she politely declined their suggestions.

Later, lying on the cot in the storage room, she

let the tears fall. She didn't want to be here. She didn't want to go home.

She wanted Wolf Dreamer, even if it meant being an outsider for the rest of her life.

Chapter 13

"Not here?" Wolf Dreamer exclaimed. "What do you mean, she is not here?"

Summer Moon Rising shrugged innocently. "I saw her leave the village soon after you did. She never returned."

"Why did you not stop her?"

She made no reply, only looked at him through wide, dark eyes.

Wolf Dreamer paced the floor of his lodge. Where would she go? Had she gone back to the homestead? Surely she knew it was too dangerous for her to go back there. She had said she wanted to go home, back east...

He turned to Summer Moon Rising. "Where did she go?"

"How should I..."

"Do not lie to me, woman! What have you done with her?"

"I did nothing! Only what she wished."

"Where is she?" His voice was low and filled with menace.

"I took her down the mountain," Summer Moon Rising replied defiantly. "She is gone, and you will never see her again!" She cringed as he raised his hand, frightened by the anger in his eyes.

Wolf Dreamer took a deep breath and slowly lowered his arm. "Where was she going?"

"I told her to go south. I could have killed her, but I did not." She took a step forward, one hand outstretched. "We can be together now."

"Get out."

She stared at him in disbelief, then ran out of the lodge.

He threw some pemmican and a change of clothes into his saddlebags, then hurried outside to saddle a horse, determined to find her before it was too late, before she boarded a stagecoach and rode out of his life forever.

The settlement rose up from the floor of the prairie, a handful of weathered buildings that crouched like animals sleeping in the sun.

Wolf Dreamer reined his horse to a halt a good distance from the town. He could not ride in and look for Rebecca, not now. He would wait until dark. She would not be hard to find.

Staring down the road, he saw a faint plume of dust that signaled a rider coming his way. Not wanting to be seen, he reined his horse into the cover of the trees.

"Rebecca." He whispered her name as he recognized the woman riding toward him. Never had he seen anything more welcome, or anyone more beautiful.

A wave of longing swept through him as he urged his horse onto the trail.

Rebecca drew up, startled, when a man rode out of the trees. For a moment, she simply stared at him, not believing her eyes.

"Wolf Dreamer!" she exclaimed. "What are you doing here?"

"I could ask the same of you."

"I asked you first."

"I was coming after you," he replied. "Why else would I be here?"

"And I was coming back to you," she confessed, feeling suddenly shy.

Wolf Dreamer glanced down the road, all too aware of the nearness of the *wasichu* settlement ahead.

"Come," he said, and led the way into the trees,

out of the sight of the town and anyone who might happen by.

Rebecca followed him, her heart beating wildly. He had come for her.

When he found a place he considered safe, Wolf Dreamer dismounted, then lifted Rebecca from the back of her horse.

"Were you coming to take me back?" she asked.

"No."

"No?"

He shook his head. "I could not face my life without you. If you will not live in my world, then I will live in yours."

She stared at him, unable to believe her ears. "You were going to go back east with me?"

He nodded.

"Oh, Wolf Dreamer, I love you so much!"

"Is that why you left?"

"No. I was just being foolish and afraid. I was on my way back to you."

"Were you?" he asked, disbelief strong in his voice. "I thought you wanted nothing more than to go back east to be with your people."

She didn't miss the heavy emphasis on the words *your people*.

"You are my people," she said. "There's nothing for me back there. Everything I want is right here."

He opened his arms and she moved into his embrace, feeling truly at home for the first time in her life.

Epilogue

Rebecca sat outside her lodge cradling her infant son in her arms. How handsome he was, her little warrior, with his dusky skin and thick black hair. For the first few days after his birth, she had been afraid to let him out of her sight, out of her arms, for fear she would lose him, but he was a strong healthy child.

Looking at him made her heart swell with love for him and for his father. She had married Wolf Dreamer the day after they returned to his people. Summer Moon Rising had left the village the following day.

Rebecca had come to love living in a hide lodge.

The Lakota lodge was a sacred place. The floor of the tipi represented Mother Earth, the sides, rising upward, symbolized the heavens. The tipi's round shape was a reminder that life was a circle with no beginning and no end. Sweet sage or sweet grass burned on the small altar behind the firepit. The lodge was sturdy enough to withstand winter winds and storms, yet light enough that she could put it up or take it down in minutes.

White Deer Woman had become Rebecca's good friend. She had helped Rebecca learn the Lakota language and customs, introduced her to her friends, made her feel welcome. She had been at Rebecca's side when she labored to bring her son into the world.

White Deer Woman had made an object that Rebecca had found rather curious. It was a beaded turtle amulet decorated with feathers and horsehair. White Deer Woman had explained that the Lakota revered the turtle because it lived long and was difficult to kill. Thus it was that the Lakota sought the protective power of the turtle for their children. When her son had been born, the umbilical cord had been cut, packed in herbs, and placed inside the turtle.

In the four months since then, Rebecca had found her place within the tribe. Her marriage to Wolf Dreamer had brought her a measure of acceptance. He was their shaman, the spiritual leader and healer of the People. He had told them the white woman was his destiny and none dared deny it.

She was in awe of her husband's powers. She had seen him do miraculous things. Truly, he had been blessed by the Great Spirit.

Looking up, she saw Wolf Dreamer walking toward her. As always, the sight of him filled her with a rush of love.

He smiled as he stopped in front of her, his golden brown eyes filled with love as he looked at her and then their son. "How is the little one?"

"He is well." Rebecca glanced at the large cloth-covered bundle in his arms. "What have you there?"

He removed the cloth and she saw that it was a cradleboard. The outside was covered with white doeskin and beaded in colors of blue, yellow, red, white and black in a geometric design. The inside was stuffed with cattail fluff.

"Oh, Wolf," she murmured, "it's lovely. Wherever did you get it?"

"White Deer Woman made it," he replied. "For our little one. He will rest comfortably inside."

Rebecca nodded. Lakota babies spent much of their first year inside a cradleboard. Mothers sometimes hung the boards from a tree branch, where leaves shaded them and summer breezes gently rocked them, lulling babies to sleep.

Her heart filled with love for Wolf Dreamer as

she placed their son inside the cradleboard. Rising, she slipped her arm around her husband's waist, marveling at the twist of fate that had brought her to this man, this place.

He smiled down at her as he drew her into his embrace. "So, *wastelakapi*," he said, a teasing glint in his eye. "Do you believe in dreams now?"

"Oh, yes," she murmured. "And you've made them all come true."

* * * * *

Dear Reader,

I was thrilled when I was asked to be a part of this anthology. Kathleen Eagle has long been one of my idols, and sharing a book with her, and Ruth, is a dream come true.

As some of you may know, I'm always working on more than one story at a time because my Muse isn't always reliable. Sometimes she takes a vacation, and sometimes she insists on doing things Her way! That's what happened with Wolf Dreamer. Originally, this story was going to be a fantasy set in the mountains of a distant planet. However, my Muse didn't like that idea and the next thing I knew, my hero was no longer a wizard but a warrior. But, as they say, all's well that ends well.

Thanks to all of you who wrote to tell me how much you enjoyed Dude Ranch Bride, my very first Silhouette Romance. Thanks to my wonderful agent, that was another dream come true. My second Silhouette Romance, West Texas Bride, will be out in November.

Best,
Madeline

www.madelinebaker.net

COWBOY DAYS
AND INDIAN NIGHTS

Kathleen Eagle

* * *

For my son, David,
and for my first grandchild, Piper Sky Eagle.

Dear Reader,

I've always loved Westerns, be they TV shows, movies or books, but when I was growing up, I thought cowboys and Indians stood on opposite sides of the fence. As a young woman, I discovered that some of the best cowboys are also Indians. In fact, I've been married to an Indian cowboy for thirty-three years. Little wonder that the hero of my very first Silhouette Special Edition novel was a rodeo cowboy who was part Lakota. I can't believe it's been nineteen years since that book, *Someday Soon,* was first published!

Leslie Wainger was the editor for that book and every one I've written for Silhouette since. When she invited me to contribute to *Lakota Legacy,* I jumped at the chance. I wanted to write a story about a cowboy who plays a special role, both in the rodeo arena and in one woman's newly emptied nest and lonely heart. And I loved the idea of discovering human connections through the history of a cherished heirloom. Thank you for taking this journey with us!

Sincerely,

Kathleen Eagle

Chapter 1

Meredith would not have opened the door to the trail-worn stranger on her porch if it hadn't been for the dog. The rawboned black mutt had already connected with her through the window. Head tipped to one side, tail swishing, black eyes brimming with hope, he clearly wanted to assure her that the man in the dusty jeans and threadbare plaid shirt really was a decent guy. Because he reminded her of someone she missed very much—the dog, not the man—Meredith took the risk.

"Hey, how's it goin'?" the man said as he turned toward the door. He touched the brim of his straw cowboy hat, his smile suggesting some history between them that she knew nothing about. "You wanna show me where to put my gear?"

She glanced past him at the blue pickup truck she assumed he'd parked in her driveway. "Put your gear?"

"It's not much. Mainly me and ol' Raven here." At its master's cue, the dog sniffed at Meredith's hand. "Looks like he smells his girlfriend," the man said, exchanging doleful looks with his dog. "Sorry, ol' son, but she's gone. That's why we're here."

"And…"

Don't ask, and don't pet the dog.

The dog nosed its way under her hand.

"And who would you be?"

"We'd be your new boarders, ma'am."

"Boarders?" She peered up at him, searching the bronzed, angular face for clues to his meaning. "I'm sorry, Mr.…"

"Ryder," he supplied.

"Mr. Ryder, I'm afraid this can't be the place you're looking for."

"Why can't it?" He glanced past her, trying to get a look inside the house, possibly scoping it out for a future visit.

She pulled the door closer, wedging herself in. "I don't rent rooms out. I don't have any…"

"Sure, you do," he insisted jovially. "The one where Kenny and his little boy were staying. Plus, you've got room for Raven now that they took Lydia and left you an empty doghouse. Raven tried to get her to stay, but that little boy wasn't havin' none o' that.''

"No, I'm sure he wasn't. Collin is so attached to Lydia, I just couldn't separate them, so I had to let Ken…'' Her son. The mention of his name, and she was suddenly chatting up a total stranger. She drew herself up, gripping the doorknob. "But I'm not renting their room.''

"Kenny told me you'd say that, but I insist on paying for my keep. Cash or chores, it's up to you, Miz Woodward.''

"Mr. Ryder—''

"Ryder's my first name, but hardly anybody uses it. I was hoping you would. I won't get familiar until you give me the word, but…'' His slow smile started in his eyes and worked its way to one corner of his mouth. It faded for lack of encouragement, leaving him to expound with a straight face. "It's Ryder Red Hawk, but I've got so damn many nicknames, I hardly ever hear my…''

"I don't know you,'' she reminded him quietly. "I'm not about to give you the word, Mr. Red Hawk. I'm not about to rent you a room, either.''

"You're all alone here, right?'' This time the front door protected her living room from his attempt to check things out for himself.

"Ye—no! No, I have...very close neighbors. I have..." She frowned. "How do you know Ken?"

"He saved my dog's life."

"Raven?" Her tone suddenly sympathetic, she rewarded the dog's tail-thumping rejoinder with a pat on his silky head. "What happened to Raven?"

The man chuckled. "Kind of embarrassing, you wanna know the truth. He took off into a lake after Lydia. Ran the whole length of a dock and jumped in after her. Trying to show off, I guess. She was fetching a Frisbee for Kenny, paddlin' after it pretty as you please. Ol' Raven was hooked right off, so to speak. Only there wasn't a hook, line or a sinker—nothin' to grab onto—and Raven can't swim."

"But he looks like he's part Lab."

"He is. Guess it's his other parts that hold him back."

"Did Ken pull him out of the water?" she asked, testing.

"Well, now, that boy of yours ain't much of a swimmer, either."

Meredith acknowledged the truth of this with raised eyebrows. That was Ken, all right. A swimming-lessons dropout. One thing he'd assured her he wouldn't miss about Minnesota was all the water. She'd made him promise that Collin would learn to swim better than his father.

"Neither am I," the cowboy added quickly, "but

between the two of us and Lydia, we got him out, got him resuscitated.'' He squatted on his heels and traded Raven a two-handed, flapping ear rub for a face licking—clearly working the dog as the key to Meredith's front door. ''Remember, boy? Lydia gave you some muzzle-to-muzzle, and then Kenny hauled you over to his vet clinic and pulled you through.''

Meredith folded her arms, taking her motherly stance as the man stood, his knees cracking as he pushed to his feet. ''Is any of this true?'' she asked him.

''Some of it, yeah. I know Kenny from the vet clinic.'' He took off his hat, pushed his finger through a thick shock of hat-creased salt-and-pepper hair, and glanced past her again. The door had eased itself open, as though offering an invitation on its own. His stiff denim jacket rustled as he squared his shoulders. ''Now, can we come in?''

''I'm sorry. I didn't mean to be rude, I just...'' She gave a moment's thought to the idea, and then shook her head. ''I don't know where Ken got the idea that I was going to rent his room out.''

''You're Kenny's mom, right? You sure don't look old enough to have a grown son, but I'd swear you're the lady in the picture he showed me.''

''Ken showed you...''

''Carries it in his billfold, right behind the little boy's picture.''

"Mr. Ryde—Red Hawk..." She caught the teasing sparkle in his eyes and left the warning to dangle as the name *Red Hawk* echoed, and she thought, *Native American; how interesting,* and wondered idly what pictures he carried in his wallet. "Which picture was it?"

"You had a blue-ribbon smile," he hinted.

"Oh. The one they took at the State Fair." She pushed back her hair, which had been shorter then. The art director had made her wear a silly checked apron because he thought it made her look more "Minnesota wholesome." She had hidden most of it behind a pyramid of jars of her prize-winning antipasto. "That was for the last cookbook. I didn't know he kept a copy in his wallet."

"You're the only woman he's got in there. Had to give him a bad time about being a mama's boy."

She sighed. "Ken hasn't had much luck with women lately."

"You ask me, he was lucky from day one."

Her face felt warm. She couldn't believe his country-hick charm was actually getting to her. "I had to give him a bad time about having to move back home with his mother, but I hated to see them leave."

"You can be sure he hated to leave the comforts of his mother's home. Especially when she's a blue-ribbon cook. He thought I might be able to talk you into board along with the room, but I don't wanna push my luck.''

"I'm always testing recipes. Ken was my guinea pig.''

"He mentioned that.''

"So there's always a ton of food, but it might not be to your liking.''

He laughed. "I never met a plate of food I didn't like.''

"Then you won't be much help, will you?'' She caught herself imagining him sitting at her table, eating poached salmon off her Fiestaware and complimenting her on the sauce. Instinctively she stepped back. "What am I saying? This really isn't a boarding house, and I'm not...''

"But Raven here, he's about as fussy as they come. If it ain't done right, he passes it over to me. I'm the one eats his leftovers.''

All right, she had to smile for the dog. He had no pedigree, but he was surely well-mannered. She could see him playing Tramp to her Lady Lydia, the impeccable English spaniel. They would be great together in the spaghetti scene.

"That's why I'm a little on the lean side,'' the man was saying. "He takes all the richest morsels, and I get what's left.''

"Do you get the meatballs, Raven?'' She was softening. She could feel it, and she knew darn well they could see it. "What do you do to pay for your meals, Mr. Red Hawk?"

"Whatever needs doing." She questioned him with a look, and he shrugged. "I'm a South Dakota cowboy, ma'am. Jack-of-all-trades. I'm here for the rodeo."

With a look she told him she had no idea what he was talking about.

"You got a rodeo comin' up at the Target Center this weekend."

"So you won't be here long?"

"Depends on how I do. Win or lose, I need a place to stay for about a week. Most places'll take one of us, but not both."

"Some hotels have kennels."

"Yeah, but it's a tight squeeze, and ol' Raven gets testy when I try to stretch out." He grinned. "We're kinda used to sharing whatever bed we got."

The image of the lanky cowboy tucked into a cage with his dog had her laughing easily now. How dangerous could he be, a man who shared his meals and his bed with his dog? She missed having Lydia stretched across her legs or tucked between them.

"Come on in," she said finally, swinging the door open.

The man followed the wedge of sunlight that cut

across the Persian carpet. The dog followed the man.

Meredith gestured toward the stairs. "I'll show you the room. I could use a couple of discriminating tasters this week, but my son is in for an earful when I call him tonight."

The heavy sound of his boots treading the stairs just behind her espadrilles seemed to make mockery of her judgment, first in taking him in, and then in taking the lead up the stairs. Her new khaki slacks were a size larger than most of the slacks she had in her closet—the ones that she recently had to admit were a bit too snug. Why hadn't she put on the black ones? The stairway felt unusually narrow, and he was tailgating her, probably thinking he couldn't see where he was going behind her big bumper.

The dog had the good sense to wait for a clear path up the stairs.

Meredith consciously added some spring to her step and spun on her heel as she rounded the newel post at the top of the stairs, eager to fill the silence. "What do you do in the rodeo?"

"I'm a bullfighter."

"Bulls?" She surveyed him pointedly, foot to head. "Isn't that a little dangerous for a man your age?"

He laughed. "I knew I shoulda kept my hat on."

"That's a wonderful hatband. Is that a turtle?" She pointed to the beaded amulet affixed to the beaded band on the side of the crown. "Is your umbilical cord inside?"

His almond-shaped eyes widened, coal black and glistening with merry surprise. "My *what?*"

"Isn't that part of your tradition? The turtle amulet for a baby's umbilical cord?"

"You're talking about Indian tradition?"

"What's your tribal affiliation?" she asked eagerly. "My guess is Lakota. That beadwork looks like Western Sioux."

He laughed again. "My guess is, you know more about it than I do. But, yeah, South Dakota Sioux." He slid the brim of the hat through his leathery brown hands, examining the amulet from several angles as he spoke. "As far as the turtle goes, if he ate somebody's umbilical cord, it sure as hell wasn't mine. I may be old, but not *that* old."

"You don't do that anymore?" Her question drew a puzzled glance. "Make a beaded amulet for a baby's umbilical cord?"

"I wouldn't know how to make a beaded anything. Like I said, you probably know more about it than I do. I've got the name and the face, but I'm not really a practicing Indian. I was raised by a white family."

"I'm sorry," she said softly, getting all hot in the face. "I was being presumptuous, wasn't I?"

"That you were, ma'am, but no offense taken." To prove it, he laid the hat in her hands for her own closer inspection. "I got this from a relative. An old lady gave it to me when I was real young. I think she was my grandma. This ol' turtle goes way back, probably even before her time."

"Then maybe there's something inside. Maybe we could loosen a few stitches and see."

"Why would we want to do that?" He laid a protective hand over his hat, but he didn't try to take it back. It was a gesture that pleased her in some foolish and perplexing way.

"Just to see. I think these relics are just fascinating." She smiled up at him and offered reassurance. "I could fix it, of course. Put it back exactly the way it was."

"Not exactly," he averred, answering her smile with his own. "The mystery would be gone. Now that you've planted the idea that my turtle might have a secret in his belly, I kinda like the mystery."

"He might have been an ancestor."

"Or she. I've been kinda short on blood relatives, but I guess everybody has ancestors." He glanced at the pictures of Kenneth and Collin that covered the wall of the upstairs hallway. "You've fixed your house up real nice, ma'am."

"Meredith," she said, too quickly. "Or...well, Meredith."

"First names generally mean first base to a cowboy, you know. Gettin' pretty familiar." He shrugged diffidently. "'Course, you've already tried to get into my turtle, so I guess I got some catchin' up to do.''

"*Mr.* Ryder," she admonished. "Red...Ryder. Red Ryder." She hardly recognized the sound of her own laughter, the way it bubbled up from deep in her throat.

"Don't you be toyin' with my name, now. A man's honor-bound to defend his name."

"I'm sorry. I wasn't making fun." Using his hat as a come-on, she beckoned him to follow her down the hall. "I would never do that."

"Make fun? I'll have to see what I can do to change that." He gave a soft whistle. "It's okay, Raven."

"This is Ken's room," she said, pushing the door back to the wall. The cowboy's proximity took the edge off the empty feeling she faced whenever she stepped across the threshold lately. The toys were gone, the books, the desk, the computer, the hand weights. There were no clothes piled in the chair beside the window, no keys or cookies on the bureau. A room that had long been cramped now seemed cavernous, the air stale.

"I was just about to get a big-boy bed for Collin and get rid of the crib." Meredith set his hat on the empty bureau, crossed the floor quickly, unlocked and opened one of the windows on either side of the double bed. She laid hands on the baby's bed she'd folded and left leaning against the wall. Ken had taken the mattress and mentioned a plan to use it in a youth bed. "Now all I have to do is get rid of the crib," Meredith said quietly.

"Don't change anything around on my account." He folded his brown, weathered hand around the crib rail, his thumb touching hers.

"It was Ken's crib, too." She looked up at him, saw the sympathy in his dark eyes and realized she was giving away more sentiment than she meant to. She shrugged. "I could have quite a garage sale with all the stuff they left behind."

"You need any help, you let me know. I've had some experience along those lines. My foster mother practically ran a store out of her garage every summer. Actually, she managed it, and I ran it. Got so I was a helluva wheeler-dealer when it came to junk."

"Junk? This is—"

"Vintage," he supplied. In fine wheeler-dealer mode, he turned the tables on her, gesturing with a flourish. "Now, ma'am, this bed has seen two boys through short pants and into blue jeans, but I can give you a good deal on her. Not only does she have a lot of life left in her, she's got added character."

She took to her role, examining scratches like a would-be buyer rather than the woman who knew the story behind every scar in the wood. "You'll have to knock off at least ten dollars for the teeth marks."

"Knock off? I generally add to the price for a mark like that. It's like barn wood. Everybody's lookin' for genuine barn wood these days, but how do you know what that barn was home to? You don't want to get tricked into buying chicken-coop wood, do you? You gotta look for signs of horse cribbing."

"What difference does it make?"

"The difference between the smell of horses and the stink of chicken crap."

"Of course." She laughed. "The proof is in the poop."

"You could say that, but we're talking crib here, not cribbing. Now this sweet little bed, she's got a soft luster about her. A warm finish, just like the woman who cared for those two boys."

"You're overselling, Mr. Red Hawk. Neither one of us has quite reached antique status."

He shook his head. "You don't want an antique. You can't be comfortable with an antique. This bed has proven her worth beyond dollars and cents. For an extra ten bucks, I'll throw in a mattress."

"Generous."

"To a fault, they tell me, but that's the way I was brought up. I'll load it up for you, too."

"I'll say," she said, laughing with him far too easily. "I might just take you up on your offer. I couldn't sell water in the desert."

"I might feel a little guilty about that, too." He

sat down on the bed, testing, giving a nod of approval, which Raven took as a signal to join his master. Ryder forestalled the jump with a hiss. "Not yet, boy. We still haven't settled on a rate."

The dog flopped down on the braided rug at the foot of the bed and snorted in frustration.

"I'll have to give it some thought. Trust me," Meredith said with a smile for both man and dog. "I'll be fair."

"Uh-oh. My daddy warned me about women who say, 'Trust me.'"

She tested the bedside table for dust and made a mental note to slip into the room sometime with a rag and some lemon oil. "I've never had a boarder before, so I'll have to find out what's fair."

He chuckled. "I've never had a woman ask me to trust her before, so I'll have to find out what's not to trust."

She feigned surprise. "Your daddy didn't say?"

"I never had a daddy." His knees cracked as he pushed off the bed. "But I've got this voice in my head that sounds like one."

"Really?" She glanced at the dog. "Voices in your head?"

He waited until she looked up at him. He had that naughty twinkle in his summer's night eyes, and he was working hard on damming up a laugh.

"I wouldn't be teasing me too much if I were you. My sense of humor is fairly limited."

"Meaning the jokes sail right over your head?"

"Meaning you have to give me some hint that you're joking."

"Doesn't everybody hear voices?"

She stared at him until he couldn't hold back any longer. He laughed, and she joined in, uncertain just what was tickling her typically very well-protected funny bone.

Raven didn't seem to find the people in the room terribly amusing, either. He was snooping around the door off the bedroom.

"That's the bathroom," Meredith said, settling back into herself. "There are towels on the shelf. The closet and drawers are all empty. If you need any—"

"Mind your manners in there, Raven," Ryder told the dog, who had disappeared into the dark room.

"He can't…" She smiled. "I mean, everything's quite in order in there."

"I don't doubt it."

"I'll have a recipe for you to sample tonight if you haven't made other plans for supper."

"Raven and I never made a plan we couldn't change at the drop of a hat." He reached over to the bureau, flipped his hat over on its crown, and flashed Meredith a charming smile. "Trust me."

Chapter 2

Ryder couldn't remember the last time he'd caught a glimpse of himself buck naked in a full-length mirror.

Okay, not quite *buck*. Parts of him were wrapped as though he'd been mummified. He was still babying a cracked rib along, wearing a tight chest bandage. His bum left knee was back into the Ace knee brace, and he'd managed to get himself hooked in the shoulder by a horned Hereford, worth half a dozen stitches his last time out. He was still hurting, but he'd be good to go by the weekend.

The stock contractor for the big Target Center rodeo had offered him other options, but working the chutes or riding a pickup horse wouldn't cover the health insurance premium he had due. He could get his stitches free from an Indian Health Service clinic, but ambulance drivers didn't ask a guy which emergency room he preferred. He had to keep those premiums paid up.

Indian Health Service reminded him of his new landlady's interest in his Indian heritage, whatever that meant. He took his hat off the dresser and turned it slowly, sliding the straw brim through his dark hands as he studied it in the new light the woman had shed on Old Man Turtle. His old friend might be more than decoration. He might connect him up with somebody, somewhere, some time. The thought that he might be wearing something like that on his head kinda gave him the creeps, but it sure excited the hell out of the lady downstairs.

She'd invited him to call her Meredith.

Well…Meredith.

Was she called something else? Something like Merry? She didn't seem real merry. She had a natural elegance about her, soft beauty burnished by the good life she had clearly made for herself and her family. He took her for a private woman, but not the kind who ought to be left completely alone. She needed a little companionship. Kenny should have left the dog, he thought. He had the boy, and they could always get another dog. But Meredith couldn't, not right away. She was that kind of woman. Rather than replace what was missing, she would simply go on without it.

He glanced from the hat to the mirror, then up, up some more until he caught the reflection of his chagrin in his eyes. He quickly lowered the hat a few notches. He was a modest man, after all. Didn't much like being pointed at, even by his own personal member, which gloried in such rudeness. It struck him as more than a little disrespectful to be standing there naked and thinking about a lady he'd just met.

And in front of a head-to-toe mirror to boot.

He had to laugh as he headed into the bathroom for a shower, which would start out with cold water.

He was fully lathered and enjoying the switch from cold to hot when he heard Raven's soft whine. "Sorry," he called out. "This shower's too small for two."

More whining.

"Hell, you'll be shaking all over the place, and we'll be in trouble right off the bat."

Above the whining and the running water, he thought he heard something else. He opened the glass door and stuck his head out. Someone was tapping insistently, knocking, finally pounding on the bedroom door.

"Mr. Red Hawk! Ryder! Turn the shower off!"

He did. It sounded like an emergency, so he pulled his jeans over his wet butt, grabbed a towel, and skidded across the wood floor on wet heels until he hit the scatter rug. He jerked the door open.

She didn't look hurt, and she sure wasn't merry.

"What's wrong?"

"I have a flood in the kitchen," she complained, sidling into the room past him. "I forgot about the shower. I should have gotten that fixed, but it wasn't being used, so the problem—" she peeked into the bathroom, undoubtedly expecting to see a man's mess "—sort of went away."

He thought he detected a gleam of new respect in her eyes when she turned to him with an apologetic smile.

"I forgot to warn you. I'm sorry to interrupt, but the water leaks through the kitchen ceiling for some reason." She sighed, maybe with a touch of personal regret for what she was about to say. "This is a mistake. I have no business offering you a room without a fully functional private bathroom."

"You didn't exactly offer, and you weren't expecting to be in the business." He hung the towel around his neck and buttoned the jeans he'd hurriedly zipped. "How bad is the flood?"

"Well, that's not really the problem. The problem is that there's only one other bathroom, which we'd have to share."

"Just you and me?" He conjured an image that made him merry.

"That just doesn't seem wise."

"I agree. We'd get in each other's way." He rewarded her admonishing glance with a wink and a smile. "How about if we take turns?"

"No, that's not what I meant. I meant that—"

"I don't mind going first or last, either way. Just be sure you pick up your underwear. If you leave underwear on the floor, I can't be held responsible."

Again she took his bait. "For what?"

"For their whereabouts."

"What about your underwear? I've never met a man who didn't leave his clothes all over the floor."

"Sounds like you've only known the kind of man who keeps more clothes around than he needs. That wouldn't be me."

"I just meant that..." Flapping her arms, slapping her hands to her sides, she was floundering now, but he wasn't going to regret baiting a woman who was in such desperate need of a little sport. "I mean, if we each had our own space, that would be one thing, but I forgot all about the leaky shower."

"The sink works?" he asked.

She nodded.

"The john?"

Another affirmative.

"Two out of three ain't half bad. The important thing is that I won't be finding the damn toilet seat down all the time."

Her face brightened beautifully, and she permitted herself a good belly laugh. "I guess we can make do for a week," she said amid her fading chuckles.

"I'll have it fixed long before the week is over."

"I'll call a plumber," she promised, waving his offer away. "I should have done it long ago."

"It's not a plumbing problem. There's a hole somewhere. Leave it to me to find it and fix it. You've got a cowboy on the place now, which means you've got a carpenter, electrician, plumber, animal specialist—generally a caretaker for anything that needs taking care of."

"I don't mean to take advantage of..."

"I'm not a guest." He took an end of the towel in each hand and pulled the terrycloth tight against the anchor of his neck, challenging her with stance and stare. "You know how many times you've said you *didn't mean to* in the last five minutes?"

She gave a flimsy little shrug. "It's just a little awkward."

"What? You barging in when I'm takin' a shower?"

"Well, yes, but..."

"Truth is, you didn't mean to let me in your house in the first place. You think I don't know that?"

"Not at first, but..."

He shifted his weight from one bare foot to the

other. "But I'm here now, and so far, nothin' bad's happened."

She lifted her brow, allowing, "Except that my kitchen's flooded, but that's my own fault."

"It's the fault of that hole in your wall, which I'm gonna fix. But do me one favor."

She tipped her head, ready and waiting.

"Just say what you mean, straight out. I'm pretty thick-skinned. Comes the time you say something nice to me, I don't wanna be wondering what you really mean."

"You think that time will come within a week?"

"I know it will."

He finished cleaning up, put his purely practical wardrobe and other personal items away—filling a single drawer, a shelf and a foot of closet space— and stood on the landing for a moment with Raven, both of them trying to determine the next move. They heard a few kitchen noises—drawers, cupboards doors, clanging metal, running water. He'd spent his adult life staying out of kitchens, partly because his foster mother had assigned him the disgraceful role of kitchen boy, but mainly because cowboys didn't cook. They did almost every other job on the place, but no cooking.

But the kitchen noises suddenly appealed to him, and he figured she had the water cleaned up by now. He wanted to catch her in her element, doing

what she liked to do. Nobody liked scrubbing
floors.

A black-and-white cat crossed the path at the foot
of the stairs, and Raven set out to investigate. Ryder
followed, but they parted ways at the bottom of the
stairs, following their noses in different directions.

Ryder had no idea what kind of food he smelled,
but it had some fruit in it. It wasn't apple; he'd
recognize apple. Berries, maybe. Maybe she was
making a pie. Whatever it was, he hoped he'd be
offered a sample soon. His empty stomach was
rumbling. His nose drew him through a cozy living
room that felt feminine and a little old-fashioned.
He was looking for a granny-style kitchen.

He found a huge, bright, contemporary space,
outfitted on the high end for serious cooking. The
sleek stainless steel, glass and granite surely added
up to a cook's version of a racecar driver's Lam-
borghini or a jockey's Thoroughbred. The sweet
scent of the steam rising from a pot on the stove
beckoned him, but the wet gleam on the blue tile
floor warned him to walk with care.

Meredith glanced up from the chicken she was
dismembering on a butcher block.

"Is it okay if I watch?" Ryder asked.

"No, but if you know how to use a peeler, you
can take a peek between carrots."

He saw only two carrots, but they were long and

fat. "Do you have a small knife? I'm hell on horse-back with a knife."

"Do I have a knife?" Using the blade in her hand as a pointer, she drew his attention to three chunky blocks of wood housing at least two dozen matching black handles. "I happen to have a knife for every purpose under heaven."

He chose his weapon.

"That's my favorite paring knife," she warned.

"It's in good hands," he promised. He hadn't scraped a carrot in years, never voluntarily. Given a choice, he'd hawk outgrown kids' clothes and for-gotten toys all day long before he'd spend an hour doing kitchen chores.

Damn. Had it been that long since he'd actually been part of a household?

"You've got quite a fancy kitchen here," he ob-served, taking the first carrot in hand. They stood side by side, marooned together on a kitchen island in the middle of wet blue tile. Side by side was nice, but he could stand the marooned part for about a day and a night. "How much time do you spend in it?"

"I don't count the hours, but lately it's most of my day. Most days. Lately." Clearly, she didn't mind. Her smile was shaped by a measure of self-esteem along with a dollop of satisfaction. "I'm one of the lucky people who gets to do what she loves in the place she loves most. Of course, I do a lot of my work on the computer.''

''That one?'' He'd noticed the desk among the other built-in centers, each with its purpose and place in her self-contained world.

She nodded. ''Besides my cookbooks, I contribute to the newspaper and several magazines. In fact, that's how I got started.'' She slid a couple of handfuls of round, red, new potatoes his way. ''No peeling. Just one more wash.''

''Who's going to eat all this?''

She had a sweet, tinkling laugh that tickled his ears.

''This recipe serves four to six people. I've never cooked for a cowboy, but I've heard that they have hollow legs.''

''Who told you that?'' He slid her his never-fail grin. ''How long has it been since the subject of cowboys came up in your conversation?''

''I've heard that their legs are bowed because they're hollow.'' Her eyes did his grin one better, dragging the itch he'd meant for her down the length of his own body, as though she was sizing him up for her next recipe.

He shifted his legs and sucked his belly in. He was on the sinewy side, but figured he had enough meat on him to suit her needs.

''My guess is it was about thirty years ago, and you were writing fan letters to some TV cowboy.''

"They say those hollow legs straighten out after a big meal."

"You were telling him you liked the way he filled out his jeans."

"And they walk like this." Stiff-legged, she toddled side to side in place. Charlie Chaplin carrying a raw drumstick and a boning knife.

He surrendered to a fit of laughter.

"How did you get started?" she asked. Then she added, "Being a cowboy."

"I saw a notice tacked to the wall at a livestock auction house back in South Dakota," he began as he weighed a trio of potatoes in a cupped hand. "Ranch Hands Wanted in Montana. I saw a chance to get out on my own, and I jumped on it. Jumped on a semi headed in the general direction of Montana. Figured all I had to do was get there and convince Montana that I was a ranch hand. Shouldn't be too hard, I thought. Next to somebody from Montana, I should look pretty smart. Trouble was, I forgot to take the damn poster with me." Smiling to himself, he had the potatoes circling each other as he flexed his palm. "Montana's a big state."

"How old were you?"

"Eighteen was what I was claimin'. I think I was closer to sixteen. I ended up at another sale barn, lookin' for another poster. Met up with a rodeo livestock contractor. He gave me a job. Didn't take him long to figure out my only experience with livestock was in my dreams, but he kept me on anyway. He said my tall tales were a great source of amusement, which is something that's hard to come by in Montana.''

''You don't seem to have much affection for Montana.''

''It's a beautiful place. So much natural beauty there you can hardly stand it sometimes.'' He slipped her a quick smile. ''It looks especially beautiful in the rearview mirror of a pickup with a full tank of gas.''

''I take it you didn't stay long.''

''As long as it took me to earn enough money to buy that pickup.'' He popped a potato up in the air and caught it just as he popped up another one, showing off one of his real talents. ''Which was about ten years.''

''The stock contractor didn't pay very well,'' she surmised.

''He paid a fair wage for on-the-job training. I'd spend it all on a weekend. The rest of the month I was workin' for bed and board. That's part of the training—how to keep your pay from burning a hole in your pocket. I started ridin' rough stock as an amateur, started earning a few extra dollars to put toward that pickup. I wrecked the first one, so I had to start over.''

''No insurance?''

''Oh, I got it now. Like I said, Montana's a big

state. You can do a lot of drivin' before anybody comes along to remind you of details like insurance. Or a driver's license. They do get fussy about renewing your plates. They're damn proud of those plates.''

''But you'd need your own wheels to go from one rodeo to the next.''

''Cowboys are pretty generous with their transportation. If a guy needs a ride, they'll find room.'' He'd drawn nary *ooh* nor *ahh* from her with his juggling, so he thought he'd try a joke. ''Three guys in a pickup, which one's the real cowboy? The driver, the one in the passenger's seat or the guy in the middle?''

''The driver?''

He shook his head. ''Too much work. The driver has to drive. The guy next to the passenger door has to open and close the gates. The guy in the middle is the real cowboy. All he has to do is ride.''

''So, he's lazy?''

''All he *needs* to do is ride.'' He gave a don't-you-get-it double take. ''He's ready to do whatever needs doing, but right now, he's got his driver and his gate man. He's set to ride.''

''But seriously folks...'' she quipped with a look that said she was coming back at him. ''Isn't bull riding a sport for the younger man?''

''Younger than who? Younger than me? They don't get much younger than me.'' He postured, every bit the spreading peacock. "Go on. Take a guess. See what you can tell about this book from its cover."

"Guessing someone's age is just so rude." She gave him a decidedly less appreciative once-over this time. "At least forty."

"Am I that tattered?"

"Let's just say you look old enough to have better sense than to try to ride a bull."

"I am, and I do. You got my number dead-on. I just turned forty." He braced one arm on the counter and hooked the other at his hip. "You're pretty good at this game. What else can you tell from my cover?"

"Nothing, really." Turning her attention to the arranging of chicken parts, she added off-handedly, "Obviously, you've spent a lot of time outdoors."

"I already told you that."

"Even if you hadn't, it's something I could tell from your cover."

"Leather-bound, am I? That oughta tell you something about what's inside. Maybe I'm a classic."

She eyed him critically. "I'd need more evidence before I could make that assumption."

"You got a week. Can you do a whole book in a week?"

"If it's interesting enough," she allowed as she poured dark, fruit-scented sauce over the chicken.

"If you can get past the dusty old leather cover?"

"You're not dusty anymore." She took over on the potatoes he'd done nothing more than play with, reached in front of him to turn the water on. "I mopped up the proof of that."

"I think I know where that leak is, by the way." He took a step back, but only a small one. "I'll have to tear into some of that tile. Are there any leftovers around?"

"I usually throw them—" She turned on him, eyes widening. "Tear into the wall of the *shower?*" She looked horrified. "Make a hole in my *wall?*"

"You've already got a hole in your wall," he reminded her as he pilfered a pinch of chopped nuts from a bowl that perfectly matched the color of the kitchen tile. "I can't fix it unless I can find it, and I can't find it unless I pull off some tile."

She pondered for a moment, as though he'd given her some numbers to add up in her head. "This sounds like more than a little repair work." She gave up on the problem with a sigh. "I think I should hire a professional."

He shrugged. "Suit yourself." It was, after all, her problem.

"Not that I don't think you could handle it." Finger to lips, she reassessed him and reconsidered. "Could you?"

Damn, he thought, what was she thinking? Those

pretty fingertips were shiny with chicken fat. But those lips, full and moist and slightly pouty...

He imagined kissing the fingertips first, then the lips. Hell, he'd slip her some tongue, even. He wasn't one to let a little chicken fat get in the way of a great kiss.

"Let me know if you're interested in finding out," he muttered as he helped himself to more nuts. He was getting hungry. "This is good stuff, Raven. Want a taste?"

"I have a bin full of dog food in that bottom cabinet." She pointed to a door on the other side of the room.

"The lady's cooking enough food for six people, and she's offering you dog food, Raven." Ryder offered chopped nuts. Raven licked them from his finger and then followed the fallen bits to the floor.

"This dish wouldn't be good for him. The spices..." She went to the dog treat bin herself and returned with a cookie. "Doesn't he eat dog food?"

"He'll eat anything. He's got an iron gut, just like mine." Ryder smiled as he watched Raven clean Meredith's fingers. No, ma'am, his dog wasn't shy. "The hollow leg is a myth. The iron gut is real."

"A lot of good you two will do me as tasters." She brushed her hands together.

It pleased him that she went back to the carrots on the cutting board without making a stop at the faucet. Her kitchen was immaculate, but she was unfazed by dog germs.

His kind of woman.

"Just because we'll eat anything, that doesn't mean we don't know our beans," he assured her. "We can sure tell you when they're fit to eat. Beans especially. We're bean experts."

"Beans are a wonderful source of protein. A fine alternative to red meat."

"What have you got against red meat?"

"My recipes rarely include red meat." She consigned the chicken dish to the oven, took a plastic dog dish from a cupboard and filled it with water, set the dish on the floor, talking all the while. "I do low-cholesterol, heart-healthy cookbooks."

"Just our luck, Raven. More beans."

"Everyone's looking for great vegetarian recipes these days. You'll be amazed at how good healthful food can be."

He grimaced. "You're a vegetarian?"

"Not strictly, but don't tell anyone. My focus is on the health angle. It sells very well. Red meat is fast losing favor, even with teenagers." She smiled at him as she dried her hands on a striped towel. "Of course, you know that buffalo meat is much better for you than beef."

"Of course."

"I do the occasional ground-turkey alternative. Maybe we could come up with a couple of dishes using lean buffalo meat. What's the best way to cook buffalo?''

"On a stick,'' he said, perfectly straight-faced.

"Buffalo kabob would be great, wouldn't it? It's time I did a new ethnic cookbook. I've never included a Native American section. Do you have any family recipes we could use as a basis for Woodwardizing?''

"You're using the word *we* pretty freely all of a sudden.''

She gave him a pert, sparkly look. "The book is getting interesting.''

"And you haven't even opened it yet.'' He returned the smile with a touch of reproach. "Like I told you, I grew up with a white family.''

"Oh, that's right.'' She flipped one end of the towel over her shoulder as she set about tidying up her kitchen island. "But you left when you were sixteen. You haven't tried to discover your roots?''

"I know my onions. Is that a root?'' Ryder chuckled as he seated himself opposite her on a padded barstool. "I discovered that being an Indian allowed me to compete in more rodeos. Indian rodeos.''

"How does the rodeo figure into Native American culture?''

"In Indian country when you have a powwow in the summer, you've got to have a rodeo. Cowboy days and Indian nights. Nothin' like it.'' He watched Raven help himself at the water dish and wondered when Meredith was going to offer him something to drink.

"I'm not sure I'd like the rodeo part, but I'd love to go to a powwow."

"They're a little different nowadays, from what I hear. The dancing is more competitive than the rodeo. That's where the big prize money is now, the dancing."

"That's the part I'd like to see anyway."

He smiled. "Are you asking me for a date?"

"No." She'd made quick work of her cleanup, and now she was posing for him, arms akimbo, head tipped to one side. "But I might consider offering *you* one if I decide to go to a powwow."

"What about if you decide to go out to supper?"

"I rarely eat out."

"Do you go to the movies?"

"I wait until they come out in video. I have a big-screen TV."

"I saw that," he said with an appreciative nod. "It's a nice one."

"It was our Christmas present to the house two years ago. I told Ken he could take it with him, but he wouldn't hear of it." She checked her watch as she added absently, "You're welcome to use it whenever I'm not..."

"How about when you *are?*" he insisted.

She had just remembered to set the timer on the

oven. That done, she gave him another turn at her divided attention the way a woman might do for a child asking a string of questions.

"Are *you* asking *me* for a date?"

"Pretty cheap date," he allowed. "Your food and your TV."

"I haven't decided on the rate yet. It might not be so cheap." She opened the refrigerator door and peered up, down and around until she spotted her objective. "Would you like some ice tea?"

"Sure." *Finally.* "I get a discounted meatless rate, don't I?"

"For my rather renowned and very highly rated cooking, you'd be getting a bargain at twice the price."

"We'll see what the tasters have to say about that." He took a long drink from the tall glass she'd set near his elbow before asking, "Where do you go when you go out?"

"Ever since my son's former girlfriend left him with a baby, I haven't been out that much." She sat down across the island from him, folded her hands primly and stared at his tea. "It's odd, isn't it? You don't anticipate the grown-offspring-moves-back-home-with-a-baby scenario when your only offspring is a son."

"Ken's a good man." He figured she was looking for some outside reassurance. "Takes his responsibilities to heart. You raised him right."

"There's the little matter of getting the girl pregnant when neither of them wanted to be married to the other. I'm sure I planted that little song in his brain way back when. 'First comes love, then comes marriage. *Then* comes Kenneth with the baby carriage.'"

"Sounds like a fine recipe."

"I think so."

"Kenny just spiced it up some."

"He left out the first two ingredients. You can't do that to a perfectly good recipe." She flattened her hands on the butcher-block inset, spreading her fingers as though she were fitting the piece into the granite for the first time. "But you're right. They'll be fine. My son is a good man, and I have a beautiful grandson. They aren't that far away. I can see them anytime."

"An easy day's drive."

"It's a long drive for a toddler. But once they get settled in, maybe I'll…" She looked up at him suddenly, her eyes betraying a flash of vulnerability. "They need time to get settled, and I need to let go."

"Which comes first?" he wondered. "The letting-go part, or the getting a life?"

"What are you talking about? I have a life. I have a good life." She scowled. "That's a terrible expression, you know. *Get a life.* It's a vulgar thing to say."

"I didn't say *get a life*." On second thought, he had to admit, "Yeah, I did. That's what it amounts to, but I'm honestly wondering how you would go about it, someone like you. It's more like getting a life *of your own*. Wouldn't that help with the letting-go part? I'm just asking."

"I've never been dependent. I have my own house, my own income, my own interests. I have everything I need, and I provide it quite nicely for myself."

"Man, that was a fast turnaround," he said with a chuckle. "A minute ago I thought I was gonna have to pull out my handkerchief and catch a few tears, but you sure got your starch back in a hurry over a little vulgarity."

"A little goes a long way." She stood quickly, pushing away from the butcher block. "I'm thinking about going to Europe."

"Now?"

She shook her head impatiently, overlooking his smile. "I haven't decided when. I should talk to a travel agent. I haven't done much traveling, but I'd love to see some of the places I've studied and read so much about. France, especially." She pulled the dishtowel off her shoulder and folded it in half. "Have you seen any interesting places in your travels? Besides Montana."

"The only other countries I've been to were Canada and Mexico. Canada's nice. I don't remember much about Mexico. I was drunk the whole time I was there.''

"I've never been out of the country," she said quietly, carefully smoothing the fold she'd made, clearly ignoring the part about him being drunk.

"There's a lot to see and do right here in the good ol' U.S. of A. Right here in the Twin Cities. You don't have to go too far to find something different." He gestured with a cocked thumb. "It might be right at your front door."

"No kidding," she said, finally jarring loose with a smile.

Chapter 3

Meredith's new chicken recipe passed muster with her boarders. Raven was allowed no more than a taste of chicken with his kibbles. Meredith deemed the sauce too rich for the dog, and Ryder claimed that it was just plain too good for him. He made her admit that she didn't change into a skirt, serve wine and light candles for every meal and that she didn't often use her mother's dishes, which he helped her clear from the table at the end of the meal.

He didn't know much about dishwashers, he said, but he could scrape and wipe with the best of them. "Just don't tell anyone," he said as he hung up the towel. "There are some chores that can ruin a guy."

"Really?" She reached for his hand as he turned from the sink. It was damp and warm. "I'd say these hands can only benefit. You've got calluses on top of calluses." She looked up, saw his discomfort, and realized, to her regret, that she'd embarrassed him. She gave his hand a quick, impulsive squeeze. "As long as you promise not to tell anyone I let you touch my remote with these hands."

"Pardon me, ma'am." The confidence restored in his smile, he kept her hand from slipping away. "You're going to let me touch your remote *what?*"

"Control."

"Your control is anything but remote, but I tell you what. If I ever get my hands on it, it's goin'—"

"In addition to the TV, I have a modest library that's always open. Come see." She started to pull him along, snatching her wineglass from the shiny granite countertop as an afterthought. "Grab the bottle," she instructed, and he did. "Let's see if we can find anything on turtles."

"That doesn't sound too remote."

"Beaded ones," she said as she ushered him into her favorite room in the house. She turned on a lamp and basked in the warmth of a room full of books. "I collect old books. I just love them. The smell, the feel, the sense that the words have been right here since…''

Setting her glass aside, she pulled an old leather-bound volume from its niche and opened it carefully to the copyright page. ''Since the turn of the century. Look,'' she whispered, marveling at the detailed drawings of cook stoves and cast-iron utensils, Hoosier cabinets for the ''modern, organized kitchen,'' and laundry tools that made a wringer washer look easy to use. ''Isn't that something? Don't you wonder how many people have read this, and who they were, where they lived?''

''And why they'd be interested in Mrs. Curtiss and her discoveries?'' He added a splash of white wine to both glasses before setting the bottle on the table beside them.

''*Household* discoveries,'' Meredith amended as she turned to a photograph of a dour-looking woman whose collar seemed to be choking her.

''I'll bet her favorite household discovery was how to get a week's work out of somebody for a day's pay.''

''Look at the list of stuff they had to do on wash day.'' She ran her finger down the page before she slapped the book closed and put it back in its place. ''Just looking at it makes me tired. I would have been a total flop as a woman back then. If Mrs. Curtiss could see my kitchen—''

"She'd want to know how you got into home-maker's heaven so easy."

"I'm a homebody, not a dead body." She moved across the room to another section of shelves. "You might find something to interest you on this shelf. Native American antiquities, artifacts, basketry, ceremonies, dwellings, pottery, treaties… Oh, here." She bent to pull a book off the bottom shelf.

"That sounded alphabetical," he muttered as he moved to her side.

"Basically, yes. This one's too tall for that shelf, so it's out of order." She pushed the book into his hands and directed him toward one of the two Morris rockers that flanked the lamp table. "This has some fabulous color photographs in it It's a museum collection." She braced one arm over the back of the chair and leaned over his shoulder, turning pages for him. "There," she said of a series of beaded moccasins. "Examples from several Plains tribes. Between this and the book of Edward Curtis photographs, I know we'll find something similar to your turtle."

"Were we looking?"

"For some examples of amulets like yours." She turned a page. "Here's a cradleboard beaded with a Western Sioux mountain motif," she pointed out, reading some of the description aloud. "Isn't this gorgeous? The pattern looks very much like your hatband. Imagine how much time and skill it took some woman to make this.''

''She wasn't foolin' with any remote control.''

''Here's one with a turtle amulet.'' The turtle in the picture was red and white, and its shape seemed less distinctive than Ryder's blue and black one, but there was an interesting footnote. ''See? It says that the turtle is a symbol for longevity, and it would have contained—''

''Don't say it,'' Ryder warned. ''If I've been carrying a piece of somebody's dried-up blood vessels around all this time, I don't wanna know about it. It gives me the willies, thinking I might be wearing some dead guy's charm for long life.''

''Maybe he had a very long life, and maybe the karma passes from him to you through this amulet.''

''Or maybe not. Anyway, now you're mixing up the traditions. Karma goes with something else.'' On his own initiative, he turned the page, uncovering more beaded amulets. ''Damn. They're everywhere.''

''The word comes from somewhere else, but if karma exists, it's everywhere, too. It doesn't matter what name we give it.'' She circled behind his chair, took up her wine, passed up the other easy chair in favor of an ottoman, which put her nearly knee to knee with him. Perched before him as though she expected him to read to her, she propped her chin on her fist. "Your turtle might be a sign of more than one person's longevity," she suggested eagerly. "Maybe it's part of a connection, Ryder."

"Like an umbilical cord?" He leaned back, leaving the book lying open across his knees. "I was cut loose twice. My connection to the Red Hawks isn't much more than a nodding acquaintance. I found a few relations when I got into the Indian rodeo circuit. I've got some cousins."

"Did they know anything about your turtle?"

"I didn't ask." He smoothed the glossy page as though he were petting one of the amulets. "Yeah, I guess I wear it for luck, and maybe I've been lucky. Once or twice I missed getting gored by this much," he told her, measuring a scant inch between his thumb and forefinger. "Maybe I got a busted rib because my turtle wasn't looking. Or maybe because he *was*." After a moment's reflection, he raised his brow, challenging her theory. "What if the guy that was connected got *dis*connected? What if somebody stole his turtle? You know, cut him off prematurely? What if he—or his spirit or karma or wandering soul—what if he has bad feelings toward the people who keep passing his turtle around?"

She stared silently, trying to read his eyes. Was he worried, or was he teasing her?

He stared back, but one corner of his mouth finally twitched. "You don't know, do you?"

"I think…" Surrendering the stare-down, she focused on the book. "I'm convinced it came off a baby's cradleboard, which means it's a gentle kind of karma. Or whatever you want to call it."

"I haven't been gentle with it. That ol' turtle has seen its share of rowdiness and hard action, graced more than a few hats."

In stark contrast with the white margins of the book pages, Ryder's brown hands looked rough, ready for hard action, not quite at ease with the book or the chair or the wineglass. He took care with these things, as he certainly had with his only heirloom. Maybe he didn't know he'd been gentle with it. Maybe his gentleness came straight from the heart without any detours through the brain for conscious fine-tuning. What would it feel like, being handled by such a man's hands?

The very thought was completely un-Meredith. She couldn't remember the last time she'd noticed anything so particular about a man as his hands. Not a real man, anyway, not…

"Are you…do you have other…attachments?"

"To a woman, you mean?"

"Yes. Girlfriend, wife, intended? Children? You know, attachments in a family way."

"No. No ol' lady, legal, common or intended. And no one in a family way, as far as I…" He looked into her eyes and let her watch the light dance in his, let her see that he knew damn well why she'd asked, but that he didn't mind that she'd asked. He finally gave a hearty laugh. "Man, when you get personal, you cover all the bases right off the bat."

"Well, I—"

He lifted a hand. "Don't spoil it, now. Don't try to say you didn't mean to."

Smiling, strangely emboldened, she sipped her wine.

"I might just go to the rodeo myself this weekend and see for myself what a turtle's share of rowdiness and hard action looks like."

"I don't know if that's such a good idea," he said, abruptly sober. "I can't hardly see the rodeo as your cup of tea."

"I wouldn't expect tea." Then she matched her tone to his. "I wouldn't want to see any animals get hurt, though."

"More likely you'd see a cowboy or two get a little banged up."

"That I can handle," she tossed out lightly. "Just no horses or bulls. Or turtles. Oh, and would you mind paying your rent before you ride your bull?"

"I'd pay right now if I knew—"

"Just kidding. If you can fix that leak upstairs, we'll call it even." Grinning, she tapped the back of his hand. "But could you do it before the rodeo?"

"You're a wise woman." He reached for his glass. "The truth is, I don't ride bulls anymore."

"I thought you said you were a—"

"Bull *fighter,* but that's an exaggeration now, too." He sipped his wine and grimaced—whether over the wine or the truth, she wasn't sure. "It used to be my specialty, but I gotta quit doin' that altogether pretty quick here."

"I thought bullfighting was a different sport."

"It is."

"They don't have bullfighting in rodeos. We don't have bullfighting in this country at all, do we? It's so…" She stood up slowly, finishing her indictment with a facial expression mirroring the one he'd made over the tart wine. "So cruel. Not that I've ever—"

"Don't worry. In rodeo bullfighting, the bull is the only one who gets to carry any sharp weapons. Like I said, you won't see bloodshed, at least not from four-legged creatures."

She was headed for the other chair, walking gingerly. The bottoms of her feet had stiffened up, and she had to stretch the kinks out.

"Did you pick up a rock in your shoe?" he asked.

"Bad feet," she explained. "They seem to be aging faster than the rest of me. By the end of the day…"

"I know what you mean." He moved to the ottoman and patted the dish he'd made in the chair cushion. "Sit down here and let me give you my treatment for happy feet."

She settled into the big chair, warmed and reshaped by his body. His gesture called for her feet in his lap. Her response—because her big, flat feet had surely never been her best feature—was tentative. Like a patient afraid to see her wounds or the look on the face of the one who would tend them, she sank back in the chair. She felt his hands slip behind her knees and slide down the back of her undoubtedly bristly calves. He was doing all the choosing, the lifting, the planting of her heels firmly on his thighs, the peeling away of her canvas shoes.

"Here's your problem," he diagnosed, and she imagined a hideous wart or boil—something new to add to her growing collection of physical imperfections. "These shoes go nice with your skirt, but they're not giving your feet the support they deserve. Got any horse liniment around?"

She laughed, absurdly relieved. "I just used the last of it, I'm afraid."

His hands gave pain before pleasure, but she knew her feet were to blame. She held her breath while he took his own pains working them over, moving slowly, end to end. It was all she could do to keep quiet.

"How about Bag Balm?"

She lifted her head from the backrest. "What's…"

"For cows' udders. Keeps the teats nice and…"

She scowled. "Those are my feet."

"You don't think I know the difference between feets and teats?" He grinned. "Are yours ticklish?"

Giggling, she jerked her feet back, but he grabbed them before they escaped.

"How can I make them happy without getting to know their little quirks?"

"Ticklish feet are normal. I don't have any quirks."

"Everybody has quirks." He winked at her as he resumed the rhythm of his massaging. "Relax. I'm only holding your foot."

"A rather intimate undertaking for someone who walked into my life just a few hours ago." She smiled with pure pleasure. "Or limped. Did I miss that? I have a feeling you're a bit more perceptive than I am, but you obviously know something… ahhhh-bout tired feet."

"Does that feel good?" He shifted his kneading, turning her heel to dough. "How about here?"

She stretched and flexed, reaching for more until his heated glance turned hers to the foot that had strayed too close to his crotch. She jerked both feet away. Their eyes exchanged hints of trepidation and reassurance. He reclaimed the foot that had escaped him, followed by the more innocent one. He smiled as he watched the tension ebb from her limbs, her shoulders, finally her face.

"You're a beautiful woman."

"I'm older than you are."

"Did I say 'for your age'?" He chuckled. "That's the worst comeback my flattery has ever gotten me." He lifted a sturdy shoulder. "Except for the time I got slapped, but I was sadly misunderstood. My vocabulary was limited to man talk back then."

"Is that a language?"

"Let me try again," he said with a warm smile. "You're a very beautiful woman, Meredith. The way you move around in the kitchen, handling your pots and plates, fixing up the food. The way you stop to pet your cat, thought to give my dog some water, put the salt and pepper out even though you don't use either one. I haven't once asked myself how old you might be, and that's the truth."

"I'm a grandmother." But her smile felt girlish and flirtatious. "A very young grandmother, but still..." She sighed, fighting off total contentment. "I don't know what to think."

"About what?"

"You. No, *me*. I can't believe I'm doing this." He questioned her with a look. "Letting you stay," she said. "I can't believe I didn't tell you that it was all a mistake, and I'm sorry and good luck at your next stop."

"You still can."

"But I don't want to," she admitted. His smile was too self-satisfied. "Be rude. I hate rudeness. I agreed to let you have the room for a week, and I'm fine with that." She tipped her head back. "This feels heavenly."

"Heaven is a safe place to be." After a moment he added, "You're safe, Meredith."

Tucking her doubts away for later, she nodded.

"But I don't think it's such a good idea for you to come to the rodeo. I think we're better off for you to forget that plan."

"Why? I can always leave if I see anything upsetting."

"Once you've seen it, you can't un-see it."

"Are you going to do something bad?"

"Maybe. You might not like it." He shrugged. "You just don't strike me as a rodeo kind of a gal, and I don't want you wastin' your time on my account."

"I'm not in the habit of wasting anything." In a test flex her feet gave her no pain. "Ahh, that was some aperitif, Ryder. I guess taking in a boarder isn't such a bad idea." She smiled. "It's just that you're such a surprise."

"That makes two of us. You're a real nice surprise." He patted her foot. "For a grandma."

She always had her morning coffee and read the newspaper on the porch. One of the advantages to

working at home was not having to rush off anywhere in the morning. She had a good life. With
Ken and Collin gone, it had become a quiet life.
Some people might call it dull. A thrill-seeker like
Ryder Red Hawk would undoubtedly come to that
conclusion after a day or two. She had not seen him
yet this morning and wondered whether he was a
late riser.

"I found it" came the sudden announcement
from the kitchen. "Come see the cause of all your
cussing."

"Good morning to you, too," she said when he
popped his head into the doorway. "What cussing?"

"Yesterday, remember? When you cussed me
outta' the shower." He motioned her out of her
comfortable wicker chair. "Come take a look at the
bugger."

"Bugger?" She followed, even though she
wasn't sure she wanted to find out what kind of a
bug caused a leaky shower. "I didn't cuss at you.
What bugger?"

"Not only do you have a hole, but I'm bettin'
you've got a mouse."

"I have a cat. Somewhere." She paused to greet
his dog, but glancing to the top of the stairs, she
saw no cat. "Kitty's been hiding since Raven arrived."

"She's also been falling down on the job." He ushered her into his room, past his neatly made bed, into the bathroom, where he presented his morning's discovery by thrusting his finger through a hole in the wall. "This is the work of a mouse right here. Somebody tried to stick some caulking around that soap thing and patch some of the grout, but it didn't hold. Your son does good work on dogs and horses, but he did a piss-poor patch-up job on this shower stall."

"How do you know this wasn't my patch-up job?"

"You would have hired it done."

Eyeing the patchwork of tile and old adhesive on the shower walls, the crumbled grout and the litter on the floor, Meredith sighed. "I didn't even think you were up yet."

"I got right to it, just like I promised. Didn't take much to track down the problem."

"You found two problems, which means I'll need to track down a carpenter who also does tile work *and* an exterminator."

"What for? You've got me." With the toe of his boot he scraped a pile of litter toward the base of the toilet. "Is breakfast ready yet?"

"Breakfast?"

"I work for food," he reminded her.

"That's right." A snap of her fingers signaled things remembered. "Real men eat breakfast." On

GET 2

HOW TO GET YOUR
2 FREE BOOKS AND FREE GIFT!

1. Peel off the MIRA® sticker on the front cover. Place it in the space provided at right. This automatically entitles you to receive two free books and an exciting surprise gift.

2. Send back this card and you'll get 2 "The Best of the Best™" books. These books have a combined cover price of $11.98 or more in the U.S. and $13.98 or more in Canada, but they are yours to keep absolutely FREE!

3. There's <u>no</u> catch. You're under <u>no</u> obligation to buy anything. We charge nothing – ZERO – for your first shipment. And you don't have to make any minimum number of purchases – not even one!

4. We call this line "The Best of the Best" because each month you'll receive the best books by some of today's most popular authors. These authors show up time and time again on all the major bestseller lists and their books sell out as soon as they hit the stores. You'll like the convenience of getting them delivered to your home at our special discount prices . . . and you'll love your *Heart to Heart* subscriber newsletter featuring author news, horoscopes, recipes, book reviews and much more!

SPECIAL FREE GIFT!
We'll send you a fabulous surprise gift, absolutely FREE, simply for accepting our no-risk offer!

5. We hope that after receiving your free books you'll want to remain a subscriber. But the choice is yours – to continue or cancel, anytime at all! So why not take us up on our invitation, with no risk of any kind. You'll be glad you did!

6. And remember...we'll send you a surprise gift ABSOLUTELY FREE just for giving THE BEST OF THE BEST a try.

Visit us online at
www.mirabooks.com

® and TM are registered trademark of Harlequin Enterprises Limited.

BOOKS FREE!

THE BEST OF THE BEST™ — Here's How it Works:

Accepting your 2 free books and gift places you under no obligation to buy anything. You may keep the books and gift and return the shipping statement marked "cancel." If you do not cancel, about a month later we will send you 4 additional books and bill you just $4.74 each in the U.S., or $5.24 each in Canada, plus 25¢ shipping & handling per book and applicable taxes if any.* That's the complete price and — compared to cover prices starting from $5.99 each in the U.S. and $6.99 each in Canada — it's quite a bargain! You may cancel at any time, but if you choose to continue, every month we'll send you 4 more books, which you may either purchase at the discount price or return to us and cancel your subscription.

*Terms and prices subject to change without notice. Sales tax applicable in N.Y. Canadian residents will be charged applicable provincial taxes and GST. Credit or Debit balances in a customer's account(s) may be offset by any other outstanding balance owed by or to the customer.

If offer card is missing write to: The Best of the Best, 3010 Walden Ave., P.O. Box 1867, Buffalo, NY 14240-1867

BUSINESS REPLY MAIL
FIRST-CLASS MAIL   PERMIT NO. 717-003   BUFFALO, NY

POSTAGE WILL BE PAID BY ADDRESSEE

THE BEST OF THE BEST
3010 WALDEN AVE
PO BOX 1867
BUFFALO NY 14240-9952

NO POSTAGE
NECESSARY
IF MAILED
IN THE
UNITED STATES

second thought, she eyed the hole in her wall. "Are you sure you can handle this? It's turning into a pretty complicated repair job."

"Real men do their own repairs."

"But this is…" She started to say *my own repair,* but something in his eyes made her smile and offer Swedish pancakes instead.

Chapter 4

Ryder had never met a woman who had her own library. It had to be the most comfortable room he'd ever experienced. It felt good to sit in a big, cushy chair surrounded by shelves full of books and classy knickknacks and nice pictures on the walls and realize that the room wasn't part of a public building. There were no hours here. No closing time. No rules against having food and drink.

He loved to read, but he never stayed in one place long enough to use the library for checking out books. He always had a few paperback books in his duffel bag. Westerns, mainly. After he read them, he'd give them away or trade them in if he ran across the right bookstore. Keeping the good ones around would be nice, he thought. He'd bought some of his favorite stories more than once.

With the shower fixed and Meredith busy at her computer, Ryder had followed her suggestion that he "retire to the library with a glass of lemonade." He had tried not to let on that the consequence of squatting in the bathtub was a knee aching to retire to a sandy beach on some no-bull island in the Caribbean. He had to wonder what kind of attention a little limping might have earned him after the foot massage he'd given Meredith last night. Wondering was one thing, but he wasn't ready to find out. In the sympathy department, dishing it out was easier than taking it. Or, stickier still, being denied.

He already liked this woman as much as her son had promised he would. Kenny got to teasing him about turning into a fussy old bachelor and asked him just what kind of woman he might be willing to settle down with. Ryder didn't remember exactly what he'd said, but Kenny's response was that he'd just described his mother. It probably wouldn't have mattered what qualities he'd listed; Kenny was all set to claim them for his mom. Ryder had been set up, pure and simple.

But it sure was nice to be able to take his hound and his lemonade and "retire" to the lady's fine library.

He set his hat on its crown on the side table,

signaled for Raven to relax, and pulled out the American Indian art book he'd looked through with Meredith the night before. He flipped to the Plains Indian beadwork and paid close attention to the cradleboards. He'd never thought much about getting married, but he'd often imagined being a dad. He wondered how Kenny was making out down in South Dakota. Some trick, being a dad without a woman around. Ryder figured Kenny would find himself a nice girl within a few months. A year, tops. She'd look something like Meredith. She'd have the blue eyes, maybe, or the fine-boned hands. Kenny wouldn't even realize it himself, but there would be some similarity between the girl he picked for himself and his mom.

"Kid stuff's gettin' to me," Ryder muttered as he fanned past the cradleboard pages and into the pottery section. But there were turtle images crawling all over those pages, too.

Chuckling, he reached across the arm of the chair and sought his own turtle. "What's inside your belly, old friend? Are you carrying any secrets in there?" He caressed its bumpy back with his thumb. "You've been ridin' up there just above my ear all this time, and you never gave me a hint. Not a whisper." He gave another chuckle, remembering Meredith's burning curiosity. "Hey, you don't have to worry about me cutting you open, ol' fella. You don't wanna say anything, your secret's safe.

"But I guess I gotta wonder if whatever you've got in there is...ever *was* any connection to somebody I might be related to. Some kind of family connection. Not that I care about droppin' any names, you understand. Ryder Red Hawk is all the name I need. But some hint that whoever came before..."

"See this?" He pulled his T-shirt up, tucked his thumb into the waistband of his jeans and pulled down. "I've got a belly button, just like everybody else. I had one of those cords once. It was attached to some woman named Elaine. Father unknown. Hell, you'd think he would've dropped his own name, but..."

Raven raised his head, nose pointed toward the door. The floor creaked. Ryder pulled his shirt down as he turned slowly in the chair.

He grimaced sheepishly. "How long have you been standing there?"

Flustered, Meredith shook her head. She was glad she was carrying a plate of the blond brownies she'd made for no particular reason. They gave her an excuse for her sudden appearance, while her rubber soles explained her silence, even though she truly regretted hitting the wrong floorboard when she had.

"I didn't mean to—" *Cut you off quite so soon.*

"There you go again, doin' stuff you don't mean to."

She shrugged. "I heard you promise the turtle you wouldn't cut him open."

"Which proves I'm harmless, right? You oughta' feel safe with a guy who wouldn't hurt a turtle."

"I oughta'?" She felt a lot of things with him, but she wasn't ready to sort those things out and figure out what they were. She set the plate between his hat and his lemonade and turned the tables. "I was just wondering whether talking to a stuffed turtle was normal behavior for a rodeo cowboy."

"Cowboys'll talk to anything that don't talk back." On his way to returning the book to its shelf, he cocked an accusatory finger at Raven. "Too slow with the warning, there, partner."

"Is it normal behavior for an Indian?"

What a dumb question.

"Now, that I couldn't tell you." He turned from the bookshelf. The look of chagrin had vanished. "If you were listening just now, you know why."

"I wasn't really, but I..." It was a white lie, she realized. Thrown out in defense, which was the supposedly best offense. But that was unnecessary, gaining her nothing, and fooling no one. "Well, I *heard.* Frankly, I thought it was cute when I realized whom you were talking to. And in case you couldn't tell, I was trying to be cute with the cowboy and Indian remarks. That's really all I know about you, so..." Sidestepping the dog, backing herself into a corner, she shook her head in disgust. "Oh, I'm such a poor tease. I always fall flat."

He laughed. "I'm the one who just made an ass of myself, and you're embarrassed. For me?"

"No," she said quickly. "For myself."

"I don't get any?" He grinned and nodded toward the brownies.

"Oh, yes. Those are for you." The sparkle in the eyes of a male coveting her sweets reassured her. "You need to bulk up a little bit to fight those bulls."

"Lack of bulk is my main advantage over them. I'm down to less than half a step ahead of them as it is. But we won't turn these down, will we, boy?" Ryder broke a brownie in half.

Raven knew an offer of food when he heard one.

"Not the chocolate part," Meredith admonished. "Chocolate is really bad for dogs."

"Yes, ma'am." Dutifully Ryder started nibbling bits of chocolate out of Raven's half.

The dog whined, every bit the kid watching his big brother "evening up" the shares.

Mouth full, Ryder muttered, "She said no chocolate for you. Mmm. Here. Oops. One more."

"Don't tease him!"

"But I'm good at it." Laughing, he tossed the trimmed treat, and the dog snatched it out of the air. "I'm a professional, right, boy? That's all you get.'' Ryder polished off his half of the brownie in one bite.

A boy and his dog, she thought.

And without thinking, she asked, ''You never knew your parents at all?''

''I think my mother died not too long after I was born. I know I was with an old lady for two or three years before I got into foster care.''

''But you said you've met some of your relatives when you went to rodeos and powwows in South Dakota. Cowboy days and Indian nights, you said. Didn't you ask them?''

''Ask them what? What happened to my mother? Hell, no, I ain't gonna ask nobody that.'' He squatted on his heels beside Raven, who presented his belly for scratching. ''Somebody says we're cousins, or they're my grandma the Indian way, I just nod and shake their hand.''

''Is that part of the Indian way?''

''It's the cowboy way. You wanna avoid trouble, you keep your eyes and ears open and your mouth shut about where you came from. You don't ask other guys where they came from, either.''

''Don't ask, don't tell?''

''Yeah, well...'' He gave Raven a parting pat before pushing off a noisy knee to stand up. ''Seems like a damn good policy on any subject that's nobody else's business.''

He seemed taller, more intimidating than he had

a moment ago. Meredith glanced away, muttering. "You've told me some things."

"That's different."

If she asked him what he meant, he wasn't sure he could explain. He picked up one of the books he'd been reading and turned to a photograph he knew would offer quick distraction.

"Here's another one of those baby boards with the beaded turtle charm. This guy could be ol' Turtle's brother."

She seemed to welcome the excuse to move in close and peer over his arm. "They really are similar," she said. "So much work was put into these cradle boards, and babies outgrow everything so fast. Look, it says the baby's paternal aunt would probably have made the cradleboard."

"If the baby's dad had a sister. What if he didn't? What if he didn't have any family?"

"Community and family were so important to them, there must have been someone." She smiled up at him. "The Indian way."

"I used to rodeo with a guy from another South Dakota reservation, said he was gonna adopt me as his brother. I thought he was puttin' me on. Like it was some Hollywood blood-brother thing, you know? He said there was a ceremony they did, and Hollywood didn't know nothin' about it."

"Did you become his brother?"

"We never got around to doing the ceremony. We're buddies, though. That's good enough."

They stood awkwardly, each holding a side of the big book, his forehead a fraction of an inch from resting in her hair as they pretended to be so absorbed in the words on the page that they could neither close the book or sit down with it.

"Oh, look," she said, pointing.

Okay, she wasn't pretending.

"They used cattail fluff in the cradleboard. I wondered about that."

"The first disposable diaper in America," he mused, gaining interest.

"Wouldn't it be fun to come up with a new brand?" She stepped away, eyes bright from the light bulb he imagined above her head. "Cattail disposable diapers. Biodegradable, all natural. We'd have a cattail logo. Beadwork design on the package. Oh, I know." She clapped her hands. "Baby turtles!"

"Not one little, two little, three little baby Indians with tiny headbands and toy bows and arrows?" he teased.

"We wouldn't want to be politically incorrect, but cuteness would be essential for the package. Baby turtles," she decided.

"With headbands. We gotta have headbands."

"If you say so." She offered a handshake. "Partners?"

"Partners," he said, taking her right hand in his left as he set the book aside. "Where do we get cattails?"

"We grow our own. That's where you come in." She squeezed his hand. "You get to herd the cats."

Their laughter made a sweet duet, background music for the subtle caressing of her hand in his.

"You miss having the baby around, don't you?" he asked softly.

She nodded. "I was upset with my son for bringing a baby home when I thought that part of my life was over. Now I'm upset with him for taking it away from me a second time. Mixed feelings." She smiled at him, almost apologetically. "Are there any other kind?"

"I sure have mixed feelings about you going to the rodeo. It's nice that you want to go, but..." He sandwiched her hand in both of his, his eyes avoiding hers. "I used to be real good at it. What I do now is..." He glanced up. "Well, it's not what you think. I'm getting too slow for the bullfighting event. I do..." Why couldn't he say the word? "What I do is I distract the animals from the cowboys on the ground."

"You're a rodeo clown?"

"You said you didn't know much about rodeo."

"I know they have clowns. Are you funny?"

"What do you think?"

"Sometimes you are." Her smile turned all

warm. No apology, no sympathy. Nothing but affection. "Do you tell jokes?"

"I've been tellin' you jokes all along. Haven't you noticed?"

"Sometimes it's hard to tell. So that settles it." She clapped her free hand on the back of his, decision made. "This is one show I don't want to miss. What's your costume like?"

He groaned, slyly slipping his hands around her waist.

"Is it funny? Do you wear makeup?" She brushed the backs of her fingers down his cheek. "Confession time," she said softly. "I've imagined your face with war paint."

"Now imagine it with greasepaint."

"Red and white?"

He tipped his head, acknowledging his colors. Her fingers felt soft on his face. The scent of baked sweets and freshly washed hair filled his head and made his mouth water. He was in no mood for clowning.

"It's a shame to cover up these interesting angles and hard…"

"Hard what?"

"Do you wear…" She touched his hair.

"You're makin' me feel pretty funny, Meredith. So funny I'm gonna make you—" enfolding her, holding her fully against him, he whispered against her lips "—forget to laugh."

Setting caution and courtesy aside, he kissed her hungrily.

Putting common sense and circumspection in a remote corner, she kissed him back, eagerly.

Nothing had ever tasted as good to either tongue as that first kiss. If the first was that good, the second would blow them away. Up the stairs and into someone's bed. He knew it, and she knew it and so they made the first kiss last, holding caution and common sense at bay. They filled themselves to the brim with the succulent blended taste and sound and scent they were creating together for the first time.

The kiss lingered in all their senses beyond its doing. They read its worth in each other's eyes. He knew it was too hot. She thought it was too soon. But it was what it was, a crazy thing between a cook and a clown, and neither of them wanted it to go away.

"Is this something you want to get into with me, Meredith?"

"Why are you asking? Can't you tell? I mean..." He was giving her a chance to think it over, damn him. She put her arms tight around his neck, her mouth close to his ear and whispered, "Can't you just tell?"

His arms tightened around her, but he said nothing.

She leaned back. "I feel funny, but I'm not laughing. That should tell you something."

"*You* should tell me something," he insisted. "You should tell me what you want from me. Is it the same as what I want to give you?"

"I wish you wouldn't ask. I wish you would just sweep me off my feet without giving me a chance to think too much."

"Ah, you're one of those. I've heard about women like you." He smiled. "But I've never actually met one."

"I don't know what you mean."

"I think you do. But in case it's still hard for you to tell, these are not the jokes, folks. This is your house, your call. You say the word, and we're headed into some serious territory."

"And the word is?"

"You know what the word is, honey. You'll have to be the one to say it."

"It's been so long," she said with a sigh. She'd been swept off her feet then, too, spared the annoyance of accountability because she was young and innocent and hopping with mysterious hormones.

"That's what I figured," he said as their embrace slowly fell away. "And that's why I had to ask. I want to hear the word. I want you to say it and mean it. I want us both feelin' funny and crazy and free to laugh out loud." He reached for her again. "Where are you going?"

"To soak my head." She was gathering the dishes. "To stew myself in the hot juices of my imagination."

"Does that mean I should take a cold shower?"

"Of course not." She extended him one last chance at a brownie, but he shook it off. She shrugged. "You haven't finished the tiling."

Chapter 5

Her behavior had been horribly childish, but Meredith had nevertheless made her desires fairly clear, she thought. She hoped. She *thought* she hoped.

Seduction wasn't her best talent. She wanted to be wooed. She certainly wasn't going to throw herself at the man. Maybe he wasn't as attracted to her as she was to him. Maybe all he really wanted was room and board. He wouldn't want to hurt her feelings. She liked that. There was so much about him that she liked. He was a little shy about some things—wanting her to think of him as a cowboy rather than a clown.

Maybe he was shy about sex.

Right. *Say the word,* he'd said. Smart clown. *You asked for it,* he could say later, and he'd be able to quote the verbal contract, chapter and verse.

Wrong. He wanted her to be as clear with him as he'd been with her. Crazy-laugh-out-loud clear. Free and clear. He would come for her soon.

Ha-ha! He would come for her. Wasn't she naughty, though?

Maybe she was setting herself up for a huge disappointment, but she was going to be ready, just in case.

The dim pink glow of the seashell nightlight in the bathroom was all the light she needed for her bedtime ritual, even though she was changing it somewhat. She'd passed over the usual pajamas in favor of her only diaphanous garment, the long white nightgown that shared the back of a drawer with a couple of pairs of satin bikini panties and several bundles of lavender sachet. What the heck, she'd told herself when she'd gone back for a pair of the bikinis, might as well go all the way. She was amazed they still fit. It had been a long time since anyone had seen her underwear.

That's what I figured.

What else had he figured? She leaned close to the bathroom mirror as she patted miracle age-defying anti-wrinkle cream around her eyes. It seemed to be working, especially in this light. She'd admitted to being older than he was, but she

didn't think she looked it. His face was pretty
craggy for a forty-year-old. In a nice weather-
beaten, sun-drenched way, of course. She, on the
other hand, had been happily grazing in the over-
the-hill pasture for almost eight years.

Happily.

The familiar patter of canine paws drew her from
the mirror into the bedroom. She almost expected
Lydia to wander through the doorway and hop up
on her bed, but she greeted Raven by the correct
name.

"Did he kick you out of his bed?" Her gown
puddled around her as she knelt to exchange pets
for licks. "You haven't been drinking from the big
white bowl, have you, Raven? Does he leave the
lid up for you?"

"Did you leave your door open for me?"

Her gaze traveled from boots to jeans to belt
buckle, bare chest, to the hat brim dipping close to
the dark eyes of the man standing in her bedroom
doorway.

"I haven't gone to bed yet," she said, her mouth
suddenly gone dry.

"Good, because I just finished the tiling, and I
could use a shower." He hung his hat on a tall
bedpost, sat on the fluffy duvet-covered comforter
she'd folded to the foot of the bed, and pulled his
boots off, tucking a sock inside each one.

"Is it okay if I put these under your bed tonight?"

"If they're made for walking, I suppose you're worried about them getting away from you while you're in the shower."

"They don't go anywhere without me and vice versa. Same goes for the dog and the hat." He cocked a finger toward the former, a thumb at the latter.

"Is that the cowboy way?"

"Damn straight. Now answer my question." He stood facing her, boots in hand, looking like a man set to wade in. "I put it as delicately as I know how."

She took his boots and slid them beneath her bed. Then she took his big, roughened hands in her small, soft ones. They would wade in together.

Was it possible after all this time, she wondered, to fall in love this quickly?

She smiled. "Once the hat and boots come off, does that mean the cowboy's day is over?"

"And the Indian's night begins," he said, his voice turning husky when he tried to make it soft. "I want to spend it here with you."

"I was hoping you would. I was afraid…"

He drew her arms around his body. "I never thought…"

"…you didn't want…" She leaned into him.

"…you'd want…"

"Yes, I do. I want us to..."

"I want us, too." Firmly he moved his hands up her sides, creating a ruching of nylon and bunching of breasts. "This is a real pretty gown."

"I wore it for you."

"I'm going to take it off you for me, but first I'm going to shower me for you." He bent to kiss the swell of each breast before he backed away. "You leave those boots where they are, okay?"

"Okay."

She got into bed and watched him disappear into the bathroom. He left the door cracked open, sending a shaft of light across the foot of the bed giving her a quick peek after he'd shed his jeans. God, he looked beautiful in the buff from the back.

Maybe it was an invitation. *Follow the light.* She'd often wondered what it would be like to make love under the shower. But not under the light. No, that would be too much exposure to suit Meredith this early in the game.

Who said *game?*

Not Meredith Woodward. She didn't play games. She didn't play peek-a-boo, I-see-you, not with her unexpected boarder. She didn't play hide-and-seek in the dark. Come find me under the covers, but don't look at me too closely because I'm past my prime, and women don't care but men do. So she'd heard.

Was it foolish to trust this soon?

Okay, but *how* foolish? On a scale of one to ten?

The water stopped running. She held her breath, watching that crack of light until it dimmed.

This was definitely level-ten foolishness.

He'd left the nightlight on, the way he'd found it, and emerged with a white towel wrapped around his slim waist.

"You should have told me you were going to dress up." She hoped she sounded clever.

"I didn't want to scare you with it, but I'm up, all right," he boasted as he planted his knee on the mattress. One cracked; the other creaked. He chuckled. "Some of my parts are rustier than others."

He placed what appeared to be a multitude of condoms on her nightstand. Rusty or not, the man clearly expected things to proceed quite swimmingly.

She gave a small laugh. "I'm not scared. Just a little nervous."

"Me, too," he whispered, hovering over her, lowering himself as though he were on the down side of a pushup. "I feel like a clown getting into bed with a princess."

He'd just knocked the foolishness level down to five.

He kissed her lips with excruciating tenderness and told her, "I'm a big boy."

"Oh?"

"You tell me to stop, I can stop."

"Oh."

"You wanna break my heart, you tell me to stop." He touched her breasts through her nightgown as he pressed his kisses and whispered his crazy promises against the side of her neck. "I could probably back off if I had to."

"I don't think...that'll be—" oh, oh, his chin between her breasts, separating them for a kiss smack dab "—necessary."

"Just so you know."

"I know so little, Ryder, please—" she drew a deep breath as he took her nipple, nightgown and all, into his mouth "—teach me."

"Touch me, and I will."

She slipped her hand between their bodies, and he sucked in his belly to ease her way to the tucked corner of the towel. He sucked in even more as she ran her fingernails lightly over his abdomen, slowly over his groin. She discovered that his desire was outstanding, while hers spun itself into a knot deep inside her.

He permitted her to caress him briefly before pulling her hand away with a deep groan. "Maybe not as big as I thought."

"Stop thinking and start teaching."

"With me, a little touching goes a long way. For you..."

"Is this a long way?" She teased his belly again. "I want to learn all about Mr. Long Way."

"You'll meet him again when you're ready to bite his head off."

"Oh, my."

"Oh, your what? Your nightgown's in the way? Pretty little thing," he whispered—to her or her nightgown—she didn't know, didn't care. Up, up, over her head, finally freed and flung into the air, it fluttered like a gauzy parachute and fell to the floor on Raven's side of the bed.

The dog sniffed, stretched and snorted with indifference.

"He doesn't know what he's missing," Ryder said, smiling down at her in the shadows.

"His 'what' is missing?"

He laughed as he rolled to his back, taking her with him so that, with a little shifting, he propped himself up against the padded headboard and had her riding him astride.

Again she whispered, "Oh, my..."

"Your what, funny lady? Your breasts?"

He lifted her, tongued her, suckled her until she rolled her hips and rocked, rubbing Ryder exactly the right way. Oh, but he had a rhythm about him. He knew all about gaits and how to work one against the other to make the ride last. "My Meredith," he whispered. His words made her shiver. "I want to make you merry."

"I want to make you wild," she said.

"I want to make you mine."

He taught her how to take him for a ride, then slow down a bit and go along for the ride, then to post him while he petted her until they couldn't tell who was riding and who was being ridden, until nothing mattered but riding all the way, all the way, all the way home.

It was a long, luxurious night. It was a night for discovering wonders, for dozing and drifting in each other's arms, and then stirring each other to discover more. When morning's first blush began to brighten the space around them, illuminating the pale cabbage roses on the wall, the creamy soft curtains and the painted glass lampshades, they were still gazing sleepily across the pillows into each other's eyes. The intimacy between them was so complete that it was expressed in the smallest gesture, the mere touch of his finger to her face, her hand on his shoulder.

She broke the silence.

"What would you like for breakfast?"

His slow smile was as sweet as sunrise.

"Besides that," she said.

"A long soak in a hot tub and a tin of that horse liniment I mentioned before."

With a sassy smile, she snuggled close. "Was I too much for you, cowboy?"

"Almost," he said, snaking his arm beneath her pillow. "But I'm already looking forward to another go-round.'' He frowned as he pulled an interloper from underneath her pillow.

"Is this what I think it is?'' He held the teddy bear aloft. "Am I being watched by a jealous bear?''

"Some people have their turtles, others have their bears.'' She tried to take the old toy, but Ryder held it out of her reach.

The well-loved brown bear bore his closer scrutiny. "Somebody blinded him.''

The pronouncement sounded harsh, considering the identity of the perpetrators. Sitting up, Meredith took the bear away from Ryder and stroked its worn face.

"Ken almost choked on one of the eyes, so I took the other one off. When I dug him out of storage and gave him to Collin, he cried and threw a fit because the eyes were missing. He wanted Daddy to fix them.''

"Makes sense,'' Ryder allowed as he propped himself up beside her. "His daddy's a veterinarian.''

"Instead, Ken came up with a story about Nosy, the bear.''

"No See? Sounds like a good Indian name.''

"His name is Nosy, not No See.'' She bumped Ryder's shoulder with hers as she posed the bear on her upraised, sheet-draped knee. "Nosy's an old bear who came with kid-unfriendly button eyes.

He's gotten along quite well most of his life without them, and that's because he has a super nose. Ken made up a wonderful story about Nosy, the super-nose bear.''

''And how did he get left behind?''

''He was a gift. A trade for Lydia.'' She smiled sadly. ''Kids don't miss a trick. When I was saying my goodbyes, Collin knew that, um…'' She glanced down at Raven, who was awake, ready, waiting for his signal to start the day, just the way Lydia had been every morning. Meredith's throat tingled. ''She sticks with Collin from the time he gets up until the time he goes to bed, but at night…''

''Nosy slept with Collin, and Lydia slept with you.''

''Yep.'' She nodded, keeping the stiff upper lip. ''So, we traded.''

''It's probably just as well ol' Nosy can't see me. I don't smell too bad, but if he saw me, he might not approve.'' He took her free hand in his, lacing brown fingers with white ones. ''We're an odd match.''

''We're a nice blend.''

''Do we smell good together, Nosy boy?'' He lifted their hands to the bear's fuzzy nose. ''I'll bet we do. Clean livin' and good lovin'.''

She laughed. ''Let's bottle it and call it 'Cowboy Days and Indian Nights.' Talk about a great blend.''

"I generally don't," he said quietly. "Talk about it, I mean. I used to try to blend, but in the family that raised me, I stood out like a fly in the milk, and they let me know it. I stood out at the wrong time in all the wrong ways. Got so I hated hearing my name called. I imagined becoming invisible, started pretending I had the power to disappear. I was there, but they couldn't see me. I could do anything I wanted, as long as I didn't make any noise." He rested his head against the headboard and stared at the screen for the projection of memories—the bedroom ceiling. He sighed. "When I left, I just slipped out the back door."

She didn't like the sound of that. "Whose way of leaving would that be?"

"The invisible kid's way." He reassured her with a smile. "I'm not a kid anymore. I've cleaned up my act, learned some manners."

"I was impressed with your winning ways almost immediately," she quipped cheerfully.

"Almost?"

"You have to admit, it took you a while to get in the door. After that..." Working hard to reject niggling doubts, she lifted one shoulder. "...things moved pretty quickly."

"Light-of-day regrets? Look at me, Meredith." He lifted her chin with his fingertips. "What do you see this morning that hasn't been there all along?"

"The man who..."

Don't say it, just because you feel different. Men don't think that way. If you say it, he'll be laughing on the inside. He won't…

"The man who made love to you last night is the same one who came looking for a place to stay."

"You don't feel anything—"

"Oh, yes, I do. I feel something." He nodded, considering. But he glanced away, echoing softly, "I feel something."

"Enough to invite me to the rodeo?"

He turned to her again and looked at her for a moment, so seriously she thought he might crack.

And then he did. He cracked a big, bright smile. "Why not?"

Chapter 6

The only pickup truck Meredith had ever ridden in belonged to her uncle Marvin, who had a small dairy farm in southeastern Minnesota. Ryder's truck might have been built the same year she had last visited Uncle Marvin's farm, when she was about twelve. It was the year she'd found out that most of the bottle calves were destined to become hamburger and that the old dairy bull that had broken her uncle's foot was in the baloney sandwiches Aunt Carol had made for lunch. Until a few days ago she had considered Uncle Marvin's farm to be adequate experience with livestock and pickup trucks for one lifetime.

But today would be different. The bulls would not be featured on the lunch menu. She understood that people would ride them and fight them, but as long as she stayed away from the hot dog stand, she didn't have to think about them being eaten.

"Do they get thrown to the ground?" she mused. Ryder had become such a persistent resident in her thoughts that she could almost feel him taking an active role.

"Who?"

Pop went her bubble.

He rolled down his window and claimed a ticket from the parking ramp machine.

"The bulls," she said, mentally lopping off the *of course.* "Isn't there a part where they grab them by the horns and throw them down?"

"Those are steers." He handed her the ticket with a gesture toward the glove box. "No, honey, the only bull that gets thrown at a rodeo is the verbal kind. Otherwise, the real bulls get to do all the throwing." Perched between them on the bench seat, Raven got a pat on the head from his master while they waited for the ramp barrier to retract. "You got some special affection for bulls?"

"Not really. Not any more than any of God's other natural, innocent creatures."

"Would that include me?"

"No." She put her arm around Raven's shoulders and scratched his chest. "You fall into the *spe-*

cial affection category. Reserved for other than natural, innocent creatures with bizarre but undeniable appeal.''

''So if it's a choice between me and the bull...''

''Hmmm.'' Squinting, she wagged her finger between imaginary alternatives. ''Eeeny, beany, who's the meany? The thing is, the bull isn't the one who chooses to be part of the show.''

''Me or him?'' he insisted. ''Who's your pick?''

''You,'' she decided. ''Definitely you. The bull has size and weight on his side. I always root for the underdog.''

''I'll take it whatever way it comes.'' He licked his forefinger and chalked one up. ''Okay, let's go up the ladder. Between me and...'' He spared her a glance as he arced the wheel sharply to claim a parking space. ''Who's your favorite Beatle?''

''Paul. Between you and Paul, I'd choose you. But I wouldn't push my luck if I were you. Pit yourself against Russell Crowe, and you're done for.''

''Wanna bet?'' He slid her a grin that made her forget where to find the door handle. ''His arena or mine?''

He had suffered Meredith's gender-biased inspection of his makeup case before they'd left home, and now he permitted her to carry it for him as far as the performers' entrance to the event center's ''backstage'' area, where he would ''prepare for battle.'' Even as he made light of it, his demeanor had begun to change, his focus shifting to a contest she had yet to fully appreciate, a task that would challenge more than his wit. She could feel his edginess.

"Say goodbye to Ryder Red Hawk for a while." He took the battered leather case from her and gave her a smile. "You've got your ticket?"

She nodded, feeling strangely bereft.

"I'll meet you right here after the show," he promised.

A twinge of jealousy taunted her as she glanced at Raven, who could barely contain his tail-wagging excitement. *I get to go with him.*

"Don't I get to watch you put on your makeup?" She practically whined.

"You do not. It's a transformation."

Her voice flew up an octave. "But how will I know it's you?"

"By my hat." Hands full, he reassured her with his cocky wink before he turned and walked away.

He'd left her with plenty of time to buy a program and read it cover to cover while she munched on popcorn. Three clowns were listed, but Ryder "Turtle" Red Hawk had top billing. It had been several years since he'd won his last bullfighting championship, but he'd taken the top honor three years in a row. Meredith couldn't tell how long ago his press picture had been taken. She might not have recognized him under the makeup if she'd passed him on her way to the seat he'd selected for her. His bio boasted a list of rodeo accomplishments he'd said nothing about, but it told so little and showed nothing of the face of the man she knew.

Meredith had never been much of a sports enthusiast. As a teacher she had attended basketball and football games, but rules and strategies held no interest for her. She enjoyed watching her students, and later her son, play their hearts out. But watching grown men try to stay on the backs of a wild horses until the timer went off was a bit like watching dough rise. Either it came through all puffed up and proud, or it fell flat.

She devoted her attention to the clowns.

The best one wore a beaded turtle on his cowboy hat. Beneath the brim was a vaguely familiar face painted in ripples of red and white, which lent a mime's visual vitality to each change of expression. He wore oversized high-water overalls over a long-sleeved red shirt, red tights and black tennis shoes. A red bandanna hung from his back pocket, and a huge red feather adorned his beaded hatband. If bulls really got angry when they saw red, Ryder was about to infuriate them.

The announcer even called him Red—or Turtle, which prompted him to move like one. Because he was not miked, the announcer relayed his jokes over the loudspeaker. Meredith wasn't particularly amused by the one about mistaking a pair of bald men for one large woman, but the audience laughed generously. Meredith preferred Raven's tricks to the silly jokes. The contrast between the sleek, smart dog and the facile fellow in the baggy pants was pure fun as Raven showed his master up at every turn.

The bull-riding event was the true test of Ryder's quickness and athleticism. As he had promised, the bulls got to do all the throwing. Once a cowboy was on the ground, it was the clowns' job to see that he had a chance to make his exit without getting run over by the bull. Their colorful costumes and antics provided entertainment for the audience and distraction for the bull. Each time a cowboy hit the dirt, the ensuing hubbub provided equal parts of terror and delight for Meredith. Ryder poked around, dragging his feet and making swimming motions with his arms, lazily doing his turtle act until the bull took a notion to make soup of him.

Suddenly Ryder turned from the tortoise into the hare, evading the charging bull by a mere hairs-breadth. Escaping to the safety of a rubber barrel painted like a turtle shell, Ryder took an occasional flight through the air courtesy of bullpower. The bull's horns served as a handy rake, used to make tossing a clown in a barrel look as easy as pitching straw. Once the pickup men had herded the animal into a pen and closed the gate on him, ol' Turtle would emerge from his shell with a tentative expression on his face, followed by a victorious grin. He would have an exchange of jokes with the announcer, find his hat, and get ready for the next bull rider.

But one red-and-white bull with particularly large horns and snake-like moves was in no mood to play. He unseated his rider so quickly, the poor cowboy had no time to free his hand from the rope, which left him flopping like a puppet tied to the bucking bull's shoulders.

Flanked by the other two clowns, Ryder instantly positioned himself within inches of the animal's hazardous head. Anticipating changes in the bull's direction, he danced away from the horns, giving horsemen and ground men the chance to free the cowboy and pull him out of harm's way. Ryder dodged the animal's head, only to be clipped in the head by a flying hoof.

It all happened so fast that Meredith didn't realize she was standing until someone behind her asked her to sit down.

Sit down? When Ryder was *facedown* in the dirt? And he wasn't moving?

She stepped on a few toes and leapt over a lap or two on her way to the aisle. The steep steps nearly served as a slide for her descent to the ground-level floor. Along the way she caught a glimpse of chaps-clad cowboys holding a gate on the far side of the arena for two clowns carrying a third. That was where she was headed.

But the Target Center was huge, and there was no direct route to the gate. She thought she'd pinpointed her personal target, but there were escalators and multiple levels and circuitous approaches to be negotiated. She lost track of her direction. Each time she asked for directions, she was told, "You can't go back there."

But she *was* going back there, come high water or bull hockey. She finally tracked down the right gate, guarded by more cowboys. It led to the locker rooms.

"I'm here with one of the performers," she explained to a beefy but approachable-looking cowboy. "The one who was injured by the bull."

"You mean Red?"

"Where is he?" she demanded, still trying to catch her breath. "Are they taking him to a hospital? Which one?"

The cowboy shouted to someone out of Meredith's limited view. "Hey, is Red Hawk still back there, or did they haul him off?"

"He's back there counting the doctor's fingers," a voice shouted back. "If he gets the answer right, they're gonna let him finish the show."

"That's crazy," Meredith said, her desperation unexpectedly mounting. "I need to see him."

"Tell Red his mama wants to see him," the gate man shouted down the hallway.

"Meredith!" she shouted, standing on tiptoe as though every inch of elevation might count for something. "My name is Meredith, and I'm a close friend, and I simply want to—"

"What'd he say?" the gateman asked the invisible messenger.

"Says it's about time she showed up." Another cowboy hat appeared, but this one shaded the reassuring smile of a messenger-cowboy, who slid the bolt on the portable steel gate. "He's okay. Come on back."

She found him sitting on a massage table, face half washed, hair sticking up here, flattened out there as though he'd just gotten out of bed. Elbows planted on his knees, hat dangling between them, he looked disgusted.

A kid, she thought. A big kid beaten up by a huge monster on Halloween night.

"Ryder, that was so awful," she blurted out.

He looked up at her, puzzled or dazed, she wasn't sure which. "The rider got away, didn't he?" He glanced at the medical technician, who was stowing the tools of his trade in an emergency kit. "He's okay, isn't he?" Ryder questioned insistently.

"I'm betting it's a sprained wrist the way it swelled up, but the X-rays will tell us for sure. You're both lucky."

"Lucky, hell. I know my job, and I do it well." He turned to Meredith, who was more concerned about how well he was than how well he'd done. "Once the cowboy loses his seat, I'm his bodyguard. That's my job."

"You might have been killed. What's under this?" She lifted her hand to the bandage on his forehead.

"I lost my feather," he grumbled.

"I don't remember any feathers growing out of your head."

"It's bad luck to lose part of your costume. Especially a feather."

"Can't prove that by you, Red. You were..." The technician raised a warning finger. "Don't say *lucky, hell.* That's what's gonna jinx you. You were lucky not to lose an—"

"I took a small hit," Ryder told Meredith. "Two little stitches."

"Three," the medic corrected as he closed the box.

"Yeah, but the extra one is just for looks. This guy agreed to tighten up the skin around my eyes while he was at it. Cowboy facelift, right, Doc?"

Meredith was not amused. "Tell me you're finished for today."

"Can't quit now," he quipped, taking her hand in his. "Gotta get the other side done or I'll look like Quasimodo."

"Whom I personally find very attractive. Esmerelda was too young and foolish to appreciate..." Laying her free hand low on his chest, she detected some kind of binding under his shirt. "What's this?"

He gave a sheepish smile. "Ace, the bandage of champions. That's just for looks."

"Nobody can see it," she pointed out.

"You can." He grinned and whispered, "Later, in private. I'll take all the sympathy you want to dish out."

"That's the house special." She squeezed his hand and tried to drag him off the table. "Let's go home so I can start dishing."

"One more event." He wouldn't be dragged. He opted for a nimble hop. "I'll take sympathy for cracked ribs, but not for a light pay envelope."

"Cracked ribs?"

"Tender," he amended. "Tender ribs, like you might cook up for me tonight. Would you do that?"

She glanced away. It was no joke. There was nothing funny about this dear man getting kicked in the head by a bucking bull. She found herself so allergic to the thought of "one more event" that it made her throat close up.

She hardly recognized her own hoarse voice saying, "I don't like seeing you get hurt."

He slipped an arm around her shoulders and planted a kiss on her forehead. "I won't get hurt.

I'd tell you to stay back here and not watch, but I want to show off for you.''

Big kid, she thought. *Big, lovable kid, I can feel that tremor in your body.*

"Show off, my foot," she muttered pointlessly.

"Like fun," he countered, weaseling a smile out of her as she mouthed his comeback incredulously, rolling her eyes. "Hey, those cute little piggies go to nobody's market but mine."

"Okay, then. Show off, my—"

"Uh-uh." He touched his finger to her lips. "You ain't showin' off nothin' of yours, and all I'm showing is my best tricks. Sure it sounds juvenile, but that's the way sports are. Games to keep grownups young. My days as a bullfighter are numbered—down to double, maybe single digits. But right now I feel like a kid, and I wanna show you what I can do."

She loved the sparkle in his eyes. It was full of hope and joy and eagerness to please. Like his bandage and his unruly hair, it lent blythe boyishness to his mature face.

He tried to lift a permission-seeking eyebrow, but the bandage weighed it down.

She nodded. She knew he was humoring her, but since there was no stopping him, she might as well go along for the ride and try to fathom the unfathomable.

The bullfighting event pitted the clown's skills at

dodging disaster against the bull that had proven most adept at toying with clowns. It was a judged event in which the clowns earned points for tempting the animal to chase, toss, lunge and plunge. They scored the most points for touching the bull without getting touched back, a feat that required quickness, agility, vigilance and raw nerve.

Ryder possessed every trait, but there was an added dimension to his performance. He was foxy. The other men in the contest were clearly younger than he was, but they wasted moves and missed cues. In the end, ol' Turtle racked up the most points and won the cash prize.

Meredith waited at the appointed place and watched the crowd stream toward the Minneapolis skyway or the sidewalks, draining away to a mere trickle by the time Raven greeted her from behind with a *woof* that translated to *found her!*

She turned to pet the dog and discovered that his master had cleaned up very nicely. He was grinning from ear to ear, striding behind his canine scout, clearly feeling his oats.

Using his arm as a shepherd's crook, he hauled her in by the neck, snugged her up close to his side, and demanded, "Was *that* so awful?"

"Yes, it was, but you were amazing."

With a firm, joyous kiss, he rewarded her lips for their honesty. "Not bad for an old man, huh?"

"The way you move? If you're old, I'm an antique.'' Putting her arm around the back of his waist she anchored herself for a walk-and-talk only he knew where. They weren't going out the way they'd come in, but she followed along happily. He was all in one piece. "There are much safer ways to make a living, you know."

He flexed his free arm in a passable Popeye impression. "I yam what I yam, and it ain't no doctor, lawyer or sailor man."

"How about an Indian chief?"

"How about a rodeo clown?" Still walking, he tipped his head toward hers and poured a promise into her ear. "You play your cards right, I might give you a roll in my barrel."

"I'm not the best card player."

"You were looking for a king, and you drew a joker," he deduced as he pushed their way through a No Admittance door.

"I didn't even know I was in the game, but if the winner gets a roll in your barrel…" She offered a coy smile. "Aren't jokers supposed to be wild? They can be anything, can't they?"

"Not a doctor, lawyer or—"

"But any card I need. I want that barrel ride."

"Get ready to rock and roll, Merry m'girl."

With a flourish, he pushed open the gate to the arena.

"Here?" She surveyed the scene in disbelief.

Workers were already dismantling the pens at the far end.

"Right here in front of Mr. Target and all his toadies. Not to mention Mr. Turtle. Unless you've got one of these at home." He laid a hand on the barrel he'd used during the performance. He'd apparently stashed it in a chute when he'd made his latest crazy plan. "A rubberized turtle shell? Way in the back of your garage, maybe?"

She laughed. "I think my last clown took all his toys with him."

"Funny girl," he said as he rolled out the barrel. "We both know I'm your first. Doctors and lawyers come a dime a dozen, but it ain't every day you find a clown on your doorstep."

She eyed the brightly painted, open-ended barrel, then the huge arena. No one seemed to notice them. A front-end loader and a dump truck were revving up at the far end. She had about two seconds to make up her mind.

She saved one to add to the two more she had for tucking herself inside the barrel before anybody besides Ryder and Raven could see who was making this ridiculous move. She positioned herself the way she had seen him do, so that she would somersault as the contraption rolled.

"Use your hands and feet to brace yourself, hon. Otherwise you'll start rattling around in there like dice in a cup."

"Start slow, okay?"

"That's always the best way."

End over end she went, but without much speed, it was a challenge to become part of the motion.

"How're you doing?" he asked.

"Can we go a little faster?"

"Already?"

"Yes! Keep it going. It's like a merry-go-round."

He laughed. "It's exactly that."

Faster, faster still, and soon it became a *bona fide* carnival ride. Meredith wasn't sure where the squeals were coming from, or the kiddish *Wheeee!* or the *Do it some more!* But she was pretty sure she was the only barrel rider in the place.

She heard a man's voice call out, "What the hell are you doing, Red?"

"Tumbling my landlady," came the answer.

"Hell of a way to pay the rent."

The rolling slowed as the laughter swelled.

"I gotta evict you both. Time to clean up the sandbox," the man said. "But I can't wait to see who's in there."

Ryder's upside-down face appeared at the end of the barrel. "Need help getting out?"

"No. Just scraping my dignity off the sides of the jar so I can..." Head spinning, she crawled out on all fours. "...put it all back in place and..." A face-licking from Raven brought her head up.

Standing over her were two grinning men. "...say hello to your little friend. Mr. Target, I presume?"

"Sam Foggerty." He and Ryder leaned down simultaneously, each with an extended hand. "I just work here."

"How do you do?" She accepted both hands for the quick, if graceless, up-hauling. Time for some wit. "I'm Merry Go-Round. You've probably heard of my cousin, Holly."

"Can't say that I have. Have you heard the one about the crazy rodeo clown who put his landlady in a fake turtle shell?"

"And there he kept her very well," Meredith recited, head wobbling woozily.

Ryder caught her when she swayed. "It's a cheap high, isn't it?"

"I don't know how you walk straight after that, never mind evade the horns of any dilemma. Do I look as silly as I feel?"

"How silly do you feel?" Ryder teased, backing away. "Don't tell me. Let me find out for myself."

She started to whap Ryder in the chest but remembered the Ace bandage and turned the whap into a wave. "Nice meeting you, Sam."

"Yeah, same here." Pausing to take another closer look at the barrel, Sam turned to Ryder. "You think I could get my wife into one of these? I want to see that look on her face."

Ryder laughed. "It helps to play with a few cards up your sleeve."

Chapter 7

It was unlike Ryder to disappear after they had shared a late, light supper. Meredith couldn't help having a peek out the front window to reassure herself that his pickup truck was still parked in her driveway. Since they were nowhere to be found downstairs, she assumed that her boarder and his faithful companion must have been too tired from their day's work even to say goodnight. But on her final window-and-door check, she discovered a black dog on her back doorstep.

"What are you doing out here, Raven?" She flipped the porch light on.

"He's asking you to come out and play," said a

voice that seemed to come from the backyard gazebo. "In the dark."

She turned the porch light off. "I'll grab a sweater."

"In the nude."

Her laughter misted in the early-autumn air. "Raven, you dog, you. You've got yourself covered."

"I'll have you covered as soon as you get yourself over here, Merry, m'girl. What do you call this thing?"

"A gazebo." She followed Raven across damp grass, past the moonlit white birdbath and the huge old maple that was just beginning to drop its leaves. "I've hardly used it since my boys left," she said. "I'll bet it's full of spider webs and dusty furniture."

"Not anymore," the voice said lazily. "Is it for rent? I think I could live here."

The screen door whined as she let herself in. Even though the octagonal interior was dark, she could see that the wicker furniture had been moved to accommodate the hammock, which she hadn't hung up in years. No wonder Ryder's voice sounded so relaxed.

"If I covered the screens, it would feel like a tipi," he went on. "'Course I'd be knocking on your door pretty often, looking for conveniences."

"Like…?"

"Well, you know, indoor plumbing. Probably food and water."

"I've spoiled you," she murmured, hanging back, wondering whether he thought of her as a convenience, too.

"That you have. Come over here and let me return the favor." He made no move to get up, but she could see him reaching out to her in the dark. "I think this is a two-passenger contraption."

She joined him under the quilt that she had left neatly folded on the foot of his bed. Immediately he enfolded her in his arms, and unless her nose was mistaken...

"I came out for a smoke and decided to make myself at home," he confessed.

"I didn't know—"

"I don't, not really—except once in a while when I'm celebrating. I used to celebrate big. Now it's just a cigarette and a 'Way to go, Red Hawk. Well, thanks, Red Hawk.'"

"Didn't I congratulate you?"

"Uh-huh." He nuzzled her temple, touched his lips to her cheek.

"Didn't I make you a special flaming dessert?"

"Very special," he whispered. "I would have offered to share my cigarette with you, but I was too busy trying to hide it from you."

"Well, don't. I'm not your *mama*."

"And I couldn't be happier." He slipped his

hand beneath the bottom of her sweater. Warm fingers on her abdomen. Warm breath against the side of her neck. "Because I have something else I want to share with you tonight. I'm betting that cherry dessert was just the first of the flaming sweets you'll want to share with me."

"Oh, Ryder," she whispered. She wanted to bet on him, too, but she was afraid of the odds. Meredith Woodward was a safe bet, but surely the odds-makers would tell her that Ryder Red Hawk was not. "I've never been so scared as I was today, watching you escape that bull by the skin of your teeth. My heart was in my throat the whole time."

"Impressed you, did I?" Talk of his triumph momentarily distracted him from feeling her up. "Who's that other guy you like? Russell who?"

"He's just an actor. You're the real gladiator."

"My hat's gonna be too small, you keep this up much longer." He turned to face her, pressing his hips to hers. "*This,* on the other hand..."

She smiled in the dark, glad she had him back. She struggled to shift her trapped arm as she slipped her fingers beneath his belt buckle.

He chuckled. "No, the other hand."

"Where's your next rodeo? Where and..." She gripped his belt, felt him growing, going harder inside his jeans. "How much longer..."

"How much can you take?"

"Of you?" Her throaty laugh sounded as

naughty as his. "I don't know. I know I haven't had enough."

"I don't know what else—"

"How much longer can you stay?" she demanded, hauling on his belt as though it gave her a real handle on him.

"I've got staying power to spare. You can count on that."

"Can I?" She tugged at him again. "How about tomorrow? Can I count on it tomorrow?"

"Are we shooting for a record or something?" A slight shift of his weight had rope noisily rubbing against rope, body quietly rubbing against body. "Hey, I'm game."

"Men and their power." She drew a slow, deep breath. "Power this, power that. I don't know about staying power, but you've all got plenty of *going* power. Always places to go." The last came on a whisper.

"We don't always have places to stay. That's the hard part, and it gets harder as time goes by. You stay in so many different places, but they all feel the same. Temporary."

"I wouldn't like that."

"No, you wouldn't."

She wouldn't, and she wished he wouldn't. Not this time. Silently she counted his buttons, imagined undoing each one as she touched it, but she was more pressed to snuggle awhile. It was a special kind of warmth they made together—all the better because it was natural, and the crisp night air was natural, and it all came together perfectly.

"Does this house feel the same to you as the others?" she asked.

"Not with you here. You made it feel different as soon as you let me in. Even when you were talking like you didn't have a spare room, I felt like you had room for me." He smoothed her hair back from her face, which followed the direction of his hand as though magnetized. She kissed his palm, and he whispered, "Ah, Meredith, I'm glad I stopped here. I came so close to driving on."

A wild thought flew from head to tongue to ear before she could clip its wings.

"You could stay."

He looked at her. She didn't have to see the look in his eyes. She could feel it. She felt him go tense in ways that had nothing to do with to the proximity of her body, in muscles that the motivation to move on would surely engage.

She was going to lose him.

She shouldn't have said it, shouldn't push it, but it was out now, and she couldn't make herself leave it at that. She had to run on. Clarify. Make it worse.

"Live here," she urged boldly, more brazen than she had ever been in her life. "Not as a boarder, but…"

"A live-in boyfriend?"

"You may be a few years younger than I am, but you're hardly a boy."

"A live-in lover, then."

Say yes, she told herself, but she swallowed the simple answer and moved, oh so foolishly, to further complicate.

"I enjoy your loving, but there's more to it than that. I enjoy your company. I would enjoy having you live here with me."

Ryder took his time.

Meredith literally had to hold her tongue between her teeth to keep it still.

"This might sound old-fashioned," he said finally, "but I don't think a man should be living with a woman rent-free unless they're married."

"Oh, all right," she blurted out. "I'll charge you rent."

"What's wrong with the other option? I've never been married, but it can't be that bad."

Of all the responses she might have predicted, she would never have been ready for that one.

"I wouldn't know," she said. "I've never been married, either."

Unless she missed her guess, it had been her turn to dish out a bit of a shocker.

"My son didn't tell you that I wasn't married to his father?"

"I don't know why he would. I sure never asked."

"But you're sure surprised. I can feel it in your bones, Ryder, so don't even try to deny it."

"I guess I assumed…"

"Prejudged?"

"Maybe, but it's not a bad judgment. Sure as hell not an unreasonable assumption."

"Sure as *hell?*" Her laugh sounded hollow. "I thought it was hell. And if it wasn't, I thought I was headed there. I was young, and I thought I was in love. He was a little older, and he said he loved me, too, but marriage would have to wait. Unlike Ken's father, I grew up pretty quickly after Ken was born. With my parents' help I was able to go to school and raise my son." She shrugged. "I guess marriage is still waiting."

"You wanna give it a try with me?"

"Oh, Ryder." She hugged him tight, grateful for the sweetest goodbye a girl could possibly hope for. "I was only kidding about the rent. Can't you tell when I'm joking?"

"Can't you tell when I'm not?" He drew back as though they might have gotten too close to see the forest. "I'm ready for a home, and you're ready for a husband. The way I feel about you, Meredith, I know I'll make you a good one."

"This is crazy," she whispered, slowly realizing that he meant every word he was saying. There was no hook on her side, no catch on his.

"What's crazy?"

"This feeling," she said, now that she was beginning to think she could have it and hold it. "You make me feel so wild and wonderful. And funny. I've never felt this funny inside. I could make an absolute fool of myself over you right now."

"Honey, that's what I do for a living. You'll be in good company."

Company, she thought. His good company. It sounded so promising that she risked asking the big question. "What way do you feel?"

"Crazy, like. Dizzy, like you've been rolling me around in a barrel for days, and I don't know which foot to put down first." He pulled her close again. "And good. I feel so good with you that I'll probably be good for nothing without you."

"You're kind of a nomad, and I'm kind of a homebody."

"Maybe I could show you some places you haven't seen except in books."

"South Dakota?"

"Sure. We can start there."

"And then?"

"Then come home for a while." He reached down and brought his hat up from the floor. "Like my old friend here, I've always carried everything I had on my back. There was never any home to come to. You've given me a glimpse of what it's like to come home."

"Yes. We'll start here." She found the beaded

turtle by feel and petted its bumpy back with her thumb. "This friend of yours has lots of memories. Maybe the details are lost to you, but you've carried this connection a long time, a long way, to this home. We'll start here."

"Sounds like a fine plan."

"I might always be a homebody," she said, a little tentative.

"I might always be a traveler, but I've finally found the road home. I have a feeling I won't be able to stand being away from my homebody very long."

"We'll start here," she repeated. "We two." A cold, wet nose nudged her elbow, and she laughed. "Four."

"Five." Ryder put his hat on Meredith's head.

She sat up and adjusted the angle of the hat, suddenly feeling eternally young and downright cute. "Turtle has it all," she said. "Legs for going and home for staying."

"And maybe something tucked inside his belly for long living and endless loving." He laughed, simply for the joy of it. "Yes ma'am, me and Ol' Man Turtle, we've got it all."

* * * * *

SEVEN DAYS

Ruth Wind

Dear Reader,

As I was writing my short story for *Lakota Legacy*, Colorado was suffering through the worst drought in its history. Daily, the newspapers chronicled the effects— ranchers were selling off cattle who no longer had any grass to eat; farmers were throwing in the towel after another season killed their crops. In the cities our lawns seemed very foolish indeed.

What more natural setting for two love-thirsty people than the drought—and the end I visualized for it? My favorite part was writing about rain, falling and falling and falling into the drought of the earth and their lives— especially because it still hadn't rained in real life. The rain of love is the most precious thing most of us will ever experience, bringing with it the promise of new life, new dreams, new hopes, along with a rain-washed sunny day. Enjoy!

Love,

Ruth Wind

Prologue

Michael Chasing Horse stood at the end of his drive, arms loose at his sides, watching a trailer filled with the last of his cattle turn onto the highway. Dust from the heavy tires kicked up in the air, joining with smoke from a grass fire—the third in a week—consuming another unknown number of acres.

Dust and smoke. It was all there was these days. Drought lay on the Plains like death, the earth so dry that it had broken a backhoe brought in to dig a ditch for goose hunters. Michael had laughed at the time, bitterly, but laughed nonetheless. Four feet down they dug, and still found the earth bone-dry.

He imagined the concrete stretched all the way to the center of the earth. Even the yucca and cactus were looking withered and burned, and the grass had long ago crumbled and blown away on the gusts of an infernal wind that never seemed to stop blowing. He'd sold the last of his cattle because there was no feed for them, and hay was harder and harder to come by.

That cursed wind blew now across the sweat on his brow. It was filled with grit and sand and even—his nostrils quivered like those of one of his horses at the scent—the smell of rain walking down the sky. He could see it—life-giving rain pouring from dark-purple clouds. Rain that evaporated before it could reach the ground.

The old timers said it was the driest year they could remember since the Great Depression, seventy-five years before. The weathermen were reporting it as the driest year on record. Ever. To the west, the Rockies were a tinderbox, and they'd caught fire at least ten times over the past month. To the east, the cracked, burned land looked more like the Arizona desert than the usually arid, but fertile Colorado ranchland he so loved.

Even now, though, when conditions were so harsh, he could not help but love this land. He loved the sight of his home, built of timbers by his father's own hands, the sturdy old barn, the ancient cottonwoods along the banks of the river. Loved the austere beauty of the dun-colored Plains rolling toward the mountains draped in soft blue across the horizon. Loved the enormity of the sky and the emptiness stretching all around.

It had cost him, this love of this harsh and unforgiving land. Cost him his wife, who went slightly mad with the winds and the blistering summers and the freezing winters. Now he'd lost the cattle. If he was careful, he could, like the walking-stick cactus, last another year or so.

But as he looked at the sky, he could not help but send up a prayer.

Rain. Send rain.

Chapter 1

Sunny Kendricks found something she'd never seen when she emerged from the restaurant where she worked in the tiny town of Hobart, Colorado— rain dancers.

The small park at the center of town was filled with townsfolk and ranchers from the outlying areas, their faces serious as they looked on the trio of Native American dancers dancing and singing to the heavy, heartbeat rhythm of a drum. The dancers were adorned in feathers and moccasins, their athletic strength making them look like beautiful birds. For a long moment, she stood and watched, captured by the music and the beauty and the hope they brought. The town had asked them to come.

Imagine!

She did not have time to linger, and hurried across the park to the small, neat day care center across the street. The children were out in the fenced play yard, and most of them were leaning against the fence to watch the dancers. Sunny heard a bright, "Hi, Mama!" and spied her daughter Jessica, a tow-headed eighteen-month-old, to one side.

"Hi, daughter!" Sunny bent and kissed her daughter through the fence, and Jessie laughed.

"C'mon!"

"I'm coming."

The day had been a long one. Her feet hurt and she did not particularly love waiting tables. It was hard physical work, and she felt it this minute across her shoulders, down her back. But her pocket was plump with tips, and just the sight of her daughter made everything great. It had been so terrifying to nearly lose her. Any sacrifice Sunny had to make now was more than worth it.

She gathered her daughter and they headed out of town on two-lane Highway 50. Trees, their leaves muted by dust and wind and drought, lined the Arkansas River, so she didn't see the fire until she left the shelter of the trees and turned down the lane that led to her small house, perched on a hill three miles down the road. "Damn," she whispered, tightening her hands on the wheel. Smoke billowed up in columns of dirty white, much too close to her home for comfort. It was impossible to tell where it was, exactly, at this distance, but her heart squeezed.

What would they do if the fire took the house? There was no place else to go.

She glanced at Jessie in the rearview mirror. She'd fallen asleep, her cheeks rosy, her hair damp. The air conditioner on the serviceable Escort worked, but it was still pretty hot. Sunny flipped her own hair off her brow and focused on a positive image: her house, sitting in the open beneath a single old elm, protected by a wall of imaginary water. Aloud she said, "Whoever is listening, I hope you'll give me a break. You know the situation as well as I do."

The house was a loan from a friend in Denver. It had belonged to Diana's family years ago, and no one lived there anymore, or worked the small cantaloupe farm that once surrounded it. The fields were empty and dry, the water rights sold to a hungry Denver developer. Without the water rights, the land was useless, and not even the solitary rancher at the foot of the hill was interested, so the house sat empty.

It had been a godsend for Sunny and Jessica. Sunny had had a difficult pregnancy, complicated by her rat of a husband walking out when she was seven months along. Then Jessica was born with a hole in her heart, requiring surgery and a difficult six-month recovery. By the end of it, Sunny had run through every penny of her savings, lost her home and had nowhere to turn. Diana, a boutique owner who had purchased many of Sunny's one-of-a-kind creations, had offered the house.

They'd been here two months, and while it was a brutal land in many ways, Sunny was so relieved to have a home and a job that she would have scrubbed the floors with her teeth.

As she came around the turn where the road forked—going north to her house or west to her only neighbor's—a man stepped into the road and flagged her down. She slowed and rolled the window down, startled by her first up-close glimpse of him. Tall, with a rancher's lean, hard physique, he crossed the road toward her.

She'd known he was Native American because of the name painted on the mailbox: Chasing Horse. She had also seen him at a distance, riding his horses, working on things when she passed. She always waved, and she kept telling herself that she ought to come down and introduce herself. Each was, after all, the only neighbor the other had. The timing never seemed quite right, though, or maybe, Sunny thought, it was her innate shyness that kept her from doing it.

Up close, he was rather ruggedly handsome, with a hawkish nose and hard-planed cheeks turned the color of nutmeg by the sun. His hair was brush-cut, severe on some men, but right for this face. She wanted to put her hand on the top, feel the bushiness against her palm. "Hi," she said. "Is something wrong?"

"You saw the fire?" His voice was not loud. A good, husky voice with a little lilt in the words.

"Is it bad?"

A single nod. "Depending on the wind, one or the other of us could be in trouble."

Sunny frowned. "Okay. What should I do?"

"Not much you can do. Keep an eye open. Be prepared to leave if you have to." He spied the car seat. "Your daughter?"

"Yes." Sunny smiled. "Jessica."

"Keep a bag packed for her, just in case. Maybe one for you, too. If you need anything, I'm right down the road."

"Thank you." She stuck her hand through the car window. "My name is Sunny Kendricks."

"Michael Chasing Horse." He touched her hand briefly, then let it go, lifting a hand in farewell.

When she was safely up the road, she let go a breath. "Wow," she said aloud. And again. "Wow."

In the backseat, Jessie, likely awakened by the conversation, said, "Wow."

Sunny laughed.

Sunny's front window looked west to the mountains and to the ranch nestled next to the river beneath its canopy of cottonwoods, so she could keep an eye on the fire as she straightened up the small house, gave Jessie a snack, and sorted out a pile of bills that she was—she realized thankfully—going to be able to meet. It had been a good week for tips. Sometimes, the sheer enormity of the bills could overwhelm her, but the doctors and hospital had been quite willing to work out payment plans. Sitting at the small wooden table she'd covered with a flowered cloth from Goodwill, she wrote checks, subtracted the payments from the staggering totals, and grinned ruefully. Not for the meek and mild, those totals.

Jessie's hole in her heart was not an uncommon birth defect, unfortunately, but fortunately was one that was repairable with surgery. Sunny's daughter had come through the operation with flying colors, but had contracted a respiratory infection right afterward. It had been touch and go for quite some time. Many, but not all, of the resulting costs had been covered by insurance. The rest had fallen to Sunny, and she was determined to pay every penny of it. Those doctors and hospitals had saved her daughter's life.

And look at her now! Sunny glanced at the sturdy toddler, her fine blond hair growing down to silky little curls at her neck. Jessie was fiercely focused on using crayons to cover every inch of a piece of scrap paper with color. She was healthy as a horse these days—a vigorous eater, a happy kid on every level.

A gust of wind caught Sunny's attention, and she stood up to check the flames again, worry pulsing against her breastbone the smallest bit. Firefighters were stationed a few yards away from the barn down below, digging a trench. There were a lot of them, and they had to be exhausted by now, working as they had all day and half the night to stop this particular fire, which had followed on the heels of another three days before and another five days before that. Sometimes it seemed the Plains would never stop burning.

"I think, baby girl," Sunny said, "that we ought to make ourselves useful. Wanna help me cook?"

"Cook?" Jessie said, leaving the crayon on the floor. She added something more, but Sunny hadn't exactly sorted out all the words she knew yet, so she bent to scoop the girl up.

"Tell me all about it," she said, and settled the girl in her high chair. For a horde of hungry, hard-

working men, there was really only one choice—
piles of fried chicken and even bigger piles of potatoes. She'd purchased a half side of beef with a
specially priced bulk order of chicken three weeks
before. Her boss at the restaurant had recommended
it, predicting that the drought would make beef
prices skyrocket in the fall. He'd helped her track
down a used freezer, and Sunny could not believe
the amount of security she felt from that store of
meat.

Now it would have an extra benefit—commu-
nity-building for herself and her daughter. Sunny
didn't know if they'd actually stay here, but it never
hurt to be friendly to neighbors. Especially in such
trying times.

Turning on the radio and settling Jessie with a
measuring cup, a set of spoons and a bowl of water,
Sunny hummed along with the music and defrosted
the chicken, then prepared the seasoning. It was one
of the few recipes she had from her own family—
the secret spice was nutmeg—and she was proud of
it. It was also attached to one of the only really
nurturing memories she had of her own mother.
Debbie Kendricks had been beautiful and lost and
badly treated by men her whole life. The combination made her a dramatic figure and a rather poor
mother. To her horror, Sunny had realized when her
husband left her that she'd picked up her mother's

knack of trying to save men who couldn't be saved. When her daughter was born, she resolved she would not repeat the pattern. She would spend her life alone before she subjected Jessie to any of that.

As if the baby heard her thoughts, Jessica raised a cup of water. "Want some?"

Sunny laughed and bent down to take a tiny sip. "Thank you!"

Jessie beamed. "Thank you!"

Chapter 2

By late afternoon, the fire had roared within a hundred yards of the barn and corrals on Michael's land. He, along with a crew of volunteer and professional firefighters, worked frantically to keep the fire in place. Without the wind, it might have been an easier fight, but each time it seemed they had the voracious flames in check, the wind gusted along and threw sparks to some new spot.

"I hate this wind," growled Jacob Nelson, a fellow rancher who had also been forced to sell off sizeable portions of his own herd of cattle. "Like to drive a man insane."

Michael wiped his soot-and-sweat-caked face, resettled his cowboy hat and shoveled another load of dirt. "How'd you fare in that fire two weeks ago?"

"Ate up about forty acres, but it was scheduled for a controlled burn anyhow." He shrugged—none of those this year. Too unpredictable.

Michael nodded and bent wearily back to his task. After another hour, the wind shifted direction once more, and this time, it was a kindness—the flames doubled back upon themselves, eating up the edges of the blackened space and dying to nothing. Plumes of smoke, beautiful against the black, were all that was left.

His back ached from the shoveling, and his skin felt caked with grit, but he managed a smile and a high five for a firefighter who trudged up to him, his face a reverse raccoon mask. They both sighed, turning when a car horn tooted merrily from the road. The fireman said, "Your wife?"

"Neighbor," Michael said with some surprise.

"Purty."

She was that. Small and rounded, with a spill of glittery blond hair and big blue eyes. A Kewpie doll, he thought with a scowl, one of those bubble-headed women who were just hoping for a man to come along and take care of them. He was still scowling when he approached the car. She was taking out a big pan, which she handed to one of the fireman who was only too willing to help. "I know her,'' the fireman beside him said. ''She works the day shift at Mel's Diner. Sweet thing. Young, and that baby. Don't young men got any sense these days?''

''Hi,'' she said, and it was slightly shy, not the burbly Kewpie voice he expected. ''I saw everybody down here and thought maybe you could use something to eat. If that's okay?''

With an effort, he cleared the frown off his face. Hell, what kind of a jerk glared at any woman who brought food for weary men who'd been battling to save his ass all day long? ''We're about ready to eat what's left of the grass, lady. Let me help you— let's bring it in the kitchen.''

She gave him a big cold bowl. ''Nothing fancy, just fried chicken and potato salad and iced tea.'' She gave a short laugh. ''I didn't have a lot of ice, so it's actually lukewarm, but it always quenches my thirst better than water.''

He noticed her hands were rough and dry, the hands of a woman who had her hands in water all the time. No ring. ''Mine, too.''

''I'll just get the baby and the last platter and be right in.''

The men were already slumped around the table in mute exhaustion, politely waiting to dig into the platters somebody had already uncovered. His stomach growled at the smell, and he sat down beside the big bowl and ripped off the foil to show mounds of creamy potato salad. "Dig in, guys," he said, tossing down paper napkins and distributing a stack of plates he'd taken out of the cupboard. One of the men opened a drawer Michael indicated and put out some forks.

"Damn," said one, biting into a piece of chicken. "This is good."

"Sweetheart," said another, a grizzled sixty-year-old, as Sunny came into the kitchen. "I'm too old to marry you, but I'm gonna nominate you as an angel."

She laughed lightly. "Glad you like it."

The baby, a blond miniature on her mama's hip, leaned around and said to Michael, "Wow!"

The men laughed. "Guess you have that effect on women!"

"This is my neighbor," Michael said, and then could not remember her name. He started to shake his head, held out a hand and she caught the situation.

"I'm Sunny Kendricks. We just met for the first time this afternoon." Baby still on her hip, she bent and picked up the two-gallon cooler. Her hair was swept up in a loose knot, showing the back of her neck. It was smooth and white and he found himself admiring the soft look of the way the hair flowed upward from the spot.

"Michael," she said quietly, "do you have

glasses and ice? Let's get you all something to drink.''

"Right," he said, and was glad of the task.

"Why don't you let me take that girl for you," one of the younger guys said, "so you don't have to ruin your back?"

"Thank you." Sunny lifted Jessica and deposited her in the man's lap. For a minute, Jessica stared at the young man with wariness, her hands—why, Michael wondered, were babies' hands so sweet?— folded on her lap.

He seemed to meet some internal barometer after a moment. She put her hands on her knees and said, "Hi!"

"Oh, I only get a hi, huh? Michael got a wow."

The baby looked at Michael and pointed. "Wow."

They all laughed, Michael along with them. "She's a charmer," he said, handing Sunny a glass.

"She is that." Sunny kept her head ducked, and because he'd noticed her nape before, he saw there was a tinge of red to the skin now.

An almost forgotten sense of pleasure touched him, and he smiled. She thought he was a "wow." "Thanks, Sunny," he said seriously, taking another glass from her and placing it on the table. "This was a great thing to do."

"No problem. I saw you all out there and knew you'd be starving."

"I owe you one."

"Not at all." She raised her head and gave him a smile. A very sunny sort of smile. "That's what neighbors do, isn't it?"

Looking at the fine whiteness of her poreless skin, skin that would burn, never tan, under this harsh sun, looking at the guilelessness of a face as yet untouched by the truly harsh aspects of life, he wondered what the hell she was doing out here in this brutal land. She was like a tender gardenia.

But he nodded. "I reckon they do."

The men, wanting to get home to families and showers and a good, soft bed, didn't linger. Sunny collected their plates from the table, scraping bones into the trash. Michael made a move to help, and she shook her head with a smile. "I can do this in my sleep. Just sit."

His voice was ragged with exhaustion and a thin coat of grayish ash lay over his clothes and boots. Jessie sat on his lap, perfectly comfortable, gnawing on a piece of bread. "I can't let you do all that."

"Truly, my arms get tired holding her all the time. If you would just help me that much, it's a lot."

His face showed a softness. One finger moved on the baby's forearm. "That's easy."

Collecting used silverware, Sunny commented,

"You seem very comfortable around kids. You must have been around them a lot."

A shrug. "It's natural in a small community like this. All my friends have kids. They always seem to like me."

"That's because you like them."

He raised his eyes. "Think so?"

For one single second, she let herself admire the cut of his cheekbones, the bear-fur dark of his eyes, let herself feel that old, tamped-down longing to be held by arms as strong as these, her weary shoulders rubbed by hands so plainly reliable. Then she whisked the dishes to the counter, putting her back to him, and put the thoughts out of her mind. "Absolutely."

"So," he said. "Where you from?"

"Denver."

"The big city. What in the world brings you out here?"

Sunny bent to slide plates into the dishwasher. "Necessity. My daughter was pretty sick when she was born, and I lost my house, so a friend loaned me that one until I can get on my feet."

"Is she okay now?" Alarm and surprise threaded his voice. "She looks healthy as a rodent."

"She is. It was a hole in her heart. They fixed it, and she's fine."

He was silent for a minute. Then, "No husband

to help?'' He raised his eyes, almost in…what? Challenge?

Sunny straightened. ''No. He deserted me, actually, even before he knew that Jessie would be born with a problem. Just ran away in the middle of the day and I got divorce papers in the mail six months later. Just like that.'' She snapped her fingers, pretending it didn't matter.

But it *had* mattered. She'd wept bitterly that day, for all that she needed to take care of herself and her daughter—their daughter—and how badly she'd chosen a husband. ''He's pretty worthless. I'm better off without him.''

''How does a man leave a child?'' Michael asked in a quiet voice.

''How does anyone? But they do it all the time.''

He nodded, soberly.

Finished loading the dishes, Sunny wiped down the table. ''How about you? Ever been married?''

''Almost ten years.'' He said it gruffly, but as if to offer something in return for her story, he continued, ''She ran off with a cowboy from the local honky-tonk one night.'' A self-mocking smile. ''Maybe it was your husband.''

Sunny laughed. ''Good riddance, then.''

''Yeah.'' But she could tell the wound was not healed.

''You loved her.''

A nod. ''But I guess I love the land more.''

"It's more reliable," Sunny said, "in the long run."

That startled a laugh from him, and she couldn't help but notice the way it lightened his features, how it opened his throat and chest. "Some seasons, anyway. This one's been a little rough."

She folded the dishcloth neatly and punched the button to start the dishwasher. "You want to help me carry this stuff back out? Then I'll leave you alone and you can get your shower and a good night's sleep."

"Sure." He followed her with a load of Tupperware and the tea jug. Sunny settled Jessica in her car seat, and turned to take the dishes. "I really, really appreciate you doing this," Michael said. "It's an honor to meet you."

"You, too," she said, and just then she caught a whiff of rain on the air. "Do you smell that? The rain?"

He inhaled, closing his eyes. "Maybe it'll finally drip a little this far to the earth."

"You know," she said, "even this season is natural in the cycle of things, isn't it? Some times are wet, some are dry."

He was standing right in front of her, and she could see the underside of his jaw, the edge of his ear, before he looked down, right into her eyes. She suddenly realized he was close enough that he could bend in and kiss her if he was so inclined. If she was.

And something in her yearned toward it, just as the leaves stirred in hunger for the rain. But all that happened was that he said, "Good night, Sunny."

"'Night."

Chapter 3

The winds blew all night, buffeting Sunny's house on the hill, rattling the windows. It stopped and started, gusted and stopped, gathered itself up again and flung itself against the house like a rabid animal looking for a way in. Sunny woke up several times when it grew particularly noisy, but the house was cozy enough. Safe.

When she awakened at her usual time, 5:00 a.m., she discovered a fine layer of dust on the bathroom vanity, and wiped it down, swept the floors in both kitchen and living room. It came in through every little crack, the dust blown off the prairie, maybe even from as far away as the mountains. A trial, but she'd grown used to it. Maybe, if funds allowed it, she could see about sealing the windows a little better with some glazing compound. It wouldn't keep all the dirt out, but it might help a little.

She dressed herself in her uniform, a simple pair of slacks and a green polo shirt with Mel's written in script over the left breast, pinned up her hair, and got Jessica up and bathed and settled in her high chair for their breakfast of scrambled eggs. The morning was oddly still after all the winds through the night, and overcast, which meant the sun wouldn't cook them both all the way home this afternoon. A blessing.

It wasn't until she was on her way out the door that she smelled the smoke, realized that the sun trying to peek through the clouds was the color of a blood orange. "Dang," she said aloud, searching the Plains from her high perch to see if she could tell where the fire was this time. She didn't see anything, just the smoke lying in the air like a miasma. It stung her eyes. Jessie coughed a little.

"Yeah, let's get you into town, baby girl." The day care was air-conditioned, which kept some of the smoke particles out of the air.

She kept her eyes open for the fire as she drove, first down the gravel road that led past Michael's house, then onto the main road leading into town. About halfway to the bridge that crossed the Arkansas, she spied a horse and rider on the trail that

ran between the river and the road, and her heart
gave a little flip when she recognized her neighbor,
sitting easily atop a tan-colored horse with a blond
mane. A straight-brimmed hat with a silver band
was on his head, and she couldn't help thinking,
again, that he was very appealing. There was something so still or quiet or calming about him. She
thought of the way Jessie had sat on his lap last
night, and a little voice in her heart said, *maybe
he's different.*

Just to be with someone who loved her and loved
her daughter, might love future children—! In gen-
erations past, it had been an attainable goal for most
women. Why was it so hard to find good men now?
Or had she just been unlucky?

With a shake of her head, she brushed the questions away. They led nowhere. They were unan-
swerable, and her life had shown her that men did
not stay. Better to make peace with that and keep
her daughter—and her heart—safe. As long as she
never longed too much for anything, she could keep
a happy attitude.

He raised his hand in greeting as she passed, and
Sunny waved back, but she forced herself not to
look in the rearview mirror as she passed.

In the back seat, Jessie said, "Horsey!" and then
made a raspberry noise, the snuffling sound of a
horse. Sunny smiled and thought of his name again:

Chasing Horse. He loved his horses—that much was obvious just from passing by.

And what would it be like to have a name like that? Aloud she said to Jessica, "What if we had names like that? That expressed something about us. I could be Sunny Loves her Daughter. You could be Jessica Sweet as Morning. And maybe I'd be Sunny Morning." She laughed at the silliness.

Jessie laughed, too. "Morning!"

Her tires clopped over the wooden bridge spanning the tiny trickle of water in the river below, and as she came around the turn just a few short miles outside of town, she saw the fire. Her smile faded. It was burning hard, fed by a thicket of scrub oak on one side of the highway, and a line of poplar trees planted as a windbreak alongside a farm on the other. A green volunteer fire truck was parked across the road, and a man in a dirty white T-shirt with a grimy face stood in front of it, drinking from a tall thermos. He held up a hand and Sunny slowed, rolling down her window.

It was one of the men from the night before, and Sunny said, "You have to be exhausted, Joe!"

He nodded, wiped a hand across his forehead. "Sorry, but you're gonna have to turn back. Town's been evacuated until we can be sure this is under control."

Her heart sank at the thought of the lost tips, but

she took a breath and nodded. "Thanks. How can I find out when it's open again?"

"Keep your television on Channel 42."

She didn't have a television, much less the cable hook-up that would let her tune in to Channel 42. "What about radio or some place to call?"

The man frowned. "Don't know about that. Why don't you ask Chasing Horse? He'll know."

"Thanks. I hope you get a chance to rest soon."

"Me, too." He patted the hood, as if her car were an animal, a trusty steed ready to carry her home. It was the kind of thing that endeared this place to her, a sense of thoughtfulness, continuity, kindness. A reliable car was as valuable as a good horse in some ways, she supposed, turning back up the highway.

When she saw Michael, close to the turnoff to their road, she rolled the window down again and called out, "They told me town is evacuated, and I need to know what radio station to tune to so I can stay alert."

He shook his head, put a hand to his ear and pointed to the gravel road. Sunny turned in and put the car in Park, waited as he crossed the road toward her.

And again that soft yearning touched her. His shoulders were square and straight under his denim shirt, his hands sure as they handled the reins. He rode over to her. "Sorry! I couldn't hear you."

"I'm really sorry to bother you again," she said, "but the firemen told me to ask you what radio station I should tune to for information about the evacuation."

"Town's been evacuated?"

"The fire crossed the road, I guess, and they wanted to get everyone out, just in case."

He shook his head, took a breath. One hand rested against his thigh as he stared to the west, toward town. "Damn."

From the back seat, Jessie said, "Horse?" And then again, more insistently. "Horse!"

She waited, and he turned back. "Tune to 107. It's a Spanish station, but they give weather reports in English, too."

"Will do. Thanks!"

"Horse!" cried Jessie.

Michael smiled. "Is she saying horse?"

"Yeah. She's obsessed with animals of all kinds all of a sudden. She seems to have a real love for them."

"Do you have time to let her out and see him up close?"

"Oh, I wouldn't want to inconvenience you or anything."

He shook his head, very slowly. "Pull into my driveway and you can show her all the horses."

"Are you sure you don't mind?"

"Yep." He pulled the reins, and the horse turned to walk down the drive beneath the cottonwoods.

"Horse! Horse!" Jessie cried, pointing frantically.

"Yes, darlin', we're going as fast as I can." Sunny turned in behind horse and rider, and parked, then took Jessie out of her car seat. "Want to see the horses?"

The baby kicked at Sunny's side like a rider nudging that very same animal, and made a snorting noise again. Michael, dismounting, laughed. "That's pretty good. Where'd she pick that up? Do you ride?"

Sunny laughed lightly. "Never been this close to a horse in my whole life."

His dark eyes flattened the slightest bit. "You really are a city girl."

"Nobody chooses where they're born, Mr. Chasing Horse." She raised her chin. "I'm willing to learn."

Jessie grunted and strained toward Michael. "Horse!"

To Sunny's surprise, he took the baby easily, settling her on his hip as naturally as a mama. "You mind?"

She shook her head and tucked her hands in her pockets, following as Michael rounded the beast and settled his hand on his glossy sand-colored neck. "This is Two Moon," he said, ducking his head to speak quietly to Jessie, who stared up at him solemnly, her chubby little hands clasped together. "He was born on a day with a moon in the morning and a moon at night." He stroked the long hair of the gelding's mane, his fingers long and dark and graceful against the wheaten tendrils. "He's a palomino."

"Horse?" Jessie asked, pointing.

"Right. Want to touch him?"

Jessie nodded, her hand outstretched, and Sunny was pierced with that wild sense of furious love as her daughter leaned forward and kissed the horse, too. Jessie straightened and pointed again. "Who's that?"

"Horse," Michael said patiently.

Sunny stepped forward. "Is it okay if I touch him, too?"

"Sure." He angled his body so she could stand next to them.

The hair was silkier than she had imagined, the flesh warm beneath her palm. She could smell a slightly intoxicating scent of sweat and man, maybe a hint of a spicy soap, but it was hard to tell what was horse and what was human. To Jessie, she said, "Two Moon."

Jessie made her funny little concentration face. "Who that?" she asked again, making sure.

"Two Moon."

"Aw. T'Moon."

Michael smiled. "Smart."

"As a whip," Sunny agreed.

"The others are in the corral," he said, pointing. He carried Jessica easily, and Sunny hung back for a half second, admiring the look of his lean body with plump white baby legs kicking around his back and tummy. Beneath the cloudy skies, he looked as straight and strong and reliable as a tree, rooted deep into the earth.

And as he started pointing to the other horses, she felt herself hanging back for another reason. The outsider reason. Horses *were* completely alien to her. They scared her a little with their big heads and heavy hooves, and they moved quickly, a little nervously, maybe because of the smoke. Michael told Jessica all of their names and what colors they were—a reddish one was called a chestnut; another a bay. The third was the one who caught Sunny's imagination, though. "Who is that?" she asked, coming up to the fence.

Michael's chin lifted, and his eyes softened. "Beauty is her name."

"Like Black Beauty?"

He nodded, gaze still on the horse.

"It fits her," Sunny said. The horse was dancing a little, as if enjoying the wind, and the muscles in her body shifted and slid with such smooth grace beneath her shiny black skin that she took Sunny's breath away. Every inch of her was darkest black—

her body and legs and face, even her long tail and mane, blowing in the wind. A strange emotion moved in Sunny's chest, wonder and awe and something very like a crush on a boy. She laughed and put her hand on her chest. "She's making my heart race!"

He turned his head, as if surprised, started to say something, then turned back to Beauty. "These are Arabian horses, the oldest and wisest of all the breeds of horses." In his voice, Sunny heard his passion and respect. "The Bedouins, in the Arabian deserts, bred them and loved them. Imagine," he said, "how the Indians felt when they saw these creatures for the first time. Maybe one like this, running across the prairie, free and proud. And then they discovered how loyal they were, what wise creatures, and they made them their own."

"What kind of horses did they have before these?"

He grinned. "Dogs."

Sunny blinked. "Really? I always thought horses were sort of always here."

"Nope. The Spanish brought them."

"What do you think of that, Jessie-girl?"

"Horse!" she said with awe.

Both adults laughed.

"Hey, I know something even better than horses," Michael said. "Want to see some kittens?"

"I do!" Sunny said.

"C'mon!" Jessie said.

"They're in the barn." They walked across the yard, and Michael scanned the sky. "Those look like real rain clouds."

"There were rain dancers in town yesterday. Maybe it helped."

"You believe in that?" He paused, his arms clasped around Jessie so easily he looked like her father. "Rain dances?"

Sunny sensed there was more to the question than just simple curiosity. "Maybe. I mean, it's not much different from a prayer, is it?"

"You believe in prayer?"

"I believe there's something. Listening." She stroked her daughter's dewy arm, remembering the heartfelt begging she'd done late at night in hospital waiting rooms lit with greenish fluorescents. "You?"

His lips turned down the slightest bit. "Maybe. Mostly, I believe in the land."

"That works." She smiled up at him. "Probably the important thing is to believe in something."

He grunted.

The barn smelled of grass—or maybe it was hay—and the light was pale and dusty. He led them to a corner where a Siamese cat nursed four balls of fluff. "They're four weeks old," Michael said, bending down to dislodge a furry gray ball. It

squeaked at the same moment Jessie shrieked in
delight, "Kitty!" and reached for the baby in ec-
static hunger.

Michael gently held the kitten close to Jessie's
tummy, letting her kiss and rub it. "Easy," he said
quietly, and Jessie looked up. "Softly," he said.

"Shhh," Jessie said, but she seemed to understand. She kissed the kitten's head and made a noise
of love. "Rock-a-bye," she sang.

"Yeah," Sunny said, "it's such a pretty baby,
isn't it?"

"You can hold one, too, if you want. Been
around kittens before, haven't you?" His eyes twin-
kled.

"They're not so exotic, even in cities." A tubby
black one waddled over to her ankle and mewed,
and she bent down to pick it up, inhaling the laun-
dry-scent of kitten fur deep into her nostrils.
"Ooooh, you are so cute!" It curled up close to her
cheek, letting itself be rubbed, and started to purr.

"Who that?" Jessie asked, pointing to the black
one.

"He doesn't have a name." Michael squatted,
putting Jessie down so she could check out the others, now dancing out to see what the excitement
was about. He scooped up the mama and tucked
her into the crook of his elbow. "This is Ming, and
she doesn't get nearly enough attention now that
these rotten babies are stealing all of her thunder."

"Ming!" Jessie repeated. "Ming!"

He took off his hat and rubbed his head, and Sunny was pierced to see the tenderness—maybe even hunger—on his face as he looked at the little girl playing with the little cats. She shrieked with delight, squatting to look at one, her hands close to her chest, then laughing over her shoulder at him. "Wow!"

He laughed, showing strong white teeth, and it made his eyes crinkle up at the corners. "Man, she's cute."

"Miss Charming, that's for sure. I'm going to have my hands full when she gets to be about...oh...thirteen."

"Oh, yeah." He was still grinning as he glanced up at her. Light broke over his high-bridged nose, washed over his angular cheekbones, and Sunny found herself wanting just to stare at him, drink in all the details. He didn't look away, as if he were noticing things about her, too.

At the moment she would have had to decide whether to look away or be bold and keep her eyes on his, Jessie spied something else in a dark corner. "Ball!" She pointed, and looked hopefully over her shoulder at Michael. "Ball?"

He looked puzzled, then stood. "Even better than a ball." He took Jessie's hand, led her to a dry corner where a number of items were stored on a tarp, with a dusty covering over them. One side of the dust cover had come up, revealing a large drum made of animal skins. Intrigued, Sunny stepped closer. There was even a little hair left on the hide, and she wanted to touch it. From Jessie's lower angle, it probably did look like a ball.

He pulled it out a little, tossed the dust cover aside to scramble on a table in the back for a drumstick covered with hide, and banged. A deep, throaty sound came from it, and Jessie's eyes widened. She slapped a palm against it, making a hollow noise, and Michael drummed again. Lightly at first, the sound murmuring out of the body of the instrument into the stillness of the barn like a singer warming up.

"Is it yours?" Sunny asked.

He shook his head. "My father's. I played with him, but it was his, made for him a long time ago by an elder." As if in memory, his body shifted and he started to drum out a heartbeat-like rhythm with some force, and beside the drum, Jessie started to bounce. He laughed. "That's it! Dance!" He paused for a minute, reached into the darkness of the stacked items again, and brought out another stick. Holding out it out to Sunny, he said, "You want to try?"

Here it was, that moment of reaching out or holding back. It seemed she'd lived her whole life on the outskirts of everything, observing the world carefully to be sure she knew the rules of all the worlds that were not her own—which were nearly all of them—before joining in. "I don't know how."

"It's easy." He held the stick out patiently. "You'll like it, trust me."

"Okay." She accepted his offering and stepped up to the thigh-high drum. "What do I do?"

"Just keep time with me. Don't be afraid to hit it hard." He shifted his attention to his hand, caught some internal rhythm and started drumming. Hesitantly, Sunny joined in, and he said, "Harder!" so she swung it and felt the reverberating energy run up her arm into her shoulder. The resonant, deep sound of the drum moved through her, into the room, and Jessie started spinning around, singing a wordless song in time. She watched the tendons in Michael's forearm tense and relax, over and over, and a breathless excitement filled her chest. She raised her head with a beaming smile, and found him looking at her. He nodded, raised the tempo, gave one last bang and stopped.

"Wow," Sunny said, and laughed. "That's amazing."

"Make you want to shout, huh?"

She nodded. "Thank-you." Putting the stick down, she tucked her hands in her back pockets and took a step back. Her heel caught something and she managed to stop just in time before stepping down all the way and breaking it. The movement made her unbalance a little, so she was spinning around, tilting to the side, and her knee caught a piece of something and knocked it over. She made a dive for it at the same moment as Michael and their arms laced, his hand landing on hers and they kept the object from falling, but in that split-second, her nose was close to his neck and she could smell that scent again, a hint of spice and sweat and man, and it went right through her, rippling beneath the skin of her forehead, neck, breasts, belly, thighs before running through her feet into the ground.

"Sorry," she managed, and managed to extricate herself, looking for Jessie automatically, and seeing her with one drumstick in each hand.

"No big deal." He didn't look at her as he pulled the thing upright. "I need to get this cleaned up one of these days, decide what to do with it all."

"Is that a cradleboard?"

He held it in front of him, an oblong shape mounted on two boards fitted with straps. The main part was beaded in a geometric pattern in blue, yellow, red, white and black. "Yeah. It's pretty old, I think. I know my mom actually used it for me and for the baby who came after me, but he died."

"How terrible!"

He gave a single nod, braced the cradleboard on a table and touched the beadwork. "I remember him. He was a fat little baby named John." His fingers moved tenderly around the opening. "He got bit by a rattler when he was two and died before they could get him to the hospital." He raised his head. "I don't think either of my parents really got over it."

Impulsively, Sunny touched his arm. "How 'bout you?"

"I was only four," he said without emotion. "I don't remember it." But he used care in returning the cradleboard to its place. "Wonder if I could sell it on eBay?"

"That would be kind of a shame." She dropped her hand. "Maybe you could put it in your house. On a wall or something."

He lifted a shoulder. "Maybe."

Sunny sensed an ending to the moment, and stepped away. "Well, I guess we should be getting along. Didn't mean to eat up so much of your time."

"No trouble," he said, pulling the sheet down over the assorted things. "I enjoyed your daughter quite a bit."

"I'm glad. Jessica, it's time to go home now."

"Kitty?"

"No, sorry, we can't take a kitty with us. They're too little. They need their mama still." She turned back to Michael. "Are you going to give them away?"

His smile was kind. "Have your eye on a particular one?"

"Not really. But it might be nice to have a pet. She hasn't ever had one."

He nodded. "Think about it. I'd be glad to give her one."

He walked them out to the car, scanning the sky again as Sunny settled Jessie into the car seat. "That's more than smoke up there." He lifted his chin, breathing in. "Smell it?"

Sunny inhaled, and caught just the faintest whiff of rain. "Oh, wouldn't that be wonderful? It would feel so good. You have that drum—know any rain dance songs?"

He paused, one hand on the door as she straightened. It put their bodies fairly close together, and he didn't move away. Sunny dared herself not to back away, to meet his eyes. "I might," he said.

"Go sing it then, Mr. Chasing Horse. I would truly love some rain."

"Maybe I will." He hesitated a minute, and for one hot second, Sunny wondered it there might be a kiss in the offering. It seemed as though it might be in his mind, the way he swayed forward the smallest bit, the way he seemed to be looking at her mouth. But then he seemed to change his mind, and moved back to let her get in the driver seat. "See ya."

"Thanks again."

As she drove toward home, Jessica said from the back seat, "Wow."

Chapter 4

After Sunny and Jessica left, Michael found himself uncovering the pile of discarded goods in the
barn. Thanks to the sale of his cattle and his decision not to plant his forty acres of farm land this
year, he had little to do, and the time had been
weighing on him.

His parents had moved to Colorado from South
Dakota after a family rift between his father and his
only living relative, a brother. Michael had never
been able to sort it out, what exactly had happened
that would be so extreme his father would leave the
reservation and strike out on his own, so far from
his people. It had been hard on his mother, who

missed her circle of women, her sisters and cousins and friends. Once a year, usually around the sun dance, she returned to the reservation with her son, and they stayed for a week or two, then came back to the lonely ranch. Once, an old man from some extended branch of the Chasing Horse family had come to visit Michael's father. The two men had drummed and sung, had gone to sweat in a little hut they made from willow branches, smoked together on the back porch late into the night. Michael had been about eight. When the old man left, Michael's father remained unmoved about returning to South Dakota, no matter how his mother cursed him for a stubborn old fool, or wept silently and bitterly. She had hated the land, hated the loneliness, hated being so far from home. The bitterness turned into a snake in her belly, one that ate her up from within, and she had died when Michael was fifteen.

Donald Chasing Horse had gone quiet the day she died, and had spoken few words in the ten years he lived after his wife's death. He'd shown Michael the legacy of the land, shown him how to care for the animals and plant to maximize water, instilled, in his silent way, a deep and abiding love of this particular plot of land, the land that would be his legacy.

Now, looking through the things his parents had left—photos of Indian men and women who were likely his relatives or people he would have grown up with—he had to wonder if his father's stubbornness lived in him, too. What could have been so dramatic a disagreement that his father had left everything behind—hundreds of years of connection and tradition—to come out to this land that had cost him a son and his wife?

As it had cost Michael his own wife. There was a trunk full of her clothes beneath the drop cloth, for she had taken nothing when she left, not even a pair of socks. Michael, stunned and grieving, had hardly known what to do with it all except box it all up and put it out here. As he'd done with his parents' things.

And here it all sat, going unused, giving no pleasure to anyone.

There was nothing else to do this smoky, cloudy day. Without realizing he was doing it, he started sorting things into piles. The drum and cradleboard went to one side, joined by the photo album and a box of letters with return addresses in South Dakota and other things he'd hardly realized were there: a hand-carved flute, a pipe wrapped carefully in soft flannel. A medicine bag that must have been his father's.

Into another pile went things that he had no use for and never would; an end table he'd never liked and a crate of china his wife had brought with her, a boxful of her clothes, some outdated, cheap paintings.

The kittens, delighted to have human company, crawled around the piles and chased each other around his ankles. The mama cat came and sat at his feet, content to be stroked every now and then.

And as he sorted, he thought of Sunny. Often. There was a sense of a fresh wind about her, about the easy way she laughed and the wry but gentle way she flat-out adored her daughter. He liked her eyes, clear and straightforward.

Yeah, yeah, said a cynical voice in his head. *It's all about freshness, huh? Get real.*

Opening an unmarked box, he found a tangle of nightgowns and undergarments that had belonged to his wife. One silky turquoise gown caught his eye, and he tugged it out, trying to remember if Kara had ever worn it. If she had, he couldn't remember.

But he could see Sunny in it, see how the color would highlight her shoulders, the luminous quality of her skin.

The voice snorted.

He rubbed the fabric between his thumb and fingers, pulled the silkiness through his palm and admitted more. He would like to see her breasts, plump and white, ever so lightly encased in this fabric, would like to see how her round rear end would move beneath it. He'd told himself lately that what he needed was a rangy ranch woman, square of shoulder and lean of hip, a woman built to work and withstand the challenges of this country. But here came Sunny with her curvy, soft-looking body and he'd been thinking about it ever since they'd spoken the first time.

Biology, he thought. Go figure. He'd fallen for the same body type in his wife, all lush female curves, ripe as purple grapes, and look what it had gotten him. Biology wasn't a directive, it was just instinct. He'd promised himself he'd use his head as much as his heart—or sexual drives—in choosing another wife. If he ever chose one.

Sunny and her absolutely charming daughter would never last in this harsh world. He would be a good neighbor, but that was as far as it could go.

Sunny was cooking supper, filling the house with the scent of caramelized onions and tomato sauce for spaghetti, when she noticed through the front window how dark the clouds had grown the past twenty minutes. She left the sauce and went to the window. Great, low pillows of slate gray moved east from the mountains, and distant threads of lightning crackled through them. She stepped outside and inhaled—and a surge of hope went through her. It might be the real thing this time! Rain! If actual rain fell, she was going to stand in it and let it soak her to the skin, feed her dry skin and soak her staticky hair, and open her mouth and drink it into her dusty lungs.

She turned on the station Michael had told her about and they were warning of severe thunderstorms, which sent her hopes even higher. It would have to be a deluge to be heavy enough to reach the ground. Her boss at the restaurant had explained why they could see rain coming out of the clouds, but it never seemed to fall. The drought had left the air so dry and hot that the rain that built up evaporated before it actually made it to the earth, so it took a huge weight of water to break through the layer of dryness.

When the winds started kicking up, she finished cooking supper and turned off the electric stove, and carried Jessie into the living room, where they could watch it come through the big picture window. Jessie wasn't entirely thrilled by watching the sky, so Sunny started singing, all the songs Jessie loved—"Old McDonald" and "Rock-a-bye Baby" and—a very special favorite—"Bingo."

Maybe they could name their kitten Bingo. That would be kind of cute.

As the storm approached, Sunny could see long, feathery tendrils of gray coming out of the clouds, and the thunder and lightning crept closer, echoing through the enormous sky. Her spirits soared—how could anyone not find this land beautiful?—and she opened her front door to let the smell in. They stood in the yard, Jessie safely out of the reach of stinging ants and cactus and maybe even the odd snake on the small square of concrete porch in front of the door, Sunny on the ground. The yard was not the traditional yard she'd grown up with, grass and petunias all fed by sprinklers, but it was beautiful in its way. Yucca plants with swords of pale green grew in neat clumps around the prairie land, along with stands of prickly pear and walking-stick cactus that should have been in bloom by now, someone had told her. She'd been hoping to see it, and looked at them hopefully every day, but the buds stayed stubbornly closed.

The sound of the rain reached them first, a soft roar of promise, and Sunny yelped happily, picking up Jessie and swinging her around. She pointed. "Rain!"

Just then, the first drops started to fall. Big, fat drops, heavy as water-balloon bombs, splattering the size of fried eggs on the dry ground. They were slow at first, smacking Sunny's arms and head every so often. Jessie took one in the face and gave her mother a look that said she was insane. "Inside!"

Sunny ran up the steps and deposited her daughter just inside the door where she could stay dry, but she didn't go in herself. She turned back to the storm and raised her face and stretched her arms out from her sides to capture as much of it as she could. The raindrops were sporadic at first, barely dampening her clothes, the heat nearly evaporating the moisture between times.

Even if it stayed just like this, Sunny thought, she would be happy. The lush scent of earth dampening with life-giving rain filled the air with a thick perfume, and the humidity rose, feeding her starved cells.

But the sound grew, and the rain came harder, the drops still huge and coming faster, harder, soaking her face, her neck, her blouse. She laughed, opened her mouth to catch it. It was cold, cold rain, as refreshing as a plunge into a swimming pool, and she turned around to let it hit her back, soak her hair, and she was still laughing, feeling a need to shout, ''Whoo hoo!'' as the noise grew larger and larger, and the rain came harder, soaking her to the skin.

The first pellets of hail were tiny, changing the sound from a roar to a popcorn-popping sound as the ice pellets spattered against the hood of the car and the windows of the house. ''Ow!'' she cried, and ducked into the shelter of the doorway with Jessie, who peered out solemnly. Hair, clothes and skin soaked, Sunny wiped her face and breathed deeply of the perfume of rain, watching as the hail grew in diameter.

And grew.

And grew. When it got to the size of marbles,

she stepped back and closed the door in defense, a thread of alarm gaining strength as the sound doubled, tripled, then became a din so loud that Jessie started crying and covered her ears. *Slamming, pounding, roaring,* none of them were big enough words for the sound that filled the rooms as the hail gained in strength and size, and Sunny could see nothing beyond the windows but a blizzard of hail.

The first golf-ball-sized pieces broke through the front window, shattering it with a crash of falling glass, and Sunny screamed, turning away in fear. She backed into a doorway and grabbed an afghan off the couch, covering Jessie with it to protect her from flying glass, watching in both wonder and horror as the hail poured through the break, hundreds of ice balls of varying sizes, some of them as big as her fist. Jessie, terrified, howled, and Sunny gently bounced her, murmuring, over and over and over, "It's okay, baby, it'll be over soon. It's okay." She knew it wouldn't last. Even Denver, after all, had hail storms. She just hadn't ever seen one quite like this.

As quickly as it had come, the racket slowed and slowed, slipping to a pitter-patter of dinging hail, then down to only rain again. Jessie stopped crying and Sunny kissed her, taking the blanket off her head. "Everything's all right now, sweetheart."

Cautiously, she crossed the living-room floor to the front door and opened it. "Oh, my gosh!" she said in both amazement and horror. The world was completely transformed, the dry prairies running with mini-rivers cutting through piles of hail so thick it looked like snow. The rain had slowed to a trickle—the whole storm had lasted less than twenty minutes—and a bar of sunlight poked through, vividly gold, to touch the smeary, washed-clean world below.

Sunny bent down and picked up the biggest piece of hail she could find. It was nearly the size of a baseball. "Look at that!" she said to Jessie, and put it in her little hand.

"Cold!" Jessie said. "Water?"

"Right." She picked up another one for herself, and on impulse, took it to the freezer to save for some reason.

It was only then that she thought of her car, and ran back to the doorway to look at it. Hail covered it in piles that were rapidly melting and sliding off, and she dashed down the steps to get a closer look. It was obviously dented, but that wouldn't hurt anything—everybody's cars would be dented, no doubt. Saying a sharp, quick little prayer, she squeezed her eyes shut, then reached out an arm and pushed the hail off her windshield.

Her heart sank. A five-inch star, indented as deeply as if a hammer had hit it, marred the center of the glass, with radiating rivers of cracks running from it. "Damn," she said aloud, trying to keep her despair at bay. "Damn."

"Dam?" Jessie repeated.

"Ooops. Sorry. Mommy shouldn't have said that."

But she had no idea what she was going to do about this. Without a car, she couldn't get to town for work. It was definitely too far to walk, especially with a baby on her hip. Maybe—

Whatever. She would solve this problem later. Right now, she had to get the hail out of the living room and clean up the glass and get the window covered for the night. Glass for the house wouldn't cost as much as the windshield, and it would have to be first priority.

"C'mon, sweetie. Let's get you some dinner, okay? You can eat in your high chair while I clean up this mess."

"Eat?"

Sunny laughed. Some things, after all, were really important.

Michael assessed the hail damage to his house and outbuildings. The old cottonwoods, who'd outlived far worse, had taken the brunt of the storm, and a litter of branches and leaves were stuck to the ground, plastered to the walls of the house and barn, but aside from a broken window in a back bedroom of the house, that was the extent of it.

When he'd seen how severe the storm promised to be, he'd herded the horses into the barn and stayed there with them. He watered and fed them, then climbed in his truck to see how things were at the top of the hill, where his neighbor's house sat so exposed.

In spite of the violence of the storm, he felt oddly exhilarated. The air sparkled with the sunlight coming out behind the clouds, the smoke and miasma of the past few weeks simply washed away, and already the drought-savaged plants seemed to be perking up. Any fires that had been burning were certainly quenched, at least on the prairie.

Even before he parked, he saw that Sunny had not been as lucky as he. The front window gaped, and she appeared at the doorway with a shovel in her hand, her hair twisted into a wet mop on top of her head, her hands encased in sturdy rubber gloves. She dumped a load of hail on a pile beside the concrete steps leading to the doorway, spied him and gave a wave.

He got out of the truck, winced when he saw the windshield of her car. "Came to see if you needed some help."

She raised her eyebrows and then, oddly, gave him a smile. "I won't turn it down. I'm going to have to patch this window for the night, at the very least. There's glass all over everything in here and

I can't let Jessie out of her high chair until I get it all cleaned up.''

"Show me."

She inclined her head. "C'mon in."

Most of the hail had been shoveled out, and Michael whistled when he saw the pile beside the porch. "Hit just the right angle, huh?"

"'Fraid so. Better the living room than the bedroom, though."

He looked at her again, surprised. "You seem pretty calm."

A quick shrug. "Well, no sense crying over spilt milk. Mother Nature does what she does and you might as well make peace with it." She tucked a hank of hair behind her ear and gave him a wry grin. "I'm always laughing at people on flood plains who are surprised when it floods, or people on the coasts who lose everything in a hurricane and are shocked."

Michael laughed. "In Colorado, it hails."

"Right." With a sigh, she carried her shovel into the house, and he followed her inside.

As he came into the room, Jessica said from her high chair, where she was smeared with spaghetti, "Hi, there!"

For some reason, his entire chest warmed. "Hi, kiddo!"

She held out a fistful of noodles. "Want some?"

He bent and pretended to take a bite. "Yum!"

Sunny returned to her task, kneeling to sweep the last of the hailstones, now melting into a big puddle, into a shovel, along with shards of broken glass. Her arms were stronger than he had first thought, and her legs showed strong muscles. He grunted. Round and blond did not necessarily mean weak. She waited tables for a living after all. Not exactly a lightweight job. "Let me help you," he said.

"I've got this part. What I'm worried about is finding something to cover the window until I can get new glass." She shoveled another load, nearly the last of it, and carried it to the door. "Any ideas?"

"I've got some plywood. Screw it in and you'll be set for a few days, anyway."

"All right." She angled the shovel beneath the last bit of hail, and carried the dripping load to the porch. "Whew! That was a big fat mess. I guess I have to just let the hail melt and let the glass dry, sweep it up later." A shadow crossed her face as she caught sight of the car, the first real dismay he'd seen there. But she didn't say anything, just sighed and headed for the kitchen. "I'm going to get the mop."

"Hey," he said, and grabbed her arm. "Why don't you sit for a minute, dry your hair?"

"I don't want Jessie to get restless, and I can't let her down till I know all the glass is gone."

"Sit," he said, and pushed on her shoulder a little. "Where's the mop?"

"You really don't have to—"

He guessed cleaning materials would be in a small, narrow closet, and pulled it open. "You didn't have to fry chicken for ten hungry men, either, but you did."

"Want some?" Jessie said, holding out a fist of spaghetti toward her mother.

Sunny mimed taking a big bite, then raised those big blue eyes to Michael's face. "Truth is, I have a bigger favor to ask if I'm going to cash one in."

"Shoot." He took the mop out of the closet, lifted the bucket to the sink to fill it up.

"My windshield is destroyed and I can't drive to town. If I don't work, I don't eat."

"You need a ride, then?"

She lowered her eyes, nodded.

"That's not a problem, Sunny. It's not but five miles."

"I have to be to work at 6:00 a.m."

He grinned. "Maybe you city types think that's early, but 'round here, that's midmorning."

The words had the exact effect he'd hoped for— the worry and strain fell away from her sweet, pretty features, and she raised a grateful smile to him. For a minute, that's all there was in the world, just Sunny's columbine-blue eyes resting on his face gratefully, and he found himself wondering

what it would be like to have a woman around
again. Not for sex, necessarily. For company. For—

Don't, he told himself. She was a city girl. She
might be down on her luck just this minute, but he
knew it wouldn't last. There was drive and steely
ambition in a woman who could move out to the
Plains in desperation to give herself and her daughter a chance at a decent life. But the Plains, with
their trials, would never hold her.

Chapter 5

By the time they got the window covered with a sturdy plank of plywood, the sun had long gone, and Sunny felt the exhaustion in every pore in her body. Michael had insisted that she go ahead and bathe Jessica, who was getting quite cranky by the end of it, and put her to bed, and by the time the little girl dropped off, Michael was putting the last screws in the frame.

The sight of him startled her the slightest bit, maybe because she was so tired it was impossible to keep her guard up, or because it was such a relief to be able to count on a man to take care of something, to not have to do every single thing herself.

"Thank you," she said, and sank down on the couch. "I don't know what I would have done without your help."

"I bet you'd have figured something out." He tucked his drill into the case, and snapped the hinges closed. "Anything else you can think of?"

"Not tonight. Thank you. I'll have to cook something especially good for you to pay you back."

He grinned. "If everything you cook is as good as that chicken, I'll take you up on that offer. Bachelor cooking gets old fast, let me tell you."

"What's your favorite meal?"

There wasn't even a beat of hesitation. "Pork chops, gravy, mashed potatoes."

Sunny laughed. "That sounds like a hungry man. Did you have supper?"

A puzzled frown touched his brow. "I guess not."

"Me, either," she said. "If you'll give me two minutes to take a shower, I'll fix us both something to eat."

"You don't have to do that, Sunny."

"I'm going to cook for myself, anyway. What are you going to eat when you go back home? TV dinner in the microwave?" His shrug told her all she needed to know. She nodded, got to her feet. "Make yourself comfortable. I'll be back in a flash."

"Flashing?" he said, mockingly hopeful.

Sunny turned, not entirely sure he was flirting. He met her gaze with a little wiggle of eyebrows. "Can't blame a guy for trying, huh?"

She shook her head. "Tsk tsk."

The shower was heavenly. She didn't bother with any makeup or anything fancy—he'd already seen her at her worst, so clean and brushed would probably be a big improvement. When she stepped out of the small bathroom, she smelled coffee brewing. "You are an angel," she said, coming around the corner. "That smells so good!"

"I'm glad you don't mind. I needed some, all of a sudden. What a day, huh?"

She looked in the fridge, narrowed her eyes, starting putting things on the counter. Ham, eggs, a half loaf of banana bread she'd made a few days before, butter. "Sit down, cowboy. Let me wait on you for a few minutes, so I don't feel guilty in the morning about dragging you all the way to town."

He chuckled, and Sunny raised her head at the sound. It was rich and warm as an autumn noon. "Yes, ma'am."

"You really need to laugh more often," she said.

He met her gaze. "Yeah. Maybe I've forgotten about it." He waved one graceful hand. "That it's good for you, I mean."

"How long has it been?" Sunny asked, turning on the oven to warm the banana bread. She thought about turning on the radio, but crickets had started singing outside the window and it was such a peaceful song, it seemed a hundred times better than a radio.

"Since I laughed? Or since my wife left me?"

What woman in her right mind would *leave* this man? Sitting there in the bad green light from the overhead fluorescent, he still looked wonderful. Not handsome, exactly, and certainly not pretty in the way of a movie Indian, but she loved the fullness of his mouth, the angle of his bear-dark eyes, his hands, so long and graceful, the color of nutmeg, braced around his mug. Not to mention the competence factor!

Some women, she decided, had no sense at all. "Both. Either." She heated some butter in a skillet and dropped in thick slices of ham, scattered brown sugar over the top. "You pick."

"Just over a year, I guess. On both." He sipped coffee. "You?"

"Five minutes since I last laughed. About fifteen before that." She grinned over her shoulder as she broke eggs. "With Miss Jessie doing her antics every second, it's hard not to get a daily dose of good medicine."

"I can see that." They were quiet for a minute, then he asked. "How'd you get so wet, anyway? Were you standing in front of the window?"

"Oh, not then! I was taking a shower in that gorgeous rain—are you kidding? After all this time without any, how could I let it just fall right in front of my door and not feel it?''

''A shower,'' he repeated.

Sunny laughed. ''It felt great, too. You should try it sometime.'' She felt his eyes on her and looked over. ''What?''

A mix of curiosity and surprise and something quite intense was on his face. For an instant, Sunny felt her breath go still, felt the tension coming from him so clearly it couldn't be mistaken. He was looking at her the way a man looks at a woman he wants, with that look that made her know he'd been imagining how she might look naked. Or maybe it wasn't even that pretty. Men didn't think like that, did they? She flushed, looked away.

''This land will kill you, you know,'' he said conversationally.

''Hasn't killed you yet.''

''I'm tougher.''

She raised an eyebrow. ''How would you know that?''

He grunted. Putting his long legs out in front of him, he asked, ''What'd you do before you came here?''

She stirred eggs into the hot pan, scrambled them with quick, sure strokes. ''Come get a plate, cowboy. It's almost ready.''

He took down plates, one for each of them, silver out of the drawer she indicated, set the table so that

Sunny could come over and pour the eggs directly to their plates. They moved around each other easily, she noticed. He didn't have that man-weirdness in the kitchen, bumping into her every time he tried to help. Instead he moved smoothly, anticipating her movements, and they sat down together before the steaming eggs, glistening ham and warmed banana bread.

"Do you mind if I say a blessing?" Sunny asked.

"Nope."

He bowed his head while Sunny quickly said grace. "Dear Lord, for this we are about to receive, make us truly grateful. Amen."

He chuckled softly. "That gets right to the point."

"I'm starving!"

Michael was starving, too, and the food was excellent. He ate three slices of the banana bread, flavored with hints of cinnamon and something else he couldn't quite name, and there were generous chunks of walnut in it.

It wasn't just his stomach he was filling. He filled his eyes with the shine in her healthy, soft-looking hair, the dewiness of her scrubbed-clean face, the glitter in her blue eyes. She wore a simple scoop-neck T-shirt that allowed just a little bit of chest to show, just a hint of the curves beneath, and he liked that, too. Liked her nice round rear end as she cooked, her quick, efficient movements that seemed so at odds with that luscious figure. She ate as hungrily as a child, washing it down with milk, but then dabbed at her mouth carefully with a napkin between bites.

A paradox, this woman.

"So, you never said what you did for a living back in Denver."

"I was a seamstress. Designed one-of-a-kind clothing and sold it at boutiques, but I also made my own patterns, sewed costumes for stage shows and the Renaissance Festival, things like that."

"That's different. Why'd you give it up?"

"The truth is, a self-employed person has to work no matter what's going on, and I couldn't for nearly six months. It took everything I had to take care of Jessie." She put her fork and knife carefully down across her plate. "I had to sell my machines to pay off some of my debts."

"I'm sorry to hear that."

That lift of a shoulder. "It was worth it. I'm sure I'll get to a place where I can do it again one of these days."

"Were you good?"

She met his eyes. Nodded with a little smile.

Suddenly, through the windows came a sound. Michael lifted his head. "Listen. Hear that?" A rain of yips and yowls rang out, an excited, exuberant noise. "Coyotes."

Her face broke wide open with wonder. "Really?" She raised her eyes, as if seeing into the distance, and the coyotes accommodated her by singing a long, complicated song to each other. "They sound like they're laughing!"

"I'm sure they are."

"I thought ranchers hated coyotes."

"Some do." Truth was, they could be a pain in the neck, but he also knew they served a purpose, as all creatures did. How could you hate something that could laugh like that?

"But not you." Her eyes shone as the coyotes sang a little more, then faded into the distance. "I'm so glad."

And there was absolutely nothing fancy about her in that moment—her hair was stick-straight, her skin not perfect under the ugly lights, and there was weariness around her mouth, but he still felt something shift inside him in that instant. He looked at her mouth and wanted to kiss her, wanted fiercely to touch her, feel her body against his. She held his gaze for a moment, then looked away, down to her plate, where she adjusted the knife and fork a minute amount.

He knew he should stand up, make his excuses and go home now, but he didn't. He sat there, his palms itching with the wish to reach out and touch her, and stayed frozen, just looking, wishing, not acting.

Finally, she raised her head. She didn't say anything, but the smile was gone, and there was such a wary hunger in her face that it shamed him. She hadn't said much about her husband, but in that instant, he saw that she'd been very badly treated, like a horse who'd been beaten, and he didn't need to be doing anything that might add to that burden.

"Guess I need to let you get some sleep," he said, standing to carry his plate to the sink. "What time do you need to get to town?"

She picked up her dishes and carried them over, too. "I usually leave at six, and drop Jessie off at the day care."

"No problem." He started to move around her, but she started to move at the same time, and they bumped into each other lightly. He reached out and touched her arm. "Sorry."

She backed up. "My fault."

Nodding stiffly, he put on his hat and headed for the door. "Thanks for the meal. It was good."

"My pleasure."

In spite of the busy evening, Sunny found herself up very early, a little edge of excitement moving beneath the ordinary tasks of readying the house, getting breakfast together, waking Jessie, putting on her makeup, with which she found herself taking special care.

It was only as she was drawing a very, very thin

line of soft purple eyeliner beneath her left lashes that she realized what was going on. She stopped and stared herself square in the eye. "Don't do this, Sunny Kendricks. Don't start giving this man all the fantasy characteristics of a good and honest and true man. You don't know that much about him, and you don't need to gamble your security."

Last night, over their simple supper, her body had been quietly pulsing out little messages of pleasure—*Look at his eyes, how they shine! Look at his hands and how strong they are and imagine how they would feel! That mouth! Kiss that mouth!*

She'd resisted telegraphing any of it to him, but this morning, in anticipation of his arrival, of the fifteen minutes they would spend in his car together, she was all atwitter.

Just like her mother. Dressing up and getting happy every time a new man showed up, sure that this one would prove the exception to the rule. And sometimes they were nicer than others were, but it was a sad fact that Debbie had twisted herself into whatever she thought that man wanted, every time, until she got so lost in her make-believe identities that she self-destructed.

Not gonna happen, she said to herself, and wiped off the extra eyeliner, reapplied her usual one coat of mascara.

But it wasn't all that easy to stay aloof when Michael actually appeared. In the fresh light of morning, he was dressed in his usual jeans with a long-sleeved white shirt open at the collar, a simple uniform that should not have looked so delectable, but it did. "Good morning!" he said heartily, tipping his hat back from his forehead the slightest bit.

"Hi, Wow!"

Impossible not to be disarmed. Sunny laughed. "She thinks your name is Wow."

He braced his hands on his hips, very lean hips they were, too, and said, "Is that right? How'd she get that idea, I wonder?"

Grinning, Sunny shook her head. "I have no idea."

"Well, it does an old man some good."

"Old?" As he bent over to settle the car seat in the back bench seat of his massive truck, she laughed. "You can't be more than thirty."

"Way older than that. Thirty-six, as a matter of fact." He accepted Jessie and settled her. "Makes me a decade more than you, I figure."

"Yes, it does."

"Old."

Sunny didn't know where it came from. Some evil demon took over her body and made her give him a slow once-over, then say wickedly, "Still looking pretty fine to me."

It startled him, she saw, and she opened her

mouth to protest, but started laughing. "You started it last night with that crack about flashing."

He straightened, the dark eyes glittering, and stepped close. So close she could smell soap on his neck and a spicy under-note that made her think of a good fire. "I don't think I said I minded."

Sunny flushed, more from his closeness than the words. She was spared having to make a reply by Jessie's urgent, "Less *go!*"

It was a busy day at Mel's Diner. Everyone came to town to talk about the dual dramas—the fire then the hailstorm—and compare notes on damage. The hailstorm had been very destructive, no question, but the general mood was jovial anyway. One old man summed it up: "Sure needed the moisture."

By the time she got off at two, Sunny's pockets were thick with tips. Without any other resources, she asked her boss, a gruff but kindly ex-marine, if she could have a loan to replace her windshield. "I'll pay you back at whatever rate you think is fair. It'll probably be about two hundred dollars or so. But I can't even get to work without it."

"Tell you what," he said, picking up the phone. "My brother-in-law runs a junkyard in Rocky Ford. Let me give him a call and see what he can do." After a short discussion of the fire and the hail and what damage each had sustained, he said, "Hank, one of my best employees has a little problem, and I'm hoping you can help her out.''

To Sunny's amazement, he hung up the phone in five minutes. "You're covered. He'll bring his wrecker over this afternoon and bring you a loaner. He said it might take him a coupla weeks, since you're not the only one with a bad windshield, but that'll cover you for the meantime. He'll work with you on the money, twenty bucks a week. How's that?"

Sunny blinked back tears. "It's wonderful. Thank you. So much."

"My pleasure, kiddo. Now skedaddle and let me get my work done here."

Bemused, she walked out of the office, and there was Michael at the counter, his hat neatly beside him on a stool. Sunny halted, wanting this one quiet minute to calm her suddenly racing heart. It was his hands that captured her again—long and graceful and very strong. The most competent hands she'd ever seen, but they were gentle, too, as she'd seen when he touched his horses, the cat, Jessica.

She wanted them on her body. With the thought came a vivid image of exactly that, those elegantly shaped hands sliding up her tummy to—

He spied her and reached for his hat. "Hi. Ready to go?"

"Um. Yeah." She gestured toward the back

room. "Just let me get my purse. I didn't know you were coming to pick us up."

He tilted his head, eyes glittering. "You think you were just gonna walk?"

"I guess I hadn't thought that far."

"Lucky one of us did then."

"Be right back." As she turned into the back room, a waitress came up to her, whispering urgently, "You're seeing Michael Chasing Horse? Good grief!"

"No, it's not like that." Sunny grabbed her purse. She didn't always like this woman, Andi, who had the kind of petty greediness that led her to constantly grab tables from other waitresses. "He's my neighbor."

Andi raised an eyebrow.

"I have to go," Sunny said, and pushed by the other woman.

After the air-conditioned cool of the restaurant, it was blazingly hot outside. The weight of it made Sunny stagger a little, and Michael touched her back, once, right in the middle. "You okay?"

"Fine. That's just one of those transitions that's hard to make every single time."

They picked up Jessica, who had to be awakened from a nap and was cranky and flushed and irritable. "Go 'way," she said to Michael when he settled her in her car seat. Alarmed, Sunny glanced at his face, and he was smiling as he buckled her in.

"Girl with a curl. I knew it." He touched her forehead lightly, brushing away a circle of blond hair from her brow.

As they drove out of town, Sunny eyed the sky. A thin, distant line of clouds rimmed the western horizon. "So you were married ten years, you said?"

"Yep."

"You're such a natural with kids, I—" She broke off, realizing how rude she was about to be.

"My wife had a mother and a sister with schizophrenia. The sister is very ill, and Kara didn't want to take the chance."

"I'm sorry. I didn't mean to be so rude."

He shook his head, unconcerned. "It's a natural thing to wonder." He leaned over the steering wheel a little, peering at the sky. "Looks promising, huh?"

"It does. Two days in a row! Wouldn't that be wonderful?"

"With the heat, it'll be violent again, but I don't mind, either. Turn your radio on and keep an ear open for reports."

"And stay away from windows," Sunny joked.

"Also a good plan." He grinned, and for the space of a moment, Sunny let herself imagine that he could be what he seemed to be, that she could give her heart and he would hold it safely in his strong hands. He didn't look away, but put his hand on hers, lightly, once, then drew it away.

Chapter 6

As suppertime approached, the clouds grew darker and more foreboding. Michael ate a bowl of chili and eyed the sky uneasily. Something about it made him uncomfortable—a sound he couldn't quite hear, or a scent that was a little too elusive to name. Uncomfortable, he turned on the weather channel, but the only warnings were severe thunderstorms and possible hail. Not a surprise. He was probably worrying for nothing.

But he didn't like it. There was a weight to those clouds, a depth of blackness that went beyond the ordinary, and as if to underscore his concern, the horses were jumpy and restless, their manes flying in the wind that was picking up. Michael made the rounds of the outbuildings, tying down anything that might be carted away in a high wind—he'd seen winds that overturned cars when the storms turned violent. He brought the mother cat and her kittens into the house, rounded up the dogs. Horses still uneasy, he went back to the television. Still no upgrade. Some large hail spotted five miles southwest of Rocky Ford, a severe thunderstorm moving northeast at seven miles an hour, which meant it would arrive here in a quarter hour, maybe a little more.

Maybe, he thought, hands on his hips, he'd just turn off the breaker box, too, just to be safe. Damned lightning could sometimes take out—

An electronic voice, using the imperfect pronunciation of a robot, said, "Warning. A tornado has been sighted moving northwest from Rocky Ford. Residents are advised to—"

Michael didn't wait for the rest. He grabbed his keys and bolted out of the house.

Sunny heard the news at the exact same instant. A huge claw of terror squeezed her chest for one agonizing second, and she was frozen, her mind frantically tearing through previous experiences to see if it could get a close match for this situation. There was none.

A sudden, roaring blast of rain hit the kitchen

windows, followed by a crack of lightning and
thunder so loud she knew something had been
struck close by. It sent her adrenaline into over-
drive, and she grabbed Jessica, who had been startled by the noise and was howling, and ran to a
doorway.

No, it was a bathtub, right? Bathtub and couch
cushions. She dashed to the bathroom, set Jessie in
the tub, screamed, "Sit right there!" and ran back
to grab the cushions. Tears leaked out of her eyes
and she was making a strange animal sound, half
pant, half prayer—

The door burst open with a crash, and Sunny
screamed before she realized it was Michael. "Let's
go!" he roared. "Now! Now, now, now!"

Jessie was screaming in the bathroom, and Sunny
grabbed her, following Michael out at a dead run.
He'd grabbed the diaper bag that sat at the ready
by the front door at all times, and it made her want
to giggle for some reason. He was skidding down
the road the instant the truck doors were closed.
"Hang on," he yelled, and Sunny realized that Jessie was screaming at the top of her lungs, and the
sound of the storm was rising like a cluster of de-
mons. She held Jessica against her chest, her lips
against her head, and braced them both with her
other arm as Michael gunned the truck down the
road.

Something was clanging and banging as they

raced into the yard, and Sunny looked up. A huge, black *wall* was bearing down on them. She was stunned to stillness for one second, but Michael shoved her, grabbed her sleeve, and they bent into the wind and ducked into the house.

"Into the basement, to your left!" he cried. "Go, go, go."

Two dogs came skittering up to greet them, and Michael had paused to gather a handful of spitting, terrified kittens and cat. The mama scratched him and screeched as she leapt out of his arms and dove under a bench. He slammed the door closed behind him, and suddenly, it was much quieter.

"Right here," he said, gruffly. He was soaked, Sunny saw, as she was, as Jessie was. He pointed at a bench beneath a thick support beam, and Sunny sank down gratefully. Her entire body was trembling, hands, knees, intestines and she was clutching Jessica so hard she thought she might crush her. The baby was clinging just as hard back, as if she wanted to crawl inside Sunny's body and just stay there. "It's okay, sweetie," Sunny said. "It's okay. It's okay." She rocked forward and back. "It's okay."

Michael put his arm around her as a rocketing sound slammed into the house. Sunny squeezed her eyes closed, hearing what sounded like screams and screeches and a train. There was no sense of movement, no sound of things breaking overhead, just this unbelievable roar of sound that was so loud it drowned out even Jessie's cries. Sunny felt a hiccuping sensation in her throat and realized she was letting go of little sobs herself, mute and primitive, the mewling terror of a mother at the mercy of nature. "Please, please, please," she whispered.

It seemed to last a thousand years.

And then, it just stopped, as if some giant hand had squashed the bug. It took a second to sink in that it was over. Sunny slumped backward against the wall and closed her eyes. As if the storm had taken her energy with it, her limbs felt limp and beyond her control. Jessie curled against her chest, exhausted, too, by the drama, her breath coming in the short, shuddering breaths of post-hysteria. Next to them, Michael bent forward and dropped his head into his hands.

They simply sat there like that, unmoving, for long minutes. Sunny couldn't even get her mind around any thoughts—it was just images, flashing and flashing, and she finally said, "I have never been that terrified in my whole life. I didn't even know you could be that scared and live through it."

Michael straightened. Let go of a sigh. "I know exactly what you mean."

"Now what?" Sunny asked.

"Now we go see what it took and what it left behind."

Jessie startled a little when Sunny stood up. "It's okay, sweetie. We're just going upstairs."

Michael bent down to Jessie's level, touched her cheek. "You okay, kiddo?"

To Sunny's amazement, the baby reached for him, urgently. He took her gently, and cradled her close for a minute, rocking back and forth, one hand on her head. "That was pretty scary, wasn't it? Scared me, too."

Sunny bowed her head against the ache his tenderness gave her. Mutely, she followed him upstairs. The dogs' nails clicked on the stairs behind them.

"Oh, my goodness!" Sunny exclaimed, emerging into the light and following Michael into the yard.

There was so much *mess* that it was hard to sort it all out at first. Tangles of wires and wood and huge balls of hail and tree branches. One by one, she picked out details. An upended tree pointed stripped-clean roots to the sky, and there was a twist of metal she finally figured out might once have been a tractor, but she only made that much of a connection because there was a tire attached.

She turned in a slow circle. The house was fine, untouched except for a rain of leaves stuck to the sides, and most of the trees bordering the river looked fine, if a little battered. The corral was broken, missing pieces in three places, and the barn doors stood open, but from what she could see, the roof was still intact. "Looks like you got lucky," Sunny said.

He touched her arm and Sunny turned. "What?"

Gently, he slipped his hand beneath her elbow and drew her a few feet to the right, then pointed.

Sunny stared, feeling again that odd sense of disorientation, that struggle her brain was making to put the pieces back together properly. Because there was something wrong with this picture, and she couldn't figure out what it was. The angle was wrong, and she wondered if there was a tree missing, framing the view wrong.

And then it hit her. "Oh, my God," she said, and stumbled sideways, her stomach heaving. She vomited into the grass and simultaneously burst into tears.

Her house was gone.

Michael gripped her arm, gently and firmly. "Come on, let's get you some tea."

"I can't...I don't..."

"I got you. Come on. Put your arm around me."

And because he was the only solid thing to hang on to in the middle of chaos, Sunny did just that. Put her arm around him, leaned into him and let him help her into the house, where he settled her at the table, deposited Jessica in her lap, and put the kettle on. From a cupboard, he took a small bottle of brandy and poured some into a water glass. "Drink up," he said, and Sunny did.

It helped.

Jessie spied something when he opened a cupboard. "Cookie?"

"You mind?" Michael asked.

Sunny shook her head. When he gave the baby her cookie, he touched Sunny's shoulder. "It's a big loss. Don't try to take it in all at once."

She stared out the window. "Everything I had was in that house. Everything that was left, anyway. I've managed to keep going, but how do you prepare against a tornado? How can you keep believing when fate keeps taking everything away?"

Michael acted instinctively. He plucked Jessie out of her mother's lap, gave her an extra cookie, and pulled Sunny to her feet. She came like a rag doll into his arms, her body limp and lifeless, and he had to put her arms around his waist. He wrapped her close and rocked her as he'd rocked Jessie down in the basement. He said quiet things, murmuring in her ear: "It's a lot to think about," and "Don't worry just yet," and "There's always a way," and after a minute, Sunny started to cry. Her arms gripped him fiercely, her hands in fists against the small of his back, and he tightened his hold, pressing one hand to the hair at the nape of her neck, the other to the middle of her back. Steadying her.

She cried for a while, then simply leaned against his chest, her body easing. Michael closed his eyes and let himself feel whatever he felt. The sturdy softness of her, the smallness of her shoulders, the brush of her hair on his check. Breasts. Belly. Thighs. He moved his hand on her back, up and down, just letting the sensation grow, the need to touch another person like this, to hold and be held. She made a slight move, as if she'd pull away, and he tightened his grip the slightest bit. ''Now, it's you comforting me,'' he said, and heard the gruffness in his voice.

But she moved her hands, too, then. Pressed her lush softness against him and rubbed her cheek on his chest. That old familiar ache came on him, the need of a man for a woman, not just to hold, but to give and take, take and give. He moved his hand down her back, over the luscious swell of her hips, and she didn't protest.

She felt so good, so good. All that roundness. He traced her buttock, cupped his hand around it, cupped them then in both hands and pulled her closer against his growing erection and she made a soft sound, clutched his sides, and a vision of her without all the damp clothes on ran vividly through his mind. Turning his head into her neck, he opened his mouth and suckled against her, traced the edge of her ear with his tongue, felt her growing soft and taut at once, so he dared to cup then, the other curves his hand ached for, the full weight of a breast that overflowed his palm in a way that made him crazy, made him want to take everything off and see, taste, explore. He dragged his nails against the nub at the center, and she grabbed his hand. "Stop," she said.

"What?" Drugged by his own desire, it didn't sink in immediately. He drew her earlobe into his mouth, put the hand she'd taken away back on her hip, inhaled the scent of her hair.

She raised her arms and put them against him. "Not like this," she said, and pushed out of his embrace entirely. "It's all wrong like this."

Michael flushed, looking at Jessie, who stared up at them curiously, munching her cookie quite happily. "I'm sorry," he said. "I didn't think she was old enough to understand necking."

"I don't want to neck," Sunny said. The bruised look was back in her eyes, and he realized he hadn't even kissed her, just started groping her like a boy with his first girl at the county fair. "That's not what I'm about."

"I know," he said, and meant it. "I got carried away, and I apologize."

"It's all right. I just need you to know that's not who I am."

Michael started to say something else, then he

realized her breath was still coming hard, and her nipples were at full attention beneath her blouse, and she kept sneaking little glances at his mouth. He grabbed her arm and turned toward the counter. "Let me show you something here."

"What?"

Standing shoulder to shoulder, he held on to her hand. "Can I kiss you at least?"

She looked up at him, vulnerability in her blue, blue eyes. "I don't think it's a good idea."

"Yeah, but can I?"

A moment of pause while she searched his face, his eyes. Long enough that he noticed he could see nearly half of one breast down her shirt, and his member leaped like a puppy at the sight. Long enough for him to say, "I want to make love to you, but I'm willing to settle for a kiss."

"A kiss isn't enough for me," she said, and turned away.

"What does that mean?"

"It means what it means, that's all." Her voice was weary, and her neck bent.

Michael was flooded with a sense of shame, and he put his hand there, on the curve of her neck, in an offering of comfort. "I'm sorry, Sunny," he said, and meant it this time. "I guess the drama makes a man want to reaffirm life or something, and I'm very attracted to you."

She nodded without looking at him. "What am

I going to do?'' she asked, and it wasn't plaintive or whiney. It was the gut-level despair of a woman who'd been hanging on by a thread and had just seen it cut.

"We'll go see what we can salvage in the morning, but for now, you can go take a bath and wash all this disaster off you, and I'll take care of Jessie. You can stay here as long as you need to."

"I can't impose on you that way."

"It's what neighbors do. What if it had been my house? Would you let me sleep on your couch?"

A faint smile. "Yeah."

"All right then." He bent down and scooped Jessie into his arm.

"Cookie?" she asked hopefully.

"No more cookies," Sunny said. Then to Michael in explanation, "She hasn't had any supper."

"I'll hustle something up."

Sunny raised her head. "Microwave suppers?"

"How about frozen pizza? It's the good kind, with the rising crust."

She grinned. "Sounds great."

He jerked his head toward the door. "Upstairs, first door on the right. Big old claw-footed tub. And if you swear you won't tell anybody I've got 'em, I'll tell you where the bubbles are."

Sunny laughed, and he realized that he'd been waiting for the sound, trying to coax it out of her.

A light sound, like a morning wind. "My lips are sealed. You have some sweats or something I can put on afterwards?"

He winked. "Sure thing, kiddo. C'mon."

Chapter 7

Sunny shut herself in the old-fashioned bathroom with its big deep tub, and turned on the water and let herself have a good cry. A heartfelt, heart-deep release of the terror and the shock and the despair that had flooded through her upon seeing that her house and everything in it had been swept away. She didn't let herself think about what kind of man knew a woman had to have a cry after such trauma, who would take care of her daughter while she did it, who would fix her a meal. She didn't think about tomorrow or next week or what the ramifications of this latest disaster meant in terms of the great string of disasters that had been coming at her for two solid years.

Sinking into the deep, very hot water, into bubbles that smelled of a green forest, she didn't think. Blips of memory came back, and she let them. She saw herself, frozen in time as the tornado warning came over the radio in English and Spanish, the electronic warning system bleeping, and heard the strange panting sound of her terror as her brain had frantically tried to figure out what to do to keep Jessie safe. She saw the wall of the tornado itself, so immense and unbelievable that she knew she'd never forget it. Most of all, she heard the sound, over and over, the unbelievable roar of the storm.

But they were safe now, for tonight, with a kindly neighbor.

Who had touched her.

She hadn't fought any of the other memories, but she tried to fight this one. *Don't think about it.* Don't think of the long, ropy strength in his body, the sturdy sense of safety she'd felt as he held her, the gentleness of his hand smoothing her hair, all the soothing words he'd whispered in his lilting, resonant voice.

Don't think of the instant it changed and she felt it, all the way to the soles of her feet, the smallest possible shift of his body against hers, which made her suddenly aware of how her breasts were pressed into his ribs, and how that might feel if there were no clothes between them. Don't think of how it felt when he touched her bottom as if it was something wondrous, not the "bubble butt" her husband had sometimes teased her about having, how hot his mouth had been on her neck and how it had ignited every starved cell in her body, how she had nearly lost her head when he had cupped her breast with such a satisfied, soft groan.

Don't think, especially, about the look of his mouth, his eyes, hopeful and teasing and very, very hungry as he asked her for a kiss.

If he asked again to make love to her, how in the world could she possibly refuse? She wanted him, heaven knew. What woman with half an ounce of good sense could look at all that long, lean rancher body, covered as it was in the sleek, nut-brown skin she could see on his forearms and at the neck of his shirt and not imagine—no, don't—how it looked beneath that shirt. Who could resist that gorgeous face, those kind and sad eyes?

But she had to. Because she was spinning fantasies about him, spinning them in places that she didn't even allow herself to acknowledge, that maybe this man was really about something, that maybe there was one man who could be trusted. That's all you'd ever need, just one good man.

A knock sounded at the door. "Pizza's almost ready."

"I'll be right out!" She stood up, water sluicing from her naked body, and had an acute attack of hunger, thinking of him on the other side of the door. She looked at it, that simple, two-inch slab of wood and felt in her breasts and belly and through her thighs what he would do if she just opened it and invited him in.

A sudden vision of her mother, a pretty earnest woman, a little bit too dressed-up came to her. The cleavage at the neckline of her blouse, the too-bright smile she pasted on. Sunny had been about thirteen, seeing already that this new man was a loser and didn't appreciate all that he had, but Debbie had needed the attention so desperately, she'd pretended not to see.

Never, never, never. She had to get out of this house as soon as possible. That's all there was to it.

He'd set the table in the dining room, instead of the kitchen, and in spite of herself, Sunny smiled. There were checkered placemats on the big oak table, and tall glasses of ice and tea and heavy pottery plates. The steaming pizza was in the middle of the table, cut neatly into slices like a pizza parlor would do. "Very nicely done," she said, and added with a wry grin, "for a man."

"Thank you, ma'am. Can Jessie sit here, do you think?" He gestured at a pile of pillows in a chair. "Or do you want to hold her?"

"That should work fine." Sunny settled her daughter in the chair, cut a slice of pizza into little finger-sized bits, and set the plate in front of her. Impulsively, Sunny bent and kissed her daughter's head, smelling the sweetness, and a bolt of thanksgiving went through her—they'd survived. "I love you," she said.

Jessie lifted her face and grinned. "Love you." She waited for the kisses to be rained down on her face, and Sunny did it happily.

But as she settled down to her own meal, Sunny realized her daughter was just about done in. "She's got about fifteen minutes to collapse," she said with a little grin.

"Collapse?"

"Oh, yeah. See the way the eyelid on the left is drooping just a little bit? That means bedtime is going to be a collapse of weeping and she'll last about three seconds once I lie her down." Sunny chuckled. "Tired?"

Jessie shook her head vigorously.

Michael and Sunny exchanged a glance. "You'll see."

They were so hungry they ate in relative silence, and Sunny realized suddenly that she was hearing rain on the windows. "Listen to that! It's just ordinary rain now. What a blessing!"

"Maybe the rain dances did the trick," he said.

"Maybe."

Jessie reached for her cup and knocked it over, and that was the trigger. Tears of anger and frustration burst out of her noisily, and Sunny winked at Michael. "Here we go." She rounded the table, picked up the howling toddler and the diaper bag. "Where do you want me to put her down?"

"Come on." He led them upstairs to a spare room, furnished in an old-fashioned, warm way, with a plaid bedspread and a cowboy motif in the lamps.

Sunny laid the still-crying Jessie down on the bed, stripped off her clothes and diaper and washed her down with baby wipes. "It's all right, sugar plum, you're going to be okay, everything is all right," she murmured, putting on a dry diaper and clean pajamas. Jessie started to slow, her eyes drooping, as Sunny turned her over on her tummy, and started rubbing her back. Michael had ducked out and came back with a rocking chair, which he settled by the dresser. Sunny raised a finger to her lips, singing Jessie's favorite lullaby, an old camp church song, and Michael nodded.

In minutes, the baby was asleep, and Sunny piled pillows around the edges of the bed to keep her from falling off, then turned on a lamp in case she awakened suddenly, and tiptoed out. "Whew," she said, laughing as they sat back down to the pizza.

"Quite a storm," he agreed, his eyes crinkling up. "I think I've had enough. Want some coffee?"

"I would love some." She picked up her dishes.

He pushed her back down. "We're not doing dishes. Just sit."

"Yes, sir."

He grinned and ducked into the kitchen, bringing two big mugs of steaming coffee. Without ceremony, he shoved the pizza and dishes to one side, and settled the cups. "So, tell me your story, Sunny-girl," he said, kicking his stocking feet out in front of him. "Grow up in Denver?"

And for some reason, Sunny just let go. Let go of everything. She told him about the neighborhood where she'd lived in a tiny house with her mother, about playing in a little hidden creek where she'd once found the head of a deer—"I thought it was my punishment because I wasn't supposed to go there"—and the long nights lying on the screened porch staring at the sky.

"So how did you end up becoming a seamstress?"

"Ah," Sunny said. "Because my mother couldn't sew and I wanted more clothes than she would buy. A neighbor gave me a sewing machine and helped me get started, and I was very good at it." She lifted a shoulder. "Necessity is the mother of invention."

He nodded, his posture utterly relaxed, the expression on his face giving every appearance of interest.

"By the time I was in high school, I was earning

a pretty good income sewing for the rest of the girls. They came to me for one-of-a-kind prom outfits, that kind of thing, you know? You probably don't know this, but it's hard for women to wear just anything off the rack. One has big shoulders and a small rear end, another is busty with short legs, all that.''

''So d'you go to school or something for it?''

''I started at an art school, but I have to tell you, I was already doing better work than that, and I just decided that I'd strike out on my own.'' She paused, looking down into her cup, her thumbs moving on the handle. ''Hmmm. That's a bit of a lie, really. My mother died that year and I really didn't have money for school.''

''Sounds like you did all right.''

''I did,'' she said, and had to smile in wonder at the way it had all come together. ''Within a year, I had more work than I could do, and was turning people away. One thing that happened was that a couple came to me to make them costumes for the Renaissance Festival, and it just took off after that. I was able to buy a lot of new equipment and hire an assistant.''

His mouth tightened. ''The husband's gotta come into it somewhere along here.''

Sunny looked away from the hard set of his mouth. ''Yes, unfortunately, I inherited my mother's bad judgment about men. Paul seemed like everything I wanted. He was a hard worker, and he seemed very encouraging and we got married after a whole year of dating, so I was pretty sure it was the right thing to do.''

"How long were you married?''

"Two years, officially, from wedding date to divorce date. He didn't stick around long after I started to be really pregnant.'' She lifted her chin, met his eyes. "He thought pregnancy was disgusting, what it did to my body.''

Michael's expression didn't change, but his eyes went cold and he uttered a precise epithet.

Sunny laughed. "Exactly.'' She shrugged, as if shrugging off the whole mess. "I told you the rest—Jessie was born with a hole in her heart, and the truth is, Paul had ruined our credit and finances, so I didn't have any reserves to see me through. I'm not whining. I'm grateful for my daughter, and I'm grateful I got rid of him before he took me down with him. It's just been a bit of struggle.''

"You've got a lot of courage, Sunny. A lot of character, and for that reason, I don't think you inherited bad judgment from your mother. I think you were young and naive and a bad guy took advantage of you.''

"Thank you.'' She tossed her hair out of her face, rubbed her hands against her thighs, tried not to look at the opening of his shirt, where she could see a wedge of brown chest that looked as smooth as chiffon. "Now you. Tell me your story, Michael Chasing Horse."

"Pretty much have, already. Not a lot to it. Born in South Dakota, came here with my parents when I was a little boy, lived here ever since."

"Wife. Ten years. That's a long time."

He turned his lips down a little. "Maybe. But it was just a sad story of a woman who couldn't live with the loneliness and harshness of this land, and me being too damned stubborn to leave it. I was a—"

He was interrupted by a shrill scream from upstairs. Sunny was on her feet, bolting up the steps in a split second, fearing Jessie had fallen off the bed in spite of all their precautions. Instead, she was simply sitting up, screaming, in the middle of the pillows. "Mama!" she screamed, obviously terrified, and Sunny gathered her up, close, hugging her. "It's okay, sweetie. I'm here. I'm here."

Jessie grabbed her so hard, burrowing closer and closer, her whole body shivering, and she cried softly, terrified mewings. Sunny looked over her shoulder at Michael, who stood at the door. "She's probably just processing the tornado, poor baby. I'll rock her back to sleep."

He nodded. "I'm gonna shower."

Michael took the day off him in layers, feeling grit wash out of his hair, his face, the terror he'd felt when he'd thought of Sunny and Jessie alone on that hill—

His belly clutched in memory.

Washed it away. The water eased his tight neck, and he let the spray hit hard there for long minutes. He thought of Sunny, in this very spot, naked, not even an hour ago, and a low rumbling moved through his body—need.

It had been a long, long time since he'd lain down with a woman, skin to skin, smelled her and tasted her. This afternoon, he'd been afraid that maybe he'd never have another chance, that he'd been walled off so long in his sulk that he'd screwed up all his chances.

But he had to respect her boundaries. He'd never met a warier woman, and it sounded as though she had good reason, as if Jessica wasn't reason enough.

But how long since he'd liked a woman so much, not just desired her body, but *liked* her? She was as strong as a tree, standing rooted and fierce in her own convictions, all alone against the tornadoes— metaphorical and physical—that would have made a weaker woman despair. He admired her.

He dried off and put on a pair of sweats, then padded down the hall without his shirt to go to his room for a fresh one. As he passed the door to the guest room, he heard Sunny's light voice winding around an old, old folk song. It was the tale of a

woman who stayed true to her love through all
tests, wishing him well if he'd found love in another
woman, if he'd drowned in the great salt sea, only
to find that her love was standing there in front of
her. The sound drew him gently, to the doorway,
and the picture of the mother and daughter drew
him in farther, to sit on the bed, something so big
in his chest that he was powerless against it.

Wheat-soft lamplight fell over Sunny's shoulder,
illuminating her loose, long hair from behind so she
looked like a madonna. In her arms, the beautiful
baby girl, as blond and round as her mother, shud-
dered awake every so often, her tiny hands flailing
out as she grasped for the security of her mother's
constant hand, always there.

Something grew in the room, or maybe only in
his heart, filling his lungs, his belly, his limbs. It
was a sense of rightness, of knowledge, of blessing.
He found himself examining her face, every detail
of it, the sweep of pale-brown lashes, the round
curve of a cheek, the shape of her lips, her small
white hands, and each detail made his breath
stronger, his wish more clear. This was all he'd ever
wanted, right here. A woman who wanted and
needed him, a child to love, maybe a few more, a
couple of brothers to drive her crazy. Quiet meals,
easy laughter.

It was crazy, but his blood buzzed with it, making him dizzy and hungry, and he gazed at Sunny

directly, meeting her eyes when she raised them, letting her see what was written on his heart in this minute.

She swallowed, stumbling in her song, and then looked back at her daughter, but he saw her nostrils flare, saw a faint wash of color, barely visible in the soft light, touch her cheeks.

Still, she rocked and sang. For a long time. And Michael did not move, only sat there waiting until it felt right to her, until she saw that she could trust that he wasn't moving.

At last, she whispered, "She's asleep."

He stood up, moving out of her way as she settled the loose body of her daughter on the bed, covered her securely, and then straightened, not quite meeting his eyes as she brushed a lock of hair out of her eyes. "I guess I'll go to bed now, too."

Michael didn't move. He waited, that sense of blessing growing and growing.

She looked everywhere but at his chest, at his face, at him, moving a pillow a tiny bit, twisting her hair in her fingers. He took a step toward her, then another, reached for her hand and carried it to his mouth, then pressed it against his heart. She made a soft sound, half sorrow, half release, and looked at him. "I have never seen a man as beautiful as you," she whispered, her eyes full of regret.

Gently, gently, gently, he put his hands on her face, cupped her jaw and bent in, slowly, to press his lips to hers, once, then again, and he raised his head to look at her. "I will not hurt you," he said, and kissed her again, and this time there was an explosion of light and heat that nearly knocked him sideways, and he actually swayed. As if she felt it, too, her arms flew around him and her mouth opened and their tongues were tangled and he felt that he would fly away into some faraway world, some magic place where everything was possible.

And he wanted to smooth every inch of her with his healing, wanted his skin against hers. "Not here," he managed, and took her hand, drawing her out of the room, down the hall.

His bedroom was bright with the overcast night, soft ghostly light flooding through a bank of windows that would show the mountains during the day. Sunny was trembling, and her heart was racing and she pulled out of his grip as he closed the door. "Wait!" she cried, "I'm not sure…this is rash…"

He turned, and light skimmed over his chest, over the round, strong muscles of his shoulders and arms, down the planes of chest and belly, and the sight kindled a kind of lust she didn't even know she could feel. But it was the look in his eyes that was both terrifying and compelling, a gentle, insistent light. It made her dizzy.

"I will not do anything you don't want me to, Sunny. I won't take your heart and smash it. I don't want you to promise anything, either.'' Very gently, he reached for the buttons of the shirt. she wore. ''This is affirmation, do you understand? We're celebrating that we lived.''

He undid the first button, then the second, and Sunny didn't move, aroused and frozen at once, wanting and so afraid of wanting or needing anything or anyone, especially someone who seemed to be everything she'd ever wanted. Her breath caught as he finished unbuttoning her shirt and slid it off her shoulders. His fingers on her skin caused her to shudder softly, but still she couldn't move.

He bent down to kiss her again, and Sunny found she could manage that, could lift her face, accept the sweetness of his mouth, the fullness of his lips almost sinfully delectable, his tongue teasing and dancing, tasting of toothpaste. His hands lit on her shoulders and she jumped a little, but he took a step closer, sliding his palms down her back to rest on her waist. ''Touch me, Sunny,'' he said. ''Please. I need to feel your hands.''

And somehow it wasn't so hard to *give* what he needed. She raised her hands and smoothed them over the sleekness of his skin, as smooth as she'd imagined, and supple, and she could spend a hundred years just memorizing the landscape, the shelf of collarbone, the rigid arcs of ribs, the short nubs of nipples, the play of muscles moving beneath skin. And he touched her in return, running his fingers through her hair, gliding over her shoulders, down her arms, down her sides. There he paused and pulled her back toward the bed, but didn't immediately pull her down. Instead, he sat down, put her hands on his shoulders, and reached for her bra, sliding those nimble fingers around to find the clasp. She dropped her arms and let it fall off, and Michael took a breath, closed his eyes, then opened them again.

It moved her.

And a sense of wonder seeped in, pushing away fear, so her heart was beating faster with pleasure untainted by anything but this minute, this affirmation, as he took a breast in each hand, then bent his head and put his mouth on her. It was hot and wet and felt so good her knees nearly buckled. She gripped his shoulders and bent her head into him, and he laughed lightly and did it again. And again and again, until Sunny was shivering all over and soft as melted butter, and she pushed him backward, straddling his long, beautiful body with her hips, laughing at his groan when she pushed his arms down and rode wickedly against the erection between them, covered in layers of gray sweat pants. She kissed him and brushed her breasts over his chest, and wiggled her hips until she thought they both might explode with anticipation.

With a swift movement, he reversed their positions, and the mood shifted again. He was breathing hard and so was she as they stared at each other in the darkness, chests bared but nothing else, unless you counted the hearts beating together in some new rhythm, and when he kissed her this time, it was deep and tender and full of meaning. He cradled her between his arms and kissed her mouth and her eyes, dipped to kiss her chin, rose to kiss each cheek, and Sunny felt tears seeping out of her eyes, tears of longing and release, and he even kissed those when he found them, caught a few on his tongue and bent down to kiss her lips so she could taste the saltiness.

And there was nothing to do but give herself up to so much gentle passion. To lift her hips and let him pull away her sweat pants, and watch, vulnerable and naked, as he skimmed out of his own, revealing the rest of him, and every inch of it beautiful. She touched his lower belly, taut and hard, and ran her fingers over the edge of hair, and down the length of his member, and he touched her in return, her breasts and belly and her sex, his slow fingers making her forget everything else as they slid and entered and slid out again.

Yet he did not enter her still. He kissed her neck and the valley between her breasts, his hands running down her arms, over her hands. He kissed her ribs and thighs, parted her legs and kissed her there, and Sunny cried out, "Oh, please!" but she wasn't sure what she was asking for.

Michael knew. Tongue and fingers and then, when she was on the brink of an orgasm she thought might kill her, he stopped and inched his way up her body again. "Now?" he whispered over her lips.

"Yes."

He kissed her, deeply, touched her breasts, rubbed the nipples that were so sensitive she thought it might be enough all by itself to give her the release she craved so desperately. Between her legs, she could feel his member nudging her, and she wiggled a little, and he laughed, licked her lips. "Now?"

Sunny grabbed his shoulders and pushed hard, intending to push him over and take him herself, but he caught her arms and at that instant, plunged into her, kissing her and touching her breasts, all at once, and she made a long, low, agonized noise of pleasure, and then it was a rocketing, unbelievable blister of heat that centered in the usual place but moved through her whole body, forehead to toes, as if every molecule in her body were having an orgasm, and she couldn't help the sounds that came from her as he began to move. Nothing had ever felt that good. Ever.

And he moved and he took and he gave, and she was rippling through the end, when she felt him lose control and bite her neck and fiercely shove himself home, his hands hard on her shoulders, then her bottom, gripping hard. He made his own noises, as guttural and deep as her own, and their bodies arched and pulsed. Sunny gripped him hard, arms and legs and body, and accepted the healing he'd given, hoped she had given him some, too.

He collapsed against her, his face in the hollow of her shoulder and they simply breathed together like that for a long time, allowing pieces of themselves to return to the proper places. Sunny said, softly, "Whew!"

Michael chuckled, rubbed her side. "I can't move."

"Don't. Me either."

"I know I'm heavy. One more second."

She moved against him, freed in some unnamed way to be herself, exactly herself. "Take ten. A hundred."

"Is that purring I hear?" He lifted his head to look at her face.

She started to laugh, her arms around his neck. She made noises like a cat, nudged her nose against his neck. "Yes," she whispered. "Oh, my gosh."

He turned to his side, collapsing sideways on the pillow. Sunny faced him, touched his face, tracing the line of cheekbone, the aggressive nose, his lush mouth with a sense of wonder. Completion. There were no words in her, just a soft warmth. "Thank you," she said.

His hand moved on her arm. "For what?"

"For great sex, for a good supper, for being so kind to my daughter and me." She paused, letting the knowledge fill her. "For saving our lives."

He closed his eyes, pulled her close, pressed his forehead against hers. "I've never been so scared in my life, thinking of you two up there on the hill."

"Me, either," she said, and laughed softly. "I was standing there in the kitchen, trying to figure out what to do, and my brain just shut down, I couldn't think, and my heart was racing and there was this little noise coming out of me—" she made it, a little pant "—and then you burst in, like a super hero, to save the day."

"And provide all kinds of special services."

"That, too."

He looked at her, his eyes glowing in the low light, and he touched her hair, smoothed his hand over her head, her ear. "You are so beautiful. I feel like I could just look at you for a hundred years."

It scared her, the hint of permanence in those words. "Is that purring I hear?"

He grinned.

A sense of peace enveloped Sunny as they fell into a drowsy silence. The big soft bed cradled her sated and exhausted body, and her fretting had been silenced by making love. She felt herself drifting off and thought she ought to move back to Jessica's bed, but the baby would kick her all night, and she was safe enough, just two doors down; she would hear her if she woke up. As she was drifting into an irresistible sleep, she thought she felt Michael kiss her brow, thought she heard him whisper "thank-you," but she couldn't climb back up just then. Sleep carted her away.

Chapter 8

Chapter 8

Michael awakened with a start in the middle of the night to discover the place where Sunny had lain was empty. Immediately, he thought of Jessica, and got up to see if everything was okay. Tugging on his sweat pants, he padded down the hall and peeked in, seeing the baby asleep as she'd been, but Sunny wasn't there.

He found her in the dark kitchen, sitting in front of the window, a cup of tea at her elbow. "You could turn on the light if you want to," he said.

She jumped, then shook her head. "I'm just trying to figure things out."

"You can stay here for as long as you need to, Sunny. I'm serious."

She nodded, turned her face away. "I appreciate the offer." The unspoken part of it was, *but I can't accept it.*

His heart, which had felt so light, turned thick and heavy. "It's pretty lonely out here, I guess."

"Have you always lived here?"

"Since I was six."

"Where did you live before?"

"South Dakota. My family is Indian. My mom took me back there every year for a couple of weeks, but this is home."

She inclined her head. "Do you ever go now?"

"Not for a long time. My ex used to want to go. She was sort of into all the stuff, you know, that Indian thing. I'm not."

"She was Indian?"

He shook his head, looked at his hands. "White. Not blond like you, though—black Irish, though she always said she had some Indian blood. Who knows, maybe she did." He shrugged. "Not like it matters."

"Doesn't it? Don't you ever miss being a part of something bigger than you, a whole culture that knows your name, your people, your cousins and uncles and all the stories going back into history about your family?"

There was a lot of feeling in the question and he took it seriously. "You want that for yourself?"

"I'm just so alone, you know?" Her voice was

very quiet. "If I had any family at all to turn to, I could have gone to them for help. I could have had a place to land. I never understand how people who have it let it go."

"It wasn't me who did it," he said. "It was my father." He stood up. "Want to see something?"

"Sure."

He'd carried in his parents' things from the barn and settled them in a corner of the dining room in two boxes. He brought one back in. "I need to turn on the light. Brace yourself."

The box was filled with a wide assortment of things, and Sunny bent over to look at them. "Who did the beadwork?" she asked, drawing out a clear plastic box with a rainbow of beads sorted into tiny compartments.

"My mom." He took out another box, this one a small cedar one, stamped Manitou Springs, Colo. in fading gold, and opened it. Within were beaded earrings and bracelets, a leather pouch with a geometric design beaded into it. "She made these things."

"Beautiful," Sunny said, fingering them like an expert. She turned the bracelet over. "Loom?"

"I don't know," he said with a grin.

"Yeah, it is."

"You've done this kind of work, too?"

"Not exactly like this, but I do—did—a lot of hand beading on some of the costumes. It's precise, but very satisfying." She put the bracelet down, picked up a sheaf of pictures. As she bent over, he glimpsed the swell of a naked breast beneath his oversize shirt and wanted her again instantly. An impulse he put aside. "Who are these people?"

"Relatives." He pointed to an old man with a white streak in his long, loose hair, looking at the camera with suspicion. "That's my grandpa on my mom's side."

"You look like him," she said, smiling for the first time.

There were others, cousins he could name and some he couldn't. Uncles and aunts, Chasing Horse side and Red Willow side, his mother. "And you never talk to any of them?"

"Well, not never. Sometimes one of the cousins will come visit, and I've had letters from some of the aunts, usually at special seasons, like Christmas."

She nodded, peering at the photos as if they had some magic in them, a clue to some urgent question she was asking of life. "Hey!" she said, and gave him the picture. "Isn't that your cradleboard?"

Michael nodded. It was an old photograph, taken maybe in the thirties, or even the twenties. "Wow, this is old." A pretty young woman had the cradleboard on her back, and a baby slept inside. "Yeah, this is it. This is probably my grandfather," he said with a sense of wonder, and then he saw something that made him frown. "Wow."

"What is it?"

He put the picture on the table, then went to get the cradleboard. "See the difference?"

Sunny looked from one to the other. "The turtle? What is it?"

Michael braced the cradle board between his legs, and picked up the picture. "It's an amulet with a special blessing inside, a baby's umbilical cord. My mother always said there was a curse on my father's family because the two things were separated somehow. Nobody knows where it went, and there was this feeling that if it came back, maybe the family would be healed."

"Maybe you should make a new one. Have it blessed or something, like Catholics do for things."

"I don't know how."

"How to bless it or how to make the amulet?"

He knew blessings, though they were in a rusty place in his memory. "The amulet."

She nodded, took the picture back. "I could probably do it."

For a moment, he wondered if that might be all it took. End the rift and the loneliness, bring the family back, or maybe even just his life back into balance. He looked at the woman before him, with her long hair and wary eyes and wanted it to be her who brought the balance back to him.

But he saw that she'd flown from here already, and he didn't blame her. Sadly, he shook his head. "There's some kind of special ritual you have to follow, a baby's umbilical cord, all these things. It's something women do."

"Could you find out?"

He shrugged.

She put the picture down, nodded. "I think I'm going back to bed now. But I think I'll sleep with Jessie, okay?"

He didn't look at her. Nodded. She pressed her hand to his shoulder as she passed, and he wanted to capture it, hold it there, but he didn't. Just let her go.

In the morning, everyone was quite polite, Sunny thought, and it was hard to be too stiff with the blazingly happy Jessica chattering and laughing and enjoying the attention of two adults so thoroughly. Sunny cooked omelettes and then they gathered some empty boxes and put them in the back of the truck to hold anything they might salvage. "It might have blown quite a ways, and we can just head out across the prairie as far as we need to," Michael said. "You need a hat." He found her one, a turquoise baseball hat with Las Vegas scrolled across the brim.

"You don't seem like a Las Vegas kind of guy," Sunny said.

"Naw. Went there once, just to see, but it's too noisy."

"I've never been there."

"You're not missing anything."

She picked up Jessie, and was uncomfortably considering the car seat problem when she realized that she didn't have her baby backpack anymore, either, and how could they do this work holding a baby? "Michael, we need to think of something to keep Jessie safe. She can't get down in the prairie, especially when everything has been so stirred up."

"No." He frowned.

Sunny was trying to think of some way to create a playpen when Michael held up a hand and ducked into the house and came back with the cradleboard. From his hip pocket, he took a lethal-looking knife and braced the board on the truck, then prepared to cut the leather at the bottom. "Wait!" Sunny said. "What are you doing?"

"Look, this thing has been sitting in my barn for twenty years and never had a minute of use. If I cut the leather, Jessie can stick her legs through, and we can take turns putting her on our backs."

"It's a valuable antique, Michael, and not just on the market, but to your family."

"Things are meant to be used," he said, and plunged the knife into the leather. "It's a way to keep her safe." He cut the holes, then widened them enough to fit a toddler's legs. "See? It'll even be a way to keep shade on her."

Sunny resisted the swell of love—how could she even call it that?—that filled her chest. But she resolved to see about making the amulet, anyway. "Thank you." There were straps to fit the cradle-board over a post or shoulders, and Michael put it on his back. "See if she'll fit."

Jessie protested a little, going in, but when her legs were dangling, and they found a way to stretch and bend the opening at the shoulders so that her arms were free, she settled into it fairly happily, swinging her feet. "Good idea, Michael," Sunny said. "Very resourceful."

"Well, yeah, I'm just a pretty resourceful kind of guy." He winked, and she was relieved that he was more accepting now than he seemed to be last night of her need not to get too involved with him. "Let's roll."

The path of the tornado was vividly visible as they left the sheltering circle of trees around Michael's house and outbuildings, then drove up the road. Michael whistled softly, and Sunny, holding Jessica on her lap, widened her eyes. The path was about a quarter-mile wide, and everything in that path had been pulverized. The storm had also picked up things and tossed them, willy-nilly, everywhere. Unidentified pieces of twisted metal, pieces of wood, tree branches. A road sign, pristine and perfectly upright, had been planted in the midst of some cactus, warning the coyotes that the speed limit was five miles an hour.

"What a mess!"

Michael nodded grimly, and turned up the hill to the house. Sunny felt her stomach clench, hard, as they stopped in the driveway. The car the junkyard manager brought her—had that really only been yesterday afternoon?—had been untouched and was sitting with a single cactus arm on the windshield, without so much as a dent in it. "That is so weird," Sunny commented.

The house was another story. There was nothing left but a pile of timbers and junk all tangled together, nothing immediately recognizable, except the bathtub, sitting out in the open. Sunny wondered if the couch cushions were still inside it. "Maybe we would have lived."

He squeezed her shoulder. "Put Jessie in this thing and I'll take the first round. Sooner we start, sooner we're done."

They picked around the yard first, collecting soaked, dirty clothing, and sorting through the debris for anything Sunny wanted to keep. There wasn't much. They moved on to the house, carefully stepping over fallen timbers, through ground-up rubble and a single, cockeyed roof beam, which had protected a few things beneath it. Jessie's dresser had been knocked sideways and one drawer had fallen out, spilling tiny socks into the world. Sunny imagined some housewife in Kansas weeding her garden and plucking an embroidered anklet out of her rhubarb, and it made her smile.

"Whoo-hoo," Michael said from the other side of the mess. "Looky here!"

A pair of lacy white panties, Sunny's, waved like a naughty flag from the top of a stick of wood that might once have been part of a wall. She flushed when he reached for them, felt heat move through her breasts as that dark hand captured the delicate scrap of cloth—

And for one minute, she was transported back to his bed last night, was the willing and pliant lover he had pleased so exquisitely with those hands, that mouth that was now smiling. To make it worse, he tucked the underwear into his shirt, next to that belly that had been her undoing. As if he knew her thoughts, he grinned wickedly and spread his hands. "You want 'em, you'll have to come get 'em."

She was painfully tempted. She imagined a little wrestling match, one that would bring their bodies into hot, close contact, imagined how the tussle would raise their arousal levels, how pleasing it would be to do it all again. Unconsciously, she rubbed her belly, then realized what she was doing, and darted a look at his face to see if he had noticed.

He was stepping over the rubble, evidently ignoring the little interplay, and Sunny, disappointed for some reason she couldn't name, turned back to the task of wresting baby clothes out of drawers.

Michael knelt behind her, his hands falling on her shoulders. He leaned in close and kissed her ear. "It doesn't have to be this way, Sunny. You don't have to push me away so hard."

"Yes I do," she said and even to her own ears, the words were mournful.

His hands moved, and Sunny found herself leaning backward into his body. They were kneeling, his knees bracing her sides, and his hands slid from her shoulders into the neckline of her borrowed shirt. Fierce desire woke in her. "Michael," she whispered, but she didn't stop him. His hands slid beneath her bra, to the already-eager tips of her breasts, and touched them lightly. He suckled her ear a little, making Sunny shudder. "I want you to listen to me," he said fiercely. "This isn't about sex or power. I'm not trying to trap you into a scene where you have to be a victim again. You need a father for your daughter. You need a place to live. I need a wife because I'm dying of loneliness, and I think we're pretty compatible."

She caught his hands. "Stop it!" she said.

He caught her back, and pulled her around to face him. "No, you stop it," he said, hands on her shoulders. "Look at me, damn it."

She raised furious eyes to his face, and was

stricken all over again by that elegant beauty, the high brow, the dark eyes with their fringe of lush lashes. It made her hurt everywhere to want anyone this much.

"Would it be so terrible?" he asked softly.

"I would love you," she said, and set her jaw. "I couldn't help it. And then I couldn't protect myself, and you don't understand, but I just can't do that, okay? Don't ask it. I'll leave here in the morning."

His brow blackened, and his jaw was set hard, but he let her go. "Whatever."

They retreated to separate sides of the house, and then searched outward into the fields, combing for anything that might be saved. Sunny nursed a sense of grief and wasn't sure if it stemmed from her rejection of Michael's proposal—or what had certainly sounded like one—or this new loss she had sustained. The sun beat down on her head, and she had to keep avoiding prickly pear cactus, but one bit her ankle anyway, and on the horizon a new storm built, a mockery of the drought.

In the shredded remains of a yucca plant, she found a picture of her wedding. The leaf of the plant had gone right through the center of the photo, the only one she had left from the day she'd married Paul, and now it was ruined, and for some reason, Sunny just let her arms drop and let the despair take her. She would never amount to anything. There was some evil force at work seeing to that. And with a furious growl, she raised her head and said, "You see me trying here. Could you just cut me a break once in blue moon?"

From behind her, Michael let out a shout. "Sunny!" he cried, and she turned. He held something over his head, but she couldn't make it out. He ran toward her, as lightly and gracefully as one of his horses, the weight of the cradleboard and Jessica seeming not to weigh him down at all. There was a youthful exuberance on his face as he came forward, holding the object out to her. "Look what I found!"

It was a box with moons and stars all over it, and it was wet and muddy on the outside. "Oh, my gosh!" With trembling hands, she reached for it— her most precious, precious possession. "Did you look inside?"

He nodded, beaming. "They're a little damp and you might lose a couple, but the rest are fine."

Sunny tore off the lid and looked inside at dozens and dozens, no probably hundreds, of baby pictures, chronicling Jessie's life from before she was born to now. Tears of gratitude sprung to her eyes. "This is the only thing that would have really killed me," she said.

"I know." He said over his shoulder, "Your mama got her pictures back." He swung around and Sunny saw that Jessie was sound asleep, arms folded comfortably on the top of the leather, feet dangling bare from the bottom. Her cheeks were flushed.

"Maybe we ought to call it a day," Sunny said. "She looks pretty hot."

"Pretty much got it all anyway, anything worth saving."

She nodded, clutching the box close to her body. "Michael, thank you."

"Stop thanking me," he said, a little of the glow going out of his face.

But Sunny knew what to do to thank him. She would take care of it this afternoon.

Chapter 9

They ate and Michael went outside to make some repairs the dual storms had caused. He put on his black hat, and Sunny knew he'd ride, too. "Do the horses get restless if they don't get ridden?"

"Oh, yeah. You should let me teach you. I think you'd be a natural."

She nodded noncommittally.

When he was gone, she went to the box containing his mother's things and took out the picture of the turtle amulet and the beads. There was a special way of doing it, he'd said, and she wondered what it might be. If there was an umbilical cord contained in it, then it was likely a woman who was pregnant who did it, preparing it for her coming child. That would bring hope and faith to the task, and she thought back to her own pregnancy, to the things that had been in her mind. Joy, excitement, hope.

There was obviously no umbilical cord available, but maybe she could think of an appropriate substitute. She thought of the kittens and their mother, wondering if they might provide some idea, but drew a blank.

Then she had a most perfect idea In her own things, she found the moon and stars box and took out a lock of Jessica's hair, fine and blond, a thick curl tied with ribbon. It would do.

She set to work, using the picture as her guide, and was deeply engrossed when Jessica woke up from her nap. Sunny changed her, washed her face, and settled her on the kitchen floor with a collection of plastic glasses and spoons and lids, and kept working.

It was a pleasant space, she thought idly. The table was old and scarred, but well-cared for, and it sat in a bright corner, with a view of dark-blue mountains running an uneven finger over the horizon. Sunny started to hum as she wove beads into a circular pattern, pleased when Jessie started humming along with her, and pleased that the idea she'd had to make the amulet more three-dimensional than two was working out.

As she worked, it seemed like some long-dry part

of her brain started perking up, as if there were a bunch of little girls in her brain saying to each other, ''oooh, we finally get to play again!'' She wove green and black beads in circles and it seemed to make it easier to see her own life, circling wider and wider, away from the knotty core of her beginnings. With needle and thread, she had created order for herself, had shaped the future she wanted with her own hands.

As she wove a new hope for Michael, she began to wonder what that future might look like now.

What if?

On cue, Jessie raised her head. ''Where Michael?''

''He's outside.''

''See him?''

Sunny looked through the window and saw him in the corral, grooming the beautiful mane of the horse he'd called Two Moon. He'd taken off his hat and hung it on a fence post, along with his shirt. Sunlight streamed down on them, horse and man, accenting the smooth sleek muscles of both, creatures at home in this harsh land. Jessie said, ''There he is!'' and pointed. She looked at her mother hopefully. ''See him?''

''Maybe in a little while,'' Sunny said, and went back to the amulet. It was nearly finished now. Another hour should do it.

* * *

Michael stayed out of the house all afternoon, finding a hundred things to do so he could sort out his feelings away from the narcotic influence of the two women who'd somehow managed to steal his heart in three days flat. He couldn't stand to think of them leaving, and all day he tried to think of ways to convince Sunny it would be safe to stay.

But a cynical voice in his head wanted to know if he'd lost his mind. *A woman like that, a city girl? What makes you think she would stay any better than your wife?*

He didn't know, but there was something so sure and strong about Sunny Kendricks that he felt he could trust. That rooted strength. That depth of conviction. If she gave her word, she would keep it.

He thought of their joining last night, of that sense of jubilant blessing he'd felt, the absolute rightness of it, of the two of them being in his house. The prairie had delivered him a great gift, and he did not intend to let it go.

In late afternoon, he'd finally run out of things to do. Supper smells came out of the house, and his stomach growled gratefully. She was also a great cook—almost reason alone to convince her to stay. He quirked his lips and thought maybe that wasn't one to add to his list.

His list. He realized, putting the shovel away in the shed, that he'd been out here all afternoon making up a pitch, a campaign designed to reveal his truest heart so that she would be able to let down her guard. He didn't need to have her love just yet, though his heart had soared when she'd said she would love him. It would be enough just to convince her to stay long enough that he could show her that he was a man of his word and a man of honor.

From behind him came a baby chortle, a scream of laughter, and, smiling at the joy of that sound, Michael turned to see his girls coming across the yard toward him. Jessie was bouncing in her mother's arms, and his heart squeezed when she cried, "Hi, Michael! Hi!"

Sunny smiled as she approached. "She wanted to come see you right now. No more delays."

He took the baby and gave her a kiss, nuzzling against her neck with little growls. "Whatcha been doing?"

"Beads," she said, pointing to her mom.

Sunny nodded. He noticed that her nose, which had sunburned a little this morning, was already turning tan. "Supper's almost ready if you want to come eat. Nothing fancy, just a meat loaf and some carrots and potatoes."

"Your nose is already tanning," he said. "You look like you'd burn like a lobster."

"I know," she said, "but I don't. Never did. Neither does my Jessie-girl, thank heaven."

"Sunny," he said, "I want to—"

She smiled at him. There was a strange mischief in her eyes. "I made you something," she said, and opened her hand to reveal a turtle amulet, almost perfectly shaped, with a little open pocket. "I wasn't sure what the rituals were, but you can see here—" she pointed to a spot across the turtle's back where a sheen of glittery something shone in the lowering light "—that I used some of Jessie's hair to bring that baby energy back."

He swallowed, holding it in his palm. An arrow of sunlight struck the glittery hair woven into it, and Jessie said next to him, "Pretty!" and put her finger on it.

"Thank-you," he said, and closed his hand over it. He had some sweetgrass and sacred tobacco. Maybe she would participate in blessing it. For now, he took a breath, settled Jessie more firmly on his hip and said, "Sunny, I want you to listen to me. I know this land is hard and I know you're afraid of being hurt, but I really don't want you to go."

"I don't want to go," she said.

"I know it's crazy that you could fall in love in three days, and I know that scares you, but I swear, if you'll give me a chance, I'll make you believe. Jessie can grow up here, in the fresh air, and learn to ride horses and go to 4H, and you can turn one of those rooms into a sewing room, and I'm not saying it's always gonna be easy, but this is the hardest season we've had in twenty years, and you've gotten through it, and I just—"

"I love you, Michael," she said.

He had more reasons, but he said, "What?"

She moved forward, put her hands on his chest, and raised up on her tiptoes to kiss his mouth. "I know it's crazy, but it's also true. I love you. And there isn't a bad bone in your body, and if you'll have us, we'll see to it that you have what you need. We'll take care of you."

Light blazed up in him, golden, overflowing, and he grabbed her with his free arm, baby on one hip, amulet in his fist, and kissed her, hard. Kissed her mouth, kissed her again, raised his head to look down in her eyes to be sure it was real. "Wow," he said.

"Wow," Sunny said, and touched his face. "You're a miracle, you know that? An answer to a prayer."

He closed his eyes, put his forehead against hers. "So are you, Sunny. A ray of light in my dark world."

She kissed him. "A poet."

Jessie laughed and put her head in between them, an arm around each neck. "Aw. Love you!"

Michael kissed the little girl, and her mama. A family. It was all he'd ever wanted.

As they walked up the porch steps, Jessie said, pointing toward the prairie, "Pretty!"

They stopped. "Oh, my gosh!" Sunny breathed. Michael squeezed her hand.

Because there, across the open fields, watered at last by the great, ferocious storms, were cacti in bloom. Hundreds of them, thousands, maybe, all a vivid magenta that seemed to vibrate in the gentle sunlight slanting over the plains. A brilliant display of tenacity, he thought, and kissed Sunny's hand. She raised his and kissed it back, and they went inside to supper.

* * * * *

Three full-length novels from
#1 *New York Times* bestselling author

NORA ROBERTS

S U S P I C I O U S

This collection of Nora Roberts's finest
tales of dark passion and sexy intrigue
will have you riveted from the first page!

Includes *PARTNERS, THE ART OF DECEPTION*
and *NIGHT MOVES*, all of which have been
out of print for over a decade.

Available in November 2003, wherever books are sold.

Silhouette®

Where love comes alive™

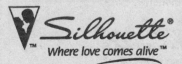
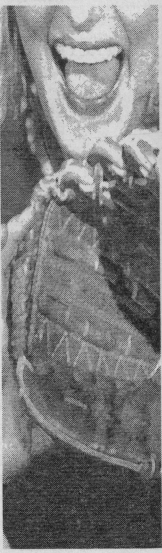

Come home to the Lone Star Country Club

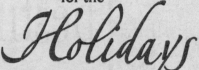

Home
for the
Holidays

**Celebrate Christmas...
Texas high-society style.**

Leanne Banks
Dixie Browning
Kathie DeNosky

Available in November 2003, wherever books are sold!